One Last Job

One Last Job

Flights and Feelings
Book Two

ANISE STARRE

Editing: Rachel Leven; Michelle Kowalski

Cover design: Bring Design

ISBN: 979-8-3909-3062-5

Also available as an ebook

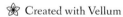 Created with Vellum

For everyone whose dream always seems just out of reach. Keep going. You'll get there. We all will.

xo

1

AMBER

THE WALLS ARE GREEN. NO, THAT'S NOT QUITE RIGHT. THE walls are *apple* green.

I turn around and hold up two paint swatches. In my left hand, *apple* green. In my right, *rye* green. Ricardo, one of my contractors, shoots me a nervous grimace as I shake the two swatches in front of his face. I like Ricardo. He's good at what he does, efficient, and, most importantly, he treats me with respect and makes sure his employees do too. We've never had any problems before. Until now.

Because the walls are *apple* green and the client requested *rye*.

"Come on, Ric," I groan. "Tell me what happened here." We're 48 hours away from install day, and the last thing I need to see right now are apple green walls in the master bedroom.

"I'm so sorry, Amber. I've got a new apprentice working with me and I thought he'd be able to handle this room alone." He runs a hand down his face and shakes his head. "It's my fault. I should've checked in on him more often. I take full responsibility."

I reach for my hair and twist a few strands around my finger. The action helps to ground me, stops me from entering a never-ending anxiety spiral as apple green walls close in on me.

"Do you think the client will notice? They do look very similar."

The laugh that bursts from my lips is borderline hysterical. *Yes*, the client is going to notice. I spent a painstaking three hours going back and forth on the pros and cons of apple versus rye with the client, and they were adamant about going with the latter.

And the colours don't look similar. Not at all.

To the untrained eye they might look identical, but there are yellow undertones in the rye green to help brighten the room, and that's why we chose it. The apple green, as beautiful a colour as it is, is too warm for a room like this and does absolutely nothing for the space.

"It's okay," I say. But it's not. We're on a tight deadline with this project, and the client is expecting their dream home to be available to them in two short days. So yeah. Definitely not okay. "How long will it take to repaint?"

"I can have it ready by this time tomorrow."

I chew the inside of my cheek. It's 3 p.m. Not ideal. "If you can have it done by 10 a.m. tomorrow, I'll pretend like this never happened."

Ricardo's face is a portrait of relief. I know he relies on the work my company gives him — we pay well, and the work is relatively steady. "Got it, boss."

Thankfully, the other rooms have all been painted correctly.

It needs a good clean, but aside from a few tiny scratches on the hardwood floors in the living room — which Ricardo assures me will easily be dealt with before he leaves today — the rest of the house is ready.

I lean against the banister and exhale the breath I've been keeping sucked in throughout my tour of the home. *We're nearly there.* I pull out my phone and fire off a quick email to my warehouse manager, Simon, giving him the go-ahead to start loading the trucks for install day. Knowing that we're nearly there, that the finish line is officially in sight, should help to ease some of the pressure I feel, but it doesn't.

There's still so much to do.

I still need to send over a final list to Simon and his team to double-check that every item is included and packed securely onto the trucks. I also need to head back to the office and print off floor plans for each room, then come *back* to the house and make sure they're pasted everywhere so nobody has any excuses for putting things in the wrong places.

I glance at my watch and groan. It's 4 p.m. I can send Simon the list while I'm on the move, but the floor plans will have to wait until tomorrow. I've got a meeting with another client — at 5.30 p.m. on a Wednesday.

Who does that?

Even as I ask myself the question, I know the answer.

Cynthia Zensi does that. My mentor, my boss, the founder of Zensi Designs, and the current bane of my life. Well, one of them.

When I first started at Zensi Designs nearly seven years ago as an assistant, Cynthia had been a completely different person. She was an icon in the British design space with a reputation for creating elegant, sophisticated, and timeless interiors for her bursting little black book full of elite clients. She was a trendsetter. Innovative, bright, and bold.

And she was my idol.

I devoured every piece of information imaginable I could find about her, fervently collecting magazine profiles and touring the country to visit the spaces she designed. I remember spending the day in the lobby of a hotel she designed in Scotland just after I turned 18, marvelling at her skill, her vision, her talent.

Three years later, and fresh from university, it felt like destiny when she announced unexpectedly that she was looking for an assistant. I spent a full week working on my application, crafting the perfect cover letter, and putting together the perfect portfolio; I felt sick when I finally hit Send. The next three weeks passed in a blur of nail biting and refreshing my inbox every few minutes and miraculously ended with an invitation to interview. I ultimately beat out hundreds of applicants and earned the job as *Cynthia Zensi's* assistant.

Sometimes I wish I could go back in time and capture the essence of excitement, joy, and trepidation I had back on my first day of work, just to remember what it felt like. Seven years on and there's no trace of it anymore. Cynthia has managed to slowly suck the life out of the one thing that has ever really brought me any happiness.

Though, to be fair, she's sucked it out of herself as well.

Seven years and two messy divorces later, the Cynthia I once looked up to no longer exists. She's a shell of her former self, and I can't remember the last time she actually worked on a project. These days, she just palms them off on me, though she's more than happy to take the credit.

Her name still holds considerable weight in the design world, but that's only because of me. I've been single-handedly managing all of Cynthia's high-profile clients for the last few years, keeping the business afloat while Cynthia swans around doing God knows what. Everyone seems to believe that she's still behind the scenes working hard and that I'm just her conduit, but they're all my designs.

My ideas.

My vision.

But on paper, I'm still a *junior* designer, and nothing I do seems to convince her to give me the promotion and the title we both know I deserve.

So it doesn't surprise me in the slightest that she's locked in a meeting for me with a high-profile client at 5.30 p.m. on a Wednesday.

It does piss me off though.

IN THE MIDDLE of rush hour, it takes me just over an hour to make it to the West End. I'm still early for the meeting, but only just. I used my time on the tube, squashed between businessmen and school kids in dire need of deodorant, to draft my final list for Simon and study up on this new client.

I've got to hand it to Cynthia. She may not be working properly anymore, but she still knows how to pull in the most lucrative clients. I'm meeting with someone called Finn Hawthorne. He's the managing director for The August Room, a private members club that was founded in New York nearly 50 years ago. It's got a reputation as being one of the most exclusive and glamorous private clubs in the world, and they're looking to branch out to new locations. Apparently, London is the first place they've chosen for their expansion.

They've purchased a stunning Georgian townhouse in the centre of the West End, and Cynthia has earned us the contract to design it.

I feel a tiny bubble of excitement as I scan through the photos of the building. It's a truly remarkable space with four floors, each ripe for a redesign. Most of my recent projects have been residential, which is fun and all, but *this*? This is a real challenge, something I can sink my teeth into and really flex my design muscles. It's a listed property, so it'll be a tricky project because I'll have to be creative to make sure we don't break any rules about maintaining the property's historical integrity, but everything about this excites me.

Maybe I won't complain about Cynthia foisting *this* client on me.

The townhouse is about a ten-minute walk from the nearest tube station, and I join the rush hour madness as we file down the crowded London streets. I'm going through some preliminary ideas for the property in my mind, when a voice cuts through my thoughts.

It's coming from a man a few paces in front of me. I can't see his face, but he's tall with a rower's physique hidden under his navy blue blazer, and he has a head of short blond hair. He's on the phone, his voice — loud, deep, and distinctly American — cutting through the noise of the city around us.

"...landed a couple hours ago. Yeah. Pretty cold. Yeah. Yeah. Uh huh. Exactly."

I try to tune him out, my focus on the Google Maps route I'm following on my phone, but his next sentence pulls me back in.

"...meeting with the designer now." A pause and a low chuckle. "That's what I'm saying. You should see how much they've quoted." Another pause. Several hums. "Exactly. It's ridiculous. All that for choosing a couple shades of paint and picking out a few pillows at IKEA?" He laughs loudly at something the person on the other end says, and I can't help but scowl at his back.

His attitude toward my career is, sadly, not an uncommon one. Annoyingly, it's one that my parents have too. Maybe that's why his words feel like a personal attack on me.

When it comes to interior design, people only see the finished product — a beautifully designed space — and assume that all we've done is throw some paint on the walls and maybe artfully placed a rug here or there. Or they watch one of those 60-minute design shows on daytime TV and think that entire home renovations can be done in an hour.

They don't see the hours and hours of work we put in behind the scenes creating floor plans, managing contractors and warehouses, sourcing items, hauling around furniture only for the client to turn their nose up at it at the very last minute.

It's hard fucking work.

"...yeah, I'm going to see if I can get the price down at this..."

He trails off and I lose him as he makes a sharp turn and dips inside a coffee shop.

Good riddance.

I wish I knew which designer he's about to meet. I'd get in touch and warn them that they've got an asshole client coming their way.

The rest of the short walk is blissfully free of assholes, and by the time I reach the listing, I've mostly pushed him from my mind.

The townhouse is as stunning up close as it was in the pictures. The four floors tower over me, and I marvel at the beautiful façade made from greying stone. Whoever the previous owners were, it's clear that they took great care of it. I step under the portico, held up by four stone columns, and lift the large circular knocker. It swings against the door with a loud *bang*, announcing my arrival.

I wait, expecting the door to open any second now. But it doesn't. I knock again, a little harder this time, and wait. And wait.

And wait.

And *wait*.

I glance at my watch, irritation practically seeping into my bloodstream. 5.45 p.m. He's late. This doesn't bode well for the project.

I'm about five seconds away from pulling my phone out and trawling through my emails to find some contact details for this Finn Hawthorne — and proof that Cynthia *did* actually schedule this appointment — when a voice catches my attention.

It's loud, deep, and distinctly American.

"Amber? Amber Wyatt from Zensi Designs?"

I glance over my shoulder. There's a man striding toward me. He's tall — easily six feet four at *least* — and even in my heels, I can tell he'll be head and shoulders over me. He's shed the blazer, opting to hang it loosely from one arm. In his other hand he's holding a paper cup with a coffee shop logo pasted across the front wrapper.

Realisation dawns on me.

Oh no.

God, please no.

He grins at me as he steps underneath the portico and offers me his coffee-free hand. "Finn Hawthorne from The August Room. Sorry I'm late, but it's lovely to meet you."

2

FINN

MY DESIGNER IS LOOKING AT ME LIKE SHE SMELLS something awful.

Her ski slope nose is scrunched, and her eyebrows are knitted together in obvious displeasure. My hand, still outstretched between us, wavers slightly.

"You *are* Amber?" I clarify, wondering if I've just given a random woman the scare of her life. "From Zensi Designs? You work with Cynthia?"

It takes her another beat or two, but her features eventually smooth and she offers me a small, strained smile. "Yes." She reaches for my hand. "It's a pleasure to meet you, Mr Hawthorne."

Despite the pleasantries, her tone is clipped and cold, and she drops my hand like I've burned her. She gives a not-so-subtle glance at her watch and then gestures to the door. "Shall we?"

"Apologies again for the delay," I say as I sidestep her and stick the key in the door. "I got turned around trying to find this place. It's my first time in London and all these streets look exactly the same." I glance behind me and flash her a smile.

It isn't returned.

Her face is like thunder and my smile falters slightly. Surely this can't be because I was a few minutes late?

The door clicks open, providing a welcome distraction, and I step over the threshold into the building that is either going to make or break my career. We step into a large foyer with high ceilings, slightly chipped hardwood flooring, and peeling wallpaper. The electricity isn't working yet — haven't gotten around to getting that sorted yet — but the room is filled with enough natural light that the absence of a lamp or two isn't really noticeable.

It's easy to imagine this foyer filled with people, laughter, and music. I picture a reception desk against the back wall and comfortable armchairs slotted into each corner. Maybe we can even turn a few of the window areas into reading nooks for our daytime guests.

The door closes behind me and the *click click* of Amber's heels as she strides across the floor interrupts my thoughts. I hear her sharp intake of breath and glance over at her. For the first time in the brief few minutes we've known each other, her irritated expression truly clears.

She looks excited. Happy even. I prefer this look on her. Her eyes are wide and shining, and her lips curve upward into a genuine smile.

"It's beautiful," she says. Her voice is barely above a whisper, and I'm not sure she even intended to say that aloud.

I jump at the chance to try to mend the rocky start we've

gotten off to. "It really is," I say. "We were lucky to spot it on the market when we did."

Her smile immediately drops at the sound of my voice, lips thinning into a displeased line. "Right. Well, let's get started so we can both get back to our homes before it gets too late."

I wince, recognising the thinly veiled jab for what it is. Still, I'm determined to keep some semblance of polite conversation going, even if she seems desperate to avoid it. "I'm in a hotel actually. Not exactly home, but it'll do."

She makes a non-committal humming noise as she digs through her bag and pulls out a tablet. "Let's take it floor by floor, room by room. I'll be taking photos and videos as we go. Cynthia has already shared your overall vision for the London location of The August Room, but let me know if there's anything extra you'd like to add to my notes as we walk around."

She doesn't wait for me to respond before she begins snapping photos of the foyer. If her commitment to disliking me wasn't so disarming, I might be impressed with her work ethic. She's meticulous as she goes, cataloguing every inch of the foyer and pausing every few seconds to jot down some notes. As she throws herself into her work, I can see her start to relax.

I wish I could do the same.

There's a familiar knot of anxiety growing in the pit of my stomach. It's been there so long it may as well be another organ at this point. I can't remember a time when I didn't feel like this. Like I'm only one wrong move away from my world crumbling down around me.

Naively, I'd assumed that the promotion would help get rid of these feelings. If anything, they've only intensified over the last few months.

Finn Hawthorne, Managing Director.

The title I've been working toward for the last ten years is finally mine. So why does it make me feel sick? It's not like I haven't earned it. I've painstakingly climbed my way up the corporate ladder, starting off at the very bottom rung. I've done the jobs nobody else wanted to touch and excelled in all of them, proving myself every step of the way. After ten years of almost nonstop seventy- and eighty-hour workweeks, barely having enough time to see my family and friends or get more than five hours of sleep every night, *nobody* can say I haven't earned this.

And yet they do.

I can't pretend like I don't hear the whispers that follow me back at the office in New York. They're not subtle about it at all, mumbling about my CEO uncle doing me a favour, or how it's my last name that gets me places.

Don't get me wrong, it absolutely does.

I'm not an idiot. I know the *Hawthorne* name still means something in certain circles, and I know that it's afforded me certain privileges in life. Like this job for example. Maybe that's why I work as hard as I do, to try to show people that I'm more than just my name.

That's the whole point of this project if I'm being honest.

I led with it in my interview for the managing director position, and, surprisingly, the board loved it. It's what tipped me over the edge compared to the other candidates. They'd been wanting to expand The August Room abroad for years now but hadn't managed to figure out a viable expansion plan yet.

Enter *me* and my plans for opening a new location in London. I'd spent weeks poring over my application, making sure I'd considered everything possible to make my vision for the London expansion a success. I learned about UK trading laws, analysed our competitors to see what they were doing right and what we could do better, found a prime location in the middle of London, worked out a marketing plan, and even found a phenomenal designer — even if they *are* wildly overpriced.

I worked hard on my presentation and the board saw the value in it.

But nobody cares about that. They can't get over fact that my uncle sits on the board.

My mood sours even further as my thoughts drift to my uncle.

It's not like we're close. Far from it actually. Ernest Belmont, CEO of The August Room, married my aunt Marion when I was fifteen, so we didn't exactly spent my formative years going on fishing trips together and bonding. Even now, I wouldn't say we have a close relationship.

Ernest has always been awkward around our family — I think it stems from an old feud he's still nursing with my father and that awkwardness extends into the workplace. He avoids me for the most part and treats me like every other employee on the rare occasions we do have to interact.

That's why it's laughable when people suggest that *he's* the reason I am where I am today. Out of everyone on the board, *he* was the one holdout when it came to my promotion. If Ernest had had his way, I think I'd still be down in the mailroom with the interns.

"All right, Mr. Hawthorne." Amber swivels around on her heels, tablet in hand. She looks noticeably less irritated now, and it's a welcome change. We're on the fourth floor and the twilight sun peeking through the windows bathes her in a golden glow. She looks almost ethereal.

"I think I've got everything I need for today," she continues. She taps something quickly onto her tablet. "Do you have any questions for me?"

I shake my head. "I think you've got everything. Cynthia has the deck I sent through earlier this week."

"Yes, I've seen it. You've got a very..." She trails off and clicks her tongue. "You've got a very strong vision for this project."

"Is that a bad thing?"

"No, definitely not. I always prefer to work with clients who know what they want." She pauses again and reaches for a few strands of the cropped, dark brown hair that frames her face. "I'd love to discuss your budget. With the vision you've shared, I think we need to lock down a number that's reasonable for both parties."

I raise a brow, surprised. It's like she's read my mind. "I do have to admit, the figures Cynthia initially sent through are a little steeper than we'd been expecting."

The side of her face twitches. "This *is* a large scale project, Mr. Hawthorne."

"I'm aware," I say. She doesn't need to tell me that. I know just how big this project is. "I just think we can reach a compromise."

She opens her mouth like she's about to respond, but then clamps it shut. Debate flashes across her face, and I find she's terrible at masking her emotions. But I don't think she knows it. The realisation makes my lips twitch.

"How about this," she says diplomatically after a few

seconds. "Send over your rough budget report and I'll work on some design concepts and some costings. One with your budget in mind. One with mine. We'll go with whichever one you're happiest with."

"That sounds fair enough."

She huffs out a quiet sigh of relief and stuffs her tablet back into her bag. "Just to let you know, we're looking at about a twelve-month time frame for a project of this scope."

My heart drops and that knot of anxiety swells in my chest. *Twelve months?*

She accurately deciphers the look of shock that must be spasming across my face because she quickly adds, "Nine months at a stretch. It'll be a challenge, but I'm confident we can—"

"We're launching this summer." I swallow, trying to take a large and surreptitious gulp of air. This is not what I need right now. *This is not what I need.* I reach for my tie and tug it loose, wondering if I'm imagining the way it's begun to suffocate me. "Cynthia assured me it could be done in three months. That's part of the reason we went with Zensi Designs."

Her jaw clenches and I can tell that this news hasn't been relayed to her.

"Well," she says, her voice strained. "If that's what Cynthia's promised, then I'm sure we can accommodate you." She's grinding her jaw so hard I'm surprised it hasn't snapped yet. She repositions her bag on her shoulder and gives me a curt nod. "It's been lovely to meet you, Mr. Hawthorne." Except, her tone makes it sound like it's been anything but. "I'll be in touch shortly with some of my— *Cynthia's* initial concepts as discussed."

"How shortly?" I ask. "Three months deadline, remember?"

There it is again. That irritated twitch on the side of her face. I'm struck with the urge to reach forward and smooth it out.

"I'll have them over to you by the end of the week," she says through gritted teeth. And then she's turning on the balls of her feet — impressive given the heels — and storming back down the stairs before I can get in another word.

3

AMBER

CYNTHIA IS UNAPOLOGETIC.

"It's The August Room, darling," she purrs down the phone.

I can hear relaxing music playing in the background, and every so often, she pulls away from the speaker to bark an order at someone. I think she might be at a spa.

"How could I say no?" she continues. "Do you know what this could do for the brand? We get this right and we'll be the most in-demand interior design company in London."

Her use of "we" irks me because we're not a "we". It's just me.

"Cynthia, I have other clients," I tell her bluntly. "I can't dedicate the amount of time a three-month job of this size would need around my current workload."

"It's fine." I can picture her waving a heavily jewelled hand in front of her, a dismissive gesture she's done to me countless times. "Kirsty can take on your slack."

"*Kirsty?*" I like the girl and everything, but she's fresh out of university and needs more mentoring. "Cynthia, those are *my* projects. My designs. I've been working hard on th—"

"And you'll take The August Room and Hawthorne as your only client until the project is finished."

I don't think she even heard my interruption.

"See, darling," she says with that trademark dismissive drawl. "You're making a problem out of nothing. It's all sorted itself out, hasn't it?"

"But—"

"Darling, I've really got to run." I can hear a muffled voice letting her know the sauna is ready. I was right. She is at a spa. "Let's discuss this in person on Friday. Book somewhere nice for lunch — *Il Pampero*, perhaps? I've been dying for a good Italian meal."

"Cynthia, I *really*—"

"Ta ta, darling. We'll chat on Friday." She hangs up without waiting for me to say goodbye and I'm left staring at her name on my phone screen.

I could call her back, but there's no point. She won't answer. And even if she did, I know she won't listen to me. Not now anyway. Friday at lunch is my best chance of getting her to change her mind on this project.

Speaking of projects...I glance at my watch. It's just gone seven. Hawthorne and I spent longer walking through the town-house than I'd expected. It was easy to get lost in the details and the potential on the walls as we slowly combed through the building.

I have to hand it to Finn Hawthorne; he really did pick a great location. And with his vision for a decadent space that uses the building's pre-existing historical architecture, I can see

The August Room fitting in easily with London's swanky roster of private members clubs.

I tap my fingers impatiently against my thigh as my train home crawls slowly along the tracks. It's late, I know, but I'm itching to start sketching out some initial concepts. I spend the journey home going through each floor in my mind, picturing the empty building filled with furniture and art, the peeling cream walls painted with sultry colours, chandeliers hanging from the high ceilings.

I can't lie. I'm excited. This project might be the one that ends up making my career. Maybe it'll be the project that finally gets Cynthia to understand just how much I do for her, how much Zensi Designs needs me, how much *she* needs me.

It's doubtful — I've had this thought before — but this is definitely the biggest project that's ever landed in my lap. If Cynthia's ever going to change her ways, it's going to be because of The August Room and Finn Hawthorne.

The fact that the future of my career potentially lies in the hands of someone like him doesn't exactly fill me with joy. His reluctance to spend what my time and effort is worth doesn't put him high up on my list of people I want to work closely with. From experience, clients who get cagey about the budget are always the worst. They're the ones who are never satisfied and always want more even though they're paying for less.

Finn Hawthorne has *nightmare client* written all over him. But I've been in this industry for seven years now and I've met plenty of men like him. He's nothing special, and I know how to handle clients like him.

By the time I get home, it's just gone nine.

I say home, but it's not *my* home. Not really.

As soon as I push open the door, my mother's voice comes floating from the living room.

"*Be quiet!* Your brother is sleeping."

I roll my eyes, thankful that she can't see me, and bite down the urge to let her know she's being louder than I am right now. I kick off my heels and pad toward the living room. My mother and her husband are curled up on the sofa together watching last week's episode of *The Apprentice*.

Patrick, her husband, glances up at me as I enter. They've been together since I was ten, so he's really my stepfather, but I've never heard him refer to me as his stepdaughter before, so I'm only returning the favour. I'm always just Amber or *Michelle's daughter* when he talks about me, so he's just Patrick or *my mother's husband* to me.

"It's late," he says, and I have to assume that's the only greeting I'm going to get from him. "Where have you been?"

How many 28-year-olds have to deal with this level of interrogation every time they come home?

"Work," I say curtly. I let my unsaid "*obviously*" hang heavy in the air.

Patrick frowns, but he doesn't say anything. Instead he nudges my mother with his elbow and she finally glances over at me.

"You left the house at seven this morning and it's just gone nine!" Her lips thin into a frown. "I just don't understand what you're doing all day. Carlton, Angeline's boy, works twelve-hour shifts, but *he's* a doctor."

"And he's bringing home good money," Patrick chimes in.

My mother nods enthusiastically. "Exactly. Do you know he bought Angeline a car for her fiftieth? A nice one too."

21

They stare pointedly at me, and I grit my teeth. "Well, I've still got six years left until your fiftieth, don't I? Plenty of time to save."

My mother snorts. "Not on that salary there isn't. And besides, you're meant to be saving for your own place."

I want to scream, *"Then why mention the fucking car?"* But I don't. Not this time anyway. I've done it before, given into my urges to throw their ridiculous logic back into their faces, and it's not ended well for me.

"We've been meaning to talk to you about that," Patrick says. "Are you still on track to be out by the end of the year?"

"Yes."

"Are you sure?" my mother asks. "Because you said that last year, and you're still here."

This is what I mean when I say this isn't my home. It can't be. Home is supposed to be where the heart is, and there's no heart in here for me.

"I don't know if you've noticed, but there's a recession going on," I say. I immediately regret the tiny ounce of sass I throw them, because Patrick's eyes narrow. "But I *am* on track, and I'll be gone by the end of the year. I promise."

I'm hoping I'll be gone in a few months actually, but they don't need to know that. I'm so close to leaving, I'm not jinxing anything.

Patrick gives me a satisfied nod and they turn back to the TV. I've been dismissed.

I dip into the kitchen and make myself a quick bowl of instant noodles and baked beans — a disgusting delicacy that I stand by — and then hurry up to my room. It's the smallest room in the house and, even though I pay rent each month,

Patrick refuses to give up his "office" and swap with me. It's irritating, but I don't really mind. The space is small, but it's *mine*. And when you don't have much, you cling to what you can get.

I pass by my younger brother's room and peek my head inside.

As expected, he's not sleeping. He's sitting up in the bed, Nintendo Switch in hand, playing what sounds like *Mario Kart*. He dives under his blanket as soon as the door squeaks open, but he's not fast enough.

I shake my head. "Gotta do better than that, kiddo. You would've been caught if it wasn't me right now."

Noah pokes his head out from underneath the blanket. His lips split into a toothy grin as he spots me. "Amber!"

"*Shush!*" I hiss, but there's no bite in it. He leaps out of bed and hurries to the door.

"You said you'd be home early today." He pouts up at me, his big brown eyes wide and sad. "I wanted to play *Mario Kart* with you. I think I know how to beat you on *Rainbow Road* now."

I bite back a laugh. "That's fighting talk right there."

"You want to play now?" he asks, waving his *Switch* in front of me.

I shake my head. "Sorry, kiddo, not today. Mum will kill me if she hears us, and I need to finish off a few things for work."

His pout deepens. "You're always working."

"I know," I say. "But how about this? This weekend, we can spend the *whole day* playing together. And, if you manage to beat me, I'll take you out for ice cream. How does that sound?"

He grins widely. "Sounds great!"

23

I shoo him back into bed and then tiptoe out of his room. I really do love him.

I lied when I said there's no heart in this place for me. There is. But only in Noah. When I eventually leave, he's the only thing I'm going to miss.

My room is about a quarter of the size of Noah's room, barely giving me enough space for my bed, a tiny desk, and a clothing rail I use as my wardrobe.

I sit at my desk and attack my noodles and beans while I scroll through my phone. There are a few email notifications from Cynthia at the top of my screen, but I can't bring myself to look at them yet. That's a problem for tomorrow's Amber to deal with. Instead, I open up my chat history with my best friend, Bailey. It's been a while since we last saw each other — we're both so busy with work — and I miss her.

AMBER

Today has been A DAY

Miss you. You free this weekend?

BAILEY

Miss you more!

I've got a PR event in central on Friday night. You want to come? I'm sure I can get you on the guest list.

AMBER

Yeah sure, why not! Could use some fun

Bailey is an influencer, and a really good one at that. She's built up her own little community of women online and has managed to sustain a career out of it. I'm so proud of her. And a little jealous too. I love that she's found something she's so passionate about *and* that it pays her bills.

Interior design is my passion, no doubt, but I don't know how long I can do this — the long hours, the endless projects, the lack of recognition — without a pay rise.

I pull out my tablet and scroll through some of the photos I took today. As I swipe, my excitement for the project builds again. This is really it.

This is going to be the project that makes my career.

I grab my pencil, open up a blank canvas on my tablet, and get to work.

4

AMBER

Cynthia's thin brows are pinched in the middle, her garish glasses sliding down her nose as she swipes through my initial design concepts.

"And you think he'll be happy with this?" She peers at me over the rim of her glasses, looking distinctly unimpressed.

"Not at all," I say cheerfully. I lean across the table, avoiding Cynthia's mostly untouched plate of pasta, and tap the screen. "*This* is the budget design. Mr. Hawthorne isn't convinced our services are worth the price you initially quoted, so I agreed to send over two design concepts and costings. He can pick between the two."

And I know which one he's going to choose. It's not like the budget concept is a bad design by any means — it's just not what he's looking for. You might see something like this in an airport lounge or a mid-market hotel lobby. Not bad, but not special.

He's going to absolutely hate it, and the thought fills me with a sadistic kind of glee.

"*This* is the actual design," I say, swiping across the screen.

My initial concept for the third floor bathroom fills the screen. I've gone for decadent pink wallpaper with bold floral prints, pastel onyx carved sinks, and floor-length ornate mirrors on either side of the room.

The vibe is different from the New York location, where the walls are painted in moody blacks and blues and the only light comes from the Edison lamps sparsely dotted around each room. It's been exquisitely designed, but members clubs using that style are a dime a dozen over here. The August Room needs something bold. Something that'll stand out from the rest and put it quickly on the map on this side of the pond.

Cynthia continues to swipe through my concepts and I bite back the smile I can feel tugging at my lips. Playful, decadent, eccentric — it's going to be a fast favourite among London's artsy upper class.

She hums quietly once she reaches the final slide. "Not bad."

My smile falters. Not bad? *Not bad?* "Is that—" I swallow. "Is that it?"

Cynthia shrugs and sets the tablet down. "You've done a fine job. Send it over to Hawthorne and get his thoughts."

This is...*odd*. Cynthia isn't shy when it comes to critiquing my work. She once spent ten minutes tearing into me because she'd disagreed with my choice of wood for a kitchen island. She's usually happy to take any opportunity to poke holes in my work all under the guise of *"helping you grow"*, so her silence now is unnerving.

I eye her warily, wondering if she's going to suddenly switch and attack me for my choice in wallpaper. "Are you sure?" I ask. "What did you think about the second floor lounge? You didn't think it was too busy? And what about the plasterwork in the reception? Did tha—"

"Like I said," she says abruptly. "The concepts are sound. Let's get Hawthorne's thoughts on them now."

This is new territory with Cynthia. I don't think I've ever come out of a design meeting with her without a notebook full of amends and my self-esteem shot to pieces.

"Send them on my behalf," she adds casually. "Let him know I'm *very* excited to be working on this. Maybe we should organise a lunch together as well. Will you sort that out?"

I sink into my seat and grit my teeth. It's not enough that she's going to steal the credit for my work *again*, I also still have to play the assistant role? "I'm sure Kirsty can organise a lunch for you two."

Cynthia shakes her head. "No, I don't want Kirsty anywhere near this project. She's got too much going on, what with taking on your extra work."

She says it like *I'm* the one who asked for this.

"I don't want to overwhelm her. That's when mistakes happen. You'll handle everything to do with Hawthorne and The August Room. Check my calendar for a lunch opening."

I nod, not trusting the words that might come out of my mouth if I open it, and jot down a reminder to schedule a lunch with Hawthorne.

We sit in silence for a few minutes. Cynthia pushes her pasta around her plate and sips her tea, seemingly unaware of the quiet fury simmering inside me. Or maybe she is aware and just doesn't care. I wouldn't put it past her.

It's only when I'm sure that the next sound out of my mouth isn't going to be a frustrated shriek that I speak again. "This is a huge project," I say, choosing my words carefully. "And I'm grateful that you think I'm up for the task."

That gets her. She glances up from her plate and there's a gleam in her eye that tells me I've hit just the right note to stroke her ego.

"Well, darling," she drawls. "I've always thought that you've got talent, you just needed the right mind to nurture you. You're a bit rough around the edges still, but you're well on your way to becoming an impressive designer in your own right."

I smile through clenched teeth. I'm pretty sure that's her version of a compliment, no matter how backhanded it might be. "Yes. Exactly. And I really appreciate your mentorship and all the advice you give me."

Her lips, painted a bright pink today, stretch into a pleased smirk.

"With a project as big as this, I think it's the perfect opportunity to prove that I'm ready for the next step," I say quickly before she can interrupt. "Once this is over, I'd love to discuss promotion opportunities."

Her smirk drops almost immediately. "A *promotion?*" She says the word like it's dirty. Like it's personally offended her in some way.

I don't say anything, letting the silence between us grow wider and wider so she can tell that I'm serious about this.

"I *suppose*," she says slowly, drawing out each syllable like it's hurting her to say it. "I suppose, given the scope of this project, that we could discuss a promotion once you've delivered."

"And a pay rise."

Her thin brows shoot into her hairline. "I don't think—"

"Cynthia, I work harder than everyone at Zensi Designs," I say, hoping she can hear my unsaid *'even you'*. "I've been here seven years and I'm still a *junior* designer. I love what I do, but I can't make it work for much longer on a salary like this."

She purses her lips. "Very well. If you can deliver this project on time and to Hawthorne's satisfaction, you'll get your promotion and a *small* pay increase to reflect your new responsibilities."

I bite the inside of my cheeks to stop a wide smile from betraying my poker face. "That sounds fair to me."

"BUT HOW MUCH IS SHE going to give you?"

I'm in a ridiculously fancy car with Bailey on our way to the launch event for a new high-end vodka brand. These kind of events aren't usually my vibe but, between our busy schedules, Bailey and I barely get a chance to see each other these days. I'll take what I can get, even if it means spending the better part of our night in a crowded bar while Bailey does her thing.

I've just finished giving her the rundown on everything that happened with Cynthia today. "I'm not sure," I say. "We didn't talk about numbers. I didn't want to scare her off. Getting her to agree to this was like pulling teeth in the first place."

"She's so weird," Bailey mutters with a roll of her eyes. "And what's with her *still* stealing your credit? You need to get out of there, babe. Start your own company. You know you'd smash it."

I snort and shake my head, dispelling any visions of the pipe dream I've held for more years than I can count now. "Cynthia may be annoying, but Zensi Designs gets brilliant jobs. It would take me years to build up trust and a client base like this. And I'd need money to start my own thing up, and I definitely don't have that. I'm stuck here, for now at least."

Bailey exhales a loud breath. "I'm sorry. But at least this project will be fun?"

I shrug. "The building is beautiful and I've got so much creative freedom, but the managing director is a bit of an asshole. I'm hoping we won't have much to do with each other beyond this initial start."

I imagine Hawthorne will jet off back to America once he's approved the designs, leaving some probably underpaid lackey here to check in every so often. I feel a brief wave of pity for this unnamed lackey, but it doesn't last long. All I can think about is how I'll be able to work in peace without Hawthorne's interference.

"Sounds great," Bailey says with a wide grin. "And how's house hunting going?"

I groan. "It's not going fast enough."

Sometimes I feel like I can't catch a break. Work is shit. Home is shit. Everything's shit.

Bailey reaches across the empty seat between us and gently squeezes my hand. We've been friends since we were kids, and she knows exactly how desperate I am to get out of my mother's house and have a place to call my own. "You're nearly there, babe," she says softly. "This year is going to be it for you, I can feel it. Promotion. Pay rise. New house." She pauses and wiggles her brows. "New man?"

That gets a giggle out of me. It's not like I'm actively opposed to dating, I've just been so busy I've not been able to devote the time to it. My last date was over half a year ago, and while we had at least a smidgen of chemistry, he'd been unimpressed with my haphazard availability, and we fizzled out after four lukewarm dates.

"We'll see," I say. "I'm not sure I'm ready to give anyone that much time just yet. Especially not with this new project."

"Just keep an open mind," Bailey says. "You never know when you might meet someone."

The car grinds to a slow halt outside a bar. Even from out here, I can tell that it's heaving inside. There's a queue that disappears all the way round the corner and the muffled sounds of music and laughter mix together to create an incomprehensible din.

I shoot Bailey a wary look. "I'm *not* standing in a queue all night."

She laughs and waves two slim, silver tickets in front of me. "Perks of the job, babe. No queuing for us."

Our driver hurries over to Bailey's door and lets us out. All eyes are on us as we bypass the queue. Bailey flashes the tickets at the bouncer, who inspects them briefly before ushering us inside.

"Is this brand any good?" I yell over the blaring techno music as we enter the main room of the bar. It's filled with people laughing, dancing, and sloshing drinks over each other.

Bailey shrugs. "I've not tried it before. The owner reached out to a bunch of us on Instagram and asked us to come down tonight and give it a go. He's trying to compete with the big names, so he needs some social media hype behind him to get started."

I nod. It makes sense, and he's certainly going to get a lot of visibility from the crowd in the room tonight. I recognise a handful of people I usually only see on my Instagram feed as we push through the crowd. They're all holding up bottles and smiling happily at the various cameras around looking, for all the world, like they're having a brilliant time.

Bailey leads me over to the bar, where we manage to slide onto two stools just as the previous inhabitants disappear onto the dance floor. We order our drinks — Bailey gets her standard cranberry and vodka, and I get a passion fruit martini — and Bailey immediately begins snapping photos.

"Sorry, sorry," she says with a grimace as she drags my glass away from me to get it into some better lighting. "I promise I won't be like this all night."

"It's fine," I say with a laugh. "It's your job; go wild."

I like watching Bailey work. She's got this confidence about her as she angles her camera in just the right position, and I love seeing it burst through. There were a few years after we finished school and I was heading to university when she didn't have this brightness to her. Her parents, as lovely as they are overall, weren't happy with her decision not to go to university. They weren't supportive of her career choices, nervous that it wouldn't amount to anything.

I'm so happy that she's proved them wrong.

Maybe it'll be my turn to prove my mother and Patrick wrong next.

You'd think that being an interior designer at one of the most sought after companies in the country would make them proud. But it doesn't.

They've never seemed to understand my job — never taken the *time* to understand it — and it doesn't help that Cynthia barely pays me above minimum wage. Patrick seems to think all

I do is *"doodle, paint, and shop"* for a living and my mother never misses the opportunity to tell me about the children of all her friends. Somehow, they all seem to be lawyers and doctors earning six figures and buying their parents cars and houses.

And my dad? My *actual* dad? To be fair to him, I have no idea what he thinks about my career choices. I only see him once or twice year if I'm very unlucky, and our conversations rarely revolve around me.

"Amber," Bailey hisses suddenly, reaching out to grab my arm. "Look lively, babe. You've got eyes on you."

I swivel around on my stool and realise that she's right. A guy is staring at me from across the room. When our eyes meet he grins sheepishly, obviously aware that he's been caught. I expect him to drop his gaze or quickly hurry away, but he doesn't.

He pushes through the crowd with surprising speed, and before I know it, he's standing in front of me. Bailey pretends to be extremely interested in the bottom of her cocktail and leaves us to it.

His name is Mark and he's handsome in a boyish kind of way. I'm pretty sure he's at least a few years younger than me, but I have to hand it to the kid: He's got game. Before I know it, I'm laughing at something he's said and then he's handing me his phone.

Bailey lets out a not so quiet *"woohoo"* under her breath behind me as I tap in my number and Mark's cheeks redden slightly. Once my number is safely saved in his phone, he grins widely, promises to message me sometime soon, and then disappears back into the crowd.

"He's definitely gone to brag to his friends," Bailey cackles as soon as he's out of hearing range. Her laughter is infectious, and I can't help but join in.

"I think that's the first time I've been hit on in months," I say as I laugh.

"That's only because it's the first time you've been *out* in months," Bailey says, and she's got a point. "But we'll discuss baby face in a minute." She nods at someone over my shoulder and then offers me an apologetic grimace. "I've got to go and do the rounds. There are a few people here I should probably be seen with."

"Go, go. I'll be right here when you get back." I wave her off and signal to the bartender for another passion fruit martini. I'm swiping through Instagram aimlessly in an attempt to avoid making eye contact with anyone while I'm alone, when someone enters my personal space.

I'm not sure why, but I assume it's Mark back again having plucked up the courage to maybe ask me for a dance, and I swivel around on my stool.

It's not Mark.

5

FINN

Even if I hadn't known who she was, I'm pretty sure Amber would've managed to drag my attention away from this incredibly dull conversation the second she walked into the room.

I nod along, not really listening as Rob — I *think* it's Rob — gives me his well-rehearsed spiel about his brand. I *should* be listening, though. Rob owns the vodka brand hosting this event, and we're currently looking for an exclusive supplier for the London location of the club.

That's the only reason I'm even here right now. I'd much rather be holed up in my hotel room going over my plans for the expansion for the nth time, but this is important. We need a supplier. Someone fresh and exciting to give us an edge over the other members clubs around. So yes, I absolutely should be listening to Rob's pitch right now, but I'm not.

I'm too busy watching Amber.

She's here with a friend, an equally pretty young woman

with a cloud of thick, curly hair. But I don't have eyes on the friend.

Just her.

She's wearing a pair of slim-fitting jeans that hug her waist, showing off a figure I hadn't noticed back at the property, a strapless black top wrapped tightly around her torso, and strappy heels. She looks stunning.

She laughs at something her friend says as they meander through the crowd and head to the bar. I don't know how, but her laugh, soft and tinkling, cuts through the loud, thumping music and hits my ears like she's standing right next to me.

What a laugh. I want to hear it again.

"...hoping to break into America. What do you think?"

I blink, reluctantly dragging my attention away from Amber and turning back to Rob. "What was that?"

"I was just saying," he yells over the music. "We'd love to branch out into the States. If things go well here, what would you think about trialling us back home?"

I frown. Have I accidentally already agreed to this? "Send me your proposal and we'll definitely look over it."

Rob's eyes light up and he immediately starts digging around in his pocket for his phone. "I'll have my assistant send it over right away."

"No rush," I say, my gaze slipping back over to Amber.

Unsurprisingly, she's been approached. I watch as she throws her head back, laughing freely and loudly at something this potential suitor has said. It's a sharp contrast to the Amber I met two days ago. It's like they're two different people, and the Amber I'm looking at right now is a stranger to me.

That irritates me more than it should. What I wouldn't give to be on the receiving end of one of those smiles. Though, that seems unlikely. She has her hackles up around me, and I'm not sure why.

Potential suitor pulls his phone out and hands it to her. On her other side, her friend grins widely and mumbles something, clearly encouraging her.

When we first met, I'd assumed that maybe she was just the kind of person who was always a bit standoffish, and I'd tried not to take it personally. But watching her now, smiling as she eagerly taps her number into his phone...I realise I've read her all wrong.

It's *me* she has the problem with.

Why does that bother me so much?

I can practically hear my sister, Nel, in the back of my mind, cackling the answer we both know to be true. I'm a people pleaser. Always have been. I want people to like me. To *see* me. To know I'm more than what their baseless assumptions might have led them to think.

Potential suitor takes his phone back and gives her a wave before disappearing back into the crowd. As soon as he's gone, Amber immediately turns to her friend and they collapse into a fit of giggles. Her friend says something, nods in the opposite direction, and then hops off her stool, leaving Amber alone.

"...work with you. What do you think?"

"Yeah, sounds good," I say absentmindedly. Before I can really give it much thought, I stand up and slide out of the booth we're sitting in. "Look, Rob, I've just seen someone I know. We'll continue this talk later, all right? You've got my number."

I don't wait for his response and immediately begin pushing

through the crowd. She's sipping on her cocktail when I approach, aimlessly tapping on her phone now that she's alone.

I sidle into the tiny gap next to her. "Fancy seeing you here."

She turns to me, that wide smile stretching her cheeks. The second she lays eyes on me, though, the smile disappears and a look of alarm replaces it.

"Mr Hawthorne?"

"Just Finn is fine," I say, flashing her a smile of my own, hoping to coax her one back out.

No such luck.

She purses her lips as a hand floats up to her hair and twists a lock around her finger. "What're you doing here?"

"I could ask you the same thing."

She doesn't respond, clearly waiting for me to go first.

All right. I'll bite.

"We're in talks with the owner about using this brand as our exclusive vodka supplier over here," I explain. "He invited me and I thought this would probably beat sitting in my hotel room alone." A lie. I'm only here out of a sense of obligation, but Amber's presence has become an unexpected bonus.

She nods, seemingly satisfied with my answer.

"And you?" I ask when it becomes clear that she's not going to offer up the information unprompted. "Is this kind of thing usually your scene?"

She snorts and shakes her head before pointing in the direction her friend disappeared. "Not at all. I'm here with my best friend as her plus-one. She's an influencer and got invited by the brand to come and do her thing."

An influencer. That's interesting and good to know. I've got an influencer strand in our marketing plan, but I've not given it much thought beyond *"should probably research some influencers"*.

"Anyone I might know?"

She shrugs and a confused look flickers across her face. Like she can't quite work out why I'm still here talking to her. An awkward silence that lasts for far too long passes between us.

"Anyway—" she begins.

"I got—" I say.

She offers me a polite smile that borders on a grimace. "You first."

"I was just going to say, I received the design concepts."

For the first time, something other than barely concealed irritation flashes across her face. She looks...excited?

"Glad to hear it," she says slowly, and I can tell she's choosing her words carefully. "Any initial thoughts on which one you'll go with?"

I level her with a look. For some reason, it feels like she's toying with me. Like this is a game for her and I'm not allowed to know all the rules just yet. "I think that's obvious."

A shadow of a smile teases her lips. "Humour me."

"The first concept wasn't bad at all, it just wasn't...It wasn't what we're looking for."

She nods and, for some reason, she looks ridiculously pleased with herself.

"The second one was much better. It was perfect, actually."

I'd been a bit put out after seeing the first concept designs and wondered if I'd made the wrong choice going with Zensi Designs. But the second concept? I've never seen anything like it. Elegant, bright, bold, eclectic — something to stand out among the sea of dark, moody members clubs with low lighting that London and New York have somehow managed to amass in droves.

"It's definitely going to cost more than I'd been expecting, but Cynthia captured my vision perfectly," I say, expecting her to be pleased. But she actually looks annoyed.

"That's Cynthia for you," she says dully. "I'm glad you liked the designs, Mr Hawthorne."

"Finn."

"*Finn*," she says pointedly, like it's a chore to say my name. "We'll get started right away on Monday booking contractors and getting samples in." She pauses, looking uncertain for a moment. "I'll be overseeing this project, just so you know. Cynthia is...Cynthia has—"

"She's busy," I finish for her. I'm no stranger to higher-ups passing their workload onto their juniors. I hate it, if I'm being honest. That's why I try to do as much of the legwork myself as possible when I'm involved in a project. But I know how corporate life works. I know how to play the game. "That's fine. If Cynthia's delegated this to you, I trust her decision. It means we'll be seeing a lot more of each other then, I suppose."

"You're not heading back to New York?"

I shake my head. To be honest, I probably should. This isn't my only project right now — the New York location is busier than ever — but this launch is my priority.

It needs to be a success and I can't trust anyone here to make sure that happens.

But I don't tell her that. Instead, I say, "I'm staying until right after the launch. I'm a hands-on kind of guy."

If *hands-on* is a synonym for "*my anxiety will quite literally not let me step away until I'm sure everything is perfect"*, then sure.

She nods and then turns back to her drink. I recognise the dismissal for what it is, but I'm not ready to let go just yet.

Something else is bothering me.

"Since we're going to be working closely for a few months," I say. "There's something I want to ask."

She looks over at me and raises an eyebrow in silent response. Her lack of desire to please me, to jump at my every command or question is oddly refreshing. I may effectively be her boss for the next three months, but it's very clear that we're playing on her turf right now.

"Is there a problem here?" I ask. "Between us, I mean."

She blinks, and I'm sure that's not the question she was expecting. "Why would there be a problem?"

"Because I'm getting the impression that you don't like me very much."

Her lips twitch almost imperceptibly. "Really."

It's not a question. She knows she's been caught and...I think that pleases her. She's *glad* that I can tell she doesn't like me.

"Yes, really." I cock my head to the side and frown. "If there's something I said or did to get on your bad side, I apologise."

I half expect her to deny it or even apologise for being so obvious, but she does neither.

"Why does it bother you so much?"

Now that's not the question *I* was expecting. Her brutal honesty and refusal to hide behind pleasantries inspires me, so I tell her the truth.

"I'm not used to having a beautiful woman dislike me. Most seem to find me charming."

"Ah," she says, clearly biting back a smile. "So it's a case of a bruised ego."

"Something like that."

"Have you ever considered that you're not as charming as you think you are?"

"I can honestly say that the thought has never crossed my mind."

She laughs at that. *Actually* laughs, like the kind of laugh that makes her throw her head back and her shoulders shake.

It's beautiful.

"Well, Hawthorne, you've yet to charm me."

She's still refusing to use my first name, but at least she's dropped the *mister*.

"I don't think that's true," I say with a grin. There's been a shift. I can feel it. Her hackles are still up, but she's definitely not as wary around me as she was before. "I think you're plenty charmed, you're just pretending otherwise."

She hums and then gives me a little shrug before she turns back to her drink. "Guess we'll never know."

I want to say more, to see how far we can go with this interesting back and forth we've developed, but her friend suddenly appears by her side. Her gaze, inquisitive and guarded, rakes over me before she jerks her head toward the back of the room.

"A girl I know has a booth back there. You want to go join them?"

Amber nods and slides off her stool. She glances briefly in my direction and gives me a perfunctory head tilt before she disappears into the crowd. They're still close enough that their voices float over to me as they make their way to their new booth.

"Who was that?" her friend asks.

Amber's response hits my ears as clearly as if she were standing right beside me. "Nobody important."

6

AMBER

One perk of having The August Room as my only client for the next three months is that I don't have to go into the office as often as before.

For the most part, my projects tend to be in residential spaces, and I can't exactly set up camp in a client's living room to work, so I usually spend a lot of time at the Zensi Designs office. Located in the loft of a converted warehouse, our office isn't particularly spacious, and even though there are only a handful of us, it can get pretty claustrophobic fast. Especially with Cynthia only a glass partition away on the days she actually bothers to come in.

But now...*Now*, I have an entire property to myself. My plan is to establish an office area on the fourth floor in the back-room where the sun hits just right in the afternoon for that extra serotonin boost. It makes sense, since Hawthorne's already earmarked this room as the office for when the club launches.

It'll be nice to have space for myself, where I can concentrate and throw myself into this project without worrying about distractions or people hovering over my shoulder nit-picking every last choice I make. My to-do list is already a mile long, and with only three months to the launch date, I don't have any time to waste.

Firstly, I need to firm up the design concepts. Along with his confirmation of the budget, Hawthorne sent a small list of suggestions over the weekend, and they're not half bad. For the most part, it seems like he just wants to bring in more of the atmosphere from the New York location so there's some continuity between the two spaces. That's an easy enough fix — a few darker shades of paint here and there and low mood lighting in the corridors — and, if I'm being honest, a fair request. But I hope it doesn't become a habit. There's nothing I hate more than having to go back and forth with a client on things we've already agreed on.

After that, I need to start contacting suppliers and contractors. It's one of the more tedious parts of the job and will likely make up the bulk of my afternoon. Not the most fun of tasks, sitting hunched over my laptop sending email after email and hoping they'll respond in a somewhat timely manner, but a necessary evil. Once that's all done, I'm free to get started on the *fun*. Sourcing furniture, decorations, and artwork to make each room in the townhouse come to life.

The sky is overcast and grim — a standard March morning here — but the property looks just as beautiful as last week as I approach it. My dream home definitely isn't in London but if it *was*, it might just be this place.

As I climb the stairs, I imagine this building filled with whispers of me. Photos of me and my friends will line the walls. The rooms will be filled with furniture and art that I've painstakingly picked out. It'll be warm and cosy, a space I've carved out with *me* in mind.

I'm a long way from owning something like this, but a girl can dream, and I'm happy to start off small. If all goes well, I'll be out of my parents' house in the next few months and into a small two-bedroom flat on the outskirts of London. Nothing too wild, and a far cry from the townhouse I'm currently in, but it'll be *mine*.

My first *real* home.

The thought always makes me smile, but today even more so than usual. I can feel it — this dream I've slowly been working toward for as long as I've been able to dream — and I'm close. *So* close. Give me three months and it'll be just like Bailey said. I'll have the promotion, a pay rise, *and* a new house.

And then I'll work on the whole *new man* thing.

Maybe.

The second I reach the fourth floor landing, my phone buzzes angrily in my pocket. I take it out and glance at it, my mood souring almost instantly. An email notification stretches across the centre of my screen.

FROM: Finn Hawthorne <fhawthorne@theaugustroom.com>
SUBJECT: Further thoughts
BODY: Hi Amber. Have had some more thoughts about the wallpaper on the third floor, can we dis…

See *this*? This is exactly what I was hoping to avoid. I swipe away the notification and barrel toward the backroom door, irritation bubbling inside me like a volcano. Maybe I can pretend I haven't seen it and tell him it's too late to make any more changes.

I throw open the door — my mind racing to figure out a professional and polite way to decline this amend — and immediately freeze.

Finn Hawthorne is sat on the floor, back pressed up against the wall. His laptop rests precariously on his thighs, and there's a sea of paper scattered around him. He doesn't notice me at first. His brows are furrowed, eyes glued to the screen in front of him as he furiously hits the keys on his laptop.

My phone vibrates again and somehow I know — just *know* — that it's another email from him.

The sound seems to pull him out of whatever trance he's in because he looks up suddenly, jolts when he spots me, and blinks.

"Amber?"

I nod, still hovering in the doorway. "Hawthorne."

He rubs at his eyes and it's only then that I notice how tired he looks. His hair is mussed, like he's been doing nothing but running his hands through it, and his eyes are dark and heavy. I wonder how well he slept last night. Judging by the two styrofoam coffee cups beside him, and the bluish purple smudges beneath his eyes, not very well.

"What're you doing here?" He runs a hand down his face and tries to stifle a yawn. "Did you get my emails?"

I ignore his first question. "The emails you *just* sent?"

He nods, apparently not seeing the problem at all. "Any thoughts?"

"I've not had the chance to look through them yet," I say.

My jaw is working overtime to stop me from saying something I'll regret. "Given that it's only just gone 9 a.m."

Either he doesn't hear the sarcasm dripping from my tone or he just doesn't care. Instead of looking even vaguely apologetic, he merely yawns again and stretches. As he leans back, the hem of his shirt rises and I catch a glimpse of taut skin and a streak of golden curls dipping into the waistband of his trousers.

I look away quickly.

"Are you going to come in?" he asks.

I'm still standing the doorway, and I hate it, but I feel like I'm intruding. This was supposed to be *my* safe space for the next few months, but he's claimed it for himself already.

I shake my head. "I was just leaving."

"You just got here," he says with a frown. "Why *are* you here?"

"No reason," I lie. "Just in the area and thought I'd get some work done. But you've clearly set up in here." I shrug, like it's no big deal. "I'll find another room."

He shakes his head and runs a hand through his hair. "This is going to be the office anyway; you might as well use it. There's plenty of space."

I can't think of an excuse that's not the verbal equivalent of a childish foot stomp. "All right."

I step into the room and make my way to the corner closest to the window. The sill stretches out just enough to make a little nook for me to sit on.

"Maybe you should do this room first?" he says, watching as I pull my laptop and tablet out of my bag. "Decorate it and get all the furniture in. I think we could both do with a desk."

"That's the plan," I grit out and remind myself that he's

trying to be helpful. That he doesn't mean to be annoying. That he doesn't realise he's talking to me like I'm an idiot.

"Great," he says brightly. "How long do you think it'll take? Do you think we could have everything in here by the end of the week?"

"Unlikely."

"Well, how long will it take?" he pushes, his brows knitting in the middle again. "It's just one room."

Just one room.

I run a hand through my hair, my fingers twisting tightly around a few strands at the front. It's ten past nine on a Monday morning and I'm already on edge. Is this how the next three months are going to be? Him making *suggestions* every few days? Me desperately trying to resist the urge to call it quits on this project before it's even really started?

"It's not *just one room*," I say, and there's more venom in my tone than I'd like.

He's a client, I tell myself. An annoying client, but a client all the same. I take a deep breath and remind myself just how much is riding on the success of this project.

"There are a lot of things I have to do first. Hire contractors, order in paint and wallpaper. Source the furniture. The list goes *on*. So forgive me if it takes me a little longer than a week to get things going."

To his credit, he looks a little contrite. He opens his mouth like he's about to say something, but then his laptop *pings* and his gaze slides down toward his screen. Frustration, clear as day, flashes across his face as he reads whatever email has just come in. I'd be lying if I said the look doesn't give me a tiny bit of satisfaction. I'm glad that he's currently feeling even a tiny fraction of the irritation I am.

I use this sudden distraction as an opportunity to go through my emails.

I was right. The one that just came in *was* another one from him.

FROM: Finn Hawthorne <fhawthorne@theaugustroom.com>
SUBJECT: RE: Further thoughts
BODY: Also the reception area rug choices...maybe a bit *too* bold?

My brow twitches. Just two days ago he was saying that I captured his vision perfectly, but now there are suddenly problems with the wallpaper and my choice in rugs?

I glance over at him. He's glaring at his laptop like it's personally wronged him. One hand drifts up from his keyboard and tugs at the salmon coloured tie around his neck. He lets out a loud groan.

A nicer person than me would ask him what's wrong, but I'm still irritated about the emails, so I ignore the obvious conflict he's going through. Instead, I pull up the design concepts on my tablet and swipe through them.

As a gesture of goodwill, I spend the next two hours making the amends he's asked for. I add the low lighting in the corridors and swap out the rug in the reception for something a little more subtle, but the wallpaper on the third floor makes me pause. It's perfect and brings the whole third floor landing together. I flick through a few other options I'd been considering, but none of them make the space pop as much as my current choice.

I make an executive decision.

I'm not changing the wallpaper. He's just going to have to deal.

"I've got the *final* designs ready," I say, hoping he hears the pointed emphasis there. "If you want to take a look."

He nods, pushes himself up from the floor, and crosses the distance between us in three long strides. I move to hand my tablet over to him but he drops onto the windowsill beside me. His arm brushes against mine as he leans over my shoulder.

Has this guy never heard of personal space?

He hums quietly as he flicks through the designs. When he reaches the slide with the third floor landing, his lips dip at the corners into a frown.

"The wallpaper's still the same."

"I'm aware."

He looks at me, dark green eyes pinning me in place. "Why?"

I swallow. His gaze is oddly arresting and throws me off for a beat or two. I force myself to hold his stare — I won't back down. Not now. Not ever. "Because the wallpaper is what brings the space together. It elevates the landing and brings it to life."

"You don't think it's too busy?"

"Clearly *you* do." It's not a question. I can read him like a book.

His lips twitch, and for a second, I think he's about to laugh. But he quickly schools his expression into something more neutral. "I'm worried it's not right for the brand. The New York location—"

"This isn't New York," I interrupt because I already know what he's going to say. "You need continuity between the two locations, yes, but you also said you want something that'll make the London location stand out. Something new. Something different." I stab at my tablet. *"This* will do that. The whole venue will be bold, bright, and busy. But still luxury. Still decadent. You're going to need to trust me on that."

He inhales deeply through his nose and I wonder if I've gone too far. If my tone was too sharp. If there wasn't enough deference in my words. I'm usually pretty good at managing egos — between Cynthia and my parents, you could say I'm a pro — but I've not got Hawthorne right just yet.

"Fine," he says after a loaded pause. "We'll go with your lead on this one."

On this one.

I swallow down my ire and decide to take this as a win. "Great. I'll get started on hiring contractors in."

I expect him to return to his spot on the floor, but he doesn't move. Instead, he closes his eyes and lets his head loll against the window. The sun is peeking through the clouds just enough to shine across his face. It hits his golden hair just right and the thought *"the sun suits him"* worms its way into my mind without my approval.

"How was your weekend?" he asks suddenly, eyes still squeezed shut.

The question startles me and it brings back memories I'd worked hard over the weekend to push aside. Hawthorne approaching me at the bar, calling me beautiful, being *far* too charming to be allowed. When I don't answer right away, he says, "Did you enjoy the event?"

I shrug, then remember he can't see the action. "It was all right." I'm reluctant to share much more about my personal life with him, but I can recognise that he's waiting for some-

53

thing more, so I add, "Did you? Have you settled on a supplier?"

His features twist into that same irritated look from before. "Not yet. We're struggling to negotiate an acceptable price point for both parties."

I can't turn my snort into a believable cough quick enough.

He peeks open an eye and I swear he looks vaguely amused. "Something funny?"

"Not at all."

He opens both eyes, clearly unconvinced. "Go on. Say it. What's so funny?"

Part of me — the *sane* part of me — knows that I shouldn't say anything. He's a client, a very important client, and I owe him at least a veil of professionalism. But there's another part of me that wonders *why bother*? He already knows I don't like him, and as far as I can tell, he doesn't seem to care. He's not brought our brief conversation at the bar up yet and he's looking at me like he's genuinely interested in knowing my thoughts.

Maybe he needs someone who's not afraid to tell him the truth.

"You're too cheap, Hawthorne," I say bluntly.

He blinks at me and...*Shit*. I've definitely fucked up. I read the room wrong. He didn't want to hear the truth.

And then he laughs. Like full on belly laughs, as if it's genuinely the funniest thing he's ever heard. I think there are tears forming in the corner of his eyes.

"*Cheap*?" He wipes his eyes and shoots me a wide smile. "I've never heard that one before."

"I find that hard to believe."

"What makes you say that?"

I glance down at my tablet pointedly. "You didn't even want to go with this concept at first," I remind him. "You thought it was too expensive."

"It *is* too expensive."

"Good work costs money."

"I know," he says, almost defensively. "I just didn't think that choosing some furniture and deciding on pink walls would cost this much."

And there it is. Again.

His words feel like a punch to the gut. Cruel, lethal, and targeted at me. I try to keep my expression neutral, but apparently I fail because he immediately starts to backtrack.

"That's not to say you and Cynthia aren't doing a great job," he says quickly. His eyes are wide and nervous, like he realises he's said the wrong thing. "It's just—"

I don't wait to hear whatever excuse he's able to come up with. Instead, I scoop my tablet and laptop in my arms and stand up. "I'll find a different room to work in."

My voice is robotic and it takes all my strength not to let the lump forming in my throat choke my words.

"You don't have to leave. I—"

"You're clearly a very busy and important man," I say as I stride toward the door. "I wouldn't want to distract you with silly things like picking out furniture or choosing the right colour for the walls."

"Amber—"

I step across the threshold and let the door slam behind me.

7

FINN

Two hours ago, I didn't think it was possible for this day to get any worse. As I watch Amber storm out of the room, I realise that I was definitely wrong.

I woke up this morning with an email from my uncle waiting for me at the top of my inbox. That, in itself, wasn't cause for concern. As CEO, my uncle is a familiar name among the sea of emails I get every day. But they usually don't come from him. More often than not, they're from his ever-rotating army of assistants contacting me on his behalf. It's rare that I get an email directly from him.

FROM: Ernest Belmont <ebelmont@theaugustroom.com>
SUBJECT: Budget
BODY: Send the revised budget report over by the end of the day.

My uncle has never been one for pleasantries, but the bluntness of the email is out of character even for him. It doesn't help that the budget report is currently my biggest nightmare. Zensi Designs is charging a lot more than my initial plans allowed for, and I'm having to move money around from other parts of the plan to make it work. It's not a huge problem, but it's definitely a growing one, and it seems like Ernest is well aware.

My chest constricts as I reread his one sentence email.

Maybe that's why I said it.

"I just didn't think that choosing some furniture and deciding on pink walls would cost this much."

I regretted it as soon as the words came out of my mouth. There was something in her eyes, a deep hurt that bubbled to the surface as soon as I said it, and it made me feel like I'm the worst person on the planet. Right up until then, I thought we'd been getting along pretty well. She'd opened up to me slightly, even had the nerve to call me *cheap* — a word I don't think has ever been used to describe me in all my 32 years.

I liked that.

I liked that she didn't care about offending me. That she was happy to tell me her truth without worrying about what I'd think.

And then I went and ruined it.

I know I should apologise — I *want* to — but the irritating *call incoming* tune starts to blare from my laptop speakers. I glance at the door, still shaking from the way she slammed it behind her, and then draw my gaze back to my laptop screen.

I should go after her. Let her know that I'm not as much of dick as I may seem. Turn on the old Hawthorne charm that's never failed me and get her to shine that beautiful smile back on me once again.

But I don't. Instead, I dial into the call and fix a strained smile onto my face as my screen fills up with the grimacing face of my uncle.

"Good morning, Ernest. You're up early," I say as lightly as I can. It's just coming up to 7 a.m. in New York, and the realisation resurrects that ball of anxiety growing in my stomach. "Has something happened?"

My mind races with every worst-case scenario possible and every single one of them ends with me being fired and blamed for everything.

"Nothing's happened. Yet." My uncle's voice is as stern and devoid of any emotion as usual. "I'd like a budget update on the London expansion."

"I just got your email this morning. I'll send the report later today."

"By midday my time."

"It might take me a little longer to firm everything up. I'll have it with you by the end of the working day."

"*Midday*, Finn."

I swallow down the ire I can feel surging up my throat. "Is there a reason you need it so urgently? I've got other priorities, and—"

"This role is new to you," Ernest cuts me off like he wasn't even listening. He probably wasn't. "And while the rest of the board are confident you'll do a satisfactory job, I'm not convinced."

Maybe I deserve that. Maybe it's my punishment for what I said to Amber earlier. Knowing that doesn't stop it from hurting, though. I've always known that my uncle didn't want me to get the managing director position, but to hear him say it is a totally different thing. A totally different kind of pain.

"The London expansion failing won't just reflect poorly on you, Finn. It'll be on me too for having vouched for you."

"But you didn't vouch for me," I say bitterly. "You were the one holdout."

If he's surprised that I know this, he doesn't let it show. The unpleasant grimace on his face doesn't shift for even a second. "Perhaps not at this stage," he concedes with a shallow nod. "But I've helped your career at many stages through the years and championed various promotions you've received. All as a favour to your aunt."

"Any promotions I've gotten, I've earned them myself," I say through gritted teeth.

He barks out a sharp laugh. "Keep telling yourself that, boy."

"Ernest, I don't—"

"Send the report by midday. I'll have it checked over and then sent to the finance department."

"I'm supposed to have final sign-off."

"Not anymore," he says. "I'll be signing off on anything budget related for the London expansion from here on out."

"That's not—"

"Midday, Finn. Midday."

He drops off the call without saying goodbye, and I'm left staring at my furious reflection on my screen.

What an *asshole*. He knows just what to say to make me feel small.

I have no idea what my aunt Marion sees in him, and every

interaction I have with him helps me understand why my father has never taken to him. Is this why he treats me so terribly? Is he living out his feud with my father by tormenting me? I wouldn't put it past him.

I count back from ten, trying to will the anger I can feel simmering on the surface to settle down, but it doesn't work. I slam my laptop shut before I do something stupid like call him back or send an angry email and push myself up onto my feet.

I need to go for a walk. Clear my mind. Try to think about anything other than my uncle's smirking face.

Like Amber?

No. Don't really want to think about her right now either.

But it's hard not to when I reach the second floor landing and find her tucked into a little alcove, her laptop and tablet scattered around her. I know she can hear me — I'm not trying to mask my footsteps — but she doesn't even so much as glance up in my direction as I come down the stairs.

She keeps her gaze locked firmly on her laptop screen as I walk past her. I have to admit, her commitment to ignoring me is impressive. The only way I can tell she's even noticed my sudden presence is by the way her fingers falter slightly on the keyboard when she hears my shoes on the hardwood floor.

I consider stopping to say something — *anything* — but the words choke in my throat. So I follow her lead and look straight ahead, pretending like I've barely noticed her. As I disappear down the staircase, I swear I see her head twitch in my direction. But when I turn around, she's back to glaring at her laptop.

Between the call with Ernest and the catastrophe that is my current working relationship with Amber, the tightness in my chest doesn't surprise me. I need to relax, take my mind off the maelstrom of thoughts swirling in my mind.

I need to *eat*.

Aside from a croissant I swiped from the hotel breakfast bar on my way out this morning, I've not eaten today. I decide to blame my foul mood on that and not the ever-growing list of things that just keep going wrong.

Has Amber eaten?

The question jumps to the front of my mind without my permission.

But *has* she eaten? I didn't hear her leave and I'm pretty sure I didn't see any signs of a home lunch in her bag. An idea pops into my head, and I feel my mood start to lift slightly as I change direction. I'm on the hunt for the small, cosy café I'd stumbled into a few days ago. The wrap I'd ordered had been delicious, and I'm in the mood for it again.

I find the café quickly enough and order two wraps to go. One for me, and one for Amber.

I'm not sure how it happens, but I end up getting lost on my way back to the club. I think I must have taken a left when it should have been a right and soon enough, I don't recognise any of the buildings near me. As I work my way down the street, trying to find anything that sparks some recognition in my memory, a store catches my eye.

It's a furniture store — a little blip of colour among a sea of cream buildings. Couches, coffee tables, lamps, and dressers spill out of the large double doors, creating a haphazard display on the street outside. I take a few steps past the entrance and then double back. Piled high in the middle of the store just beyond the entrance is a large stack of colourful beanbags.

And that's when I have my second Amber-related idea of the day.

If the owner of the store is confused as to why a six-foot-three businessman is buying two colourful beanbags on a weekday, he doesn't let it show. He happily swipes my credit card and allows me to pluck two large beanbags off the floor.

They're big, but light enough that I have no problem carrying them back to the club. I ask the owner for directions and am happy to learn I'm only a block or two away. It only takes me five minutes or so to make it back to the club.

I make my presence known by stomping loudly up the stairs, but when I reach the second floor, Amber pretends like she hasn't even noticed me.

She's still staring determinedly at her laptop like she can't sense me looming over her. I stop just in front of her and wait until she reluctantly glances up at me.

Her eyes, deep brown and incredibly expressive, rake over my body. They linger for a second on the beanbags, but then she apparently decides that's not the most pressing issue. She nods toward the wrap I'm holding out. "What's this?"

"A peace offering."

She narrows her eyes slightly.

"It's not poisonous," I say, biting down the urge to laugh. She looks so suspicious, like she's half-expecting it to explode in her face.

There's another beat of hesitation before she reaches out and takes the wrap. "Thanks. And those?" She tilts her chin at the bean bags. "Are they a peace offering too?"

"Absolutely."

Her eyes brighten and she reaches out with her free hand to

grab one. I take a step backward so the beanbag is just out of reach.

"It *is* a peace offering," I say. "But one that can only be used in the office."

"A gift with strings attached," she says, brow arched. "Why doesn't this surprise me?"

I can tell she's trying to sound irritated, but there's a curve to her lips that betrays her and spurs me on.

"Think what you'd like, but the requirement still stands." I take another step backward. "No office. No beanbag."

She glares at me for several long seconds. I'm not the kind of person to back down easily, but I can't deny I feel slightly relieved when she eventually rolls her eyes and breaks the connection. A few seconds longer and I think I would've caved and given her everything she wanted.

I still might.

"Fine," she says with a nonchalant shrug.

"Fine, as in you'll come back up to the office?"

"*Nope.*" She pops the '*p*' and levels me an unimpressed look. "I'm good here."

"On the floor?"

"*Yep.*"

"Amber."

"Hawthorne."

She's not going to budge, is she? She'll happily sit on the uncomfortable hardwood floor if it means not giving me this win. That shouldn't excite me. If anything, it should annoy the hell out of me, but it doesn't. I am tempted to push some more and see how far this can go, but then my phone buzzes in my pocket and brings me crashing back to a reality filled with endless emails and spreadsheets.

"Suit yourself," I say. "If you change your mind, you know where to find me."

She hums non-committally and I turn to leave.

"Wait."

"Yes?" And I know I'm wearing the most shit-eating grin possible, because she immediately rolls her eyes again.

"Nothing to do with the beanbags, don't worry. Cynthia's asked if you want to have lunch together this week. Send over your availability and I'll book a restaurant for you two."

I frown. "You're not coming?"

"Why would I?" Something flashes in her eyes, and I can't quite make out what it is. It looks like irritation, but it's tinged with something else.

"Because you're the one doing all the work here," I say. Isn't that obvious? "Of course you should be there. In fact, *I* want you there. It'll be good to speak to you and Cynthia at the same time."

Her jaw tightens for a brief moment, but then her expression clears and she gives me a small nod. "All right then." She pauses, looks a little unsure of herself, and then adds, "Thanks again for the wrap, by the way. I sometimes forget to bring something in the morning, and then I end up being so busy, I never end up eating."

"It's no big deal," I say. I know how it feels to lose yourself in your work that you start to neglect basic needs. Burnout comes quickly after, and I know all too well how shitty that feels. "And your beanbag will be in the office waiting for you."

Along with me.

She laughs at that and shakes her head. "It'll be waiting a long time."

It's nothing like the laugh I heard last Friday — this one is soft, breathy, and slips out of her like she barely even realises she's doing it — but it's a start.

8

AMBER

Hawthorne has bought me lunch for the last four days in a row.

I'd assumed that Monday was a one-off. His way of apologising for the unexpectedly cruel jab he threw my way. But then on Tuesday he wordlessly dropped a taco bowl into my lap on his way back up to the fourth floor. Wednesday, it was some sushi from a market stall around the corner. And on Thursday, he handed me a baguette from a nearby café.

I don't know why I keep accepting his food offerings. It would be easy to just say *"no, thanks"* and pull out the slightly squashed sandwich and bag of crisps from my bag that I've remembered to bring every day since Monday. But I don't.

I've almost started to look forward to this little routine of ours. Hawthorne is practically robotic with it. Every day at twelve he descends from the fourth floor, strides past without sparing me so much as a glance, and disappears for an hour or so. When he comes back, he's got a bag of food — and he's always got enough for me.

At first I thought he might be using the whole lunch thing as a way to try to coax me back up to the office, but he's not mentioned it since Monday. He just hands me my food, gives me a small nod, and then heads right back upstairs. I can tell he's waiting for me to make the first move. To slink back up to the office with my tail between my legs. But he's going to be waiting a long time.

If there's one thing I am, it's stubborn. You don't grow up with parents like mine, or working under someone like Cynthia, without learning how to hold your ground. Bailey says it's simultaneously my best and worst quality. She calls me *relentlessly stubborn,* but even she agrees with me on this one.

I've dubbed Hawthorne *"Asshole Client"* in my furious text rants to her, and she's firmly aboard the hate train.

I try not to think about how I've not mentioned the lunches to her, instead choosing to focus on the torrent of annoyingly pedantic emails Hawthorne sends me every day even though there's only a floor between us.

"You ready to go?" I ask.

It's Friday, and for the first time this week, Hawthorne hasn't bought me lunch. We're about to go meet Cynthia at a nearby restaurant. I'd tried to worm my way out of it, but Hawthorne had been oddly insistent, even going so far as to sign off an email to Cynthia with *"looking forward to lunch with you and Amber on Friday"* to seal the deal.

He nods and gestures to the door. "Lead the way."

The restaurant is only about a ten-minute walk from the townhouse, but it feels like an eternity with Hawthorne by my side. And, make no mistake about it, he *does* stay by my side. I try to march a few paces ahead, but he easily matches my stride and comes to walk next to me, his body acting like a barrier against me and the cars racing down the street.

It's a gentleman's move, but I can't appreciate it. The only thing I can think about is how *awkward* it is between us. We don't say much to each other when we're in the club. Hawthorne works exclusively on the fourth floor, only coming out for lunch, and I've set up my space on the second floor. Aside from our lunchtime interactions, all our conversation happens via email as if we weren't in the same building for eight hours a day. I'm not sure I know what to say to him without a computer screen between us.

I glance over at him. He's got his phone out and is tapping away at the screen as we walk. Does he ever *stop* working? I know I'm one to talk, but I think he's got even me beat when it comes to being a workaholic.

He's always there when I arrive in the morning. Even though we don't see each other until lunch, I can feel his presence when I hear his deep voice as he takes calls. He's never left before me either. I wonder how long he stays.

"Is this place any good?" he asks suddenly. He shoves his phone into his pocket and tilts his head in my direction.

I shrug. "I've not been here before."

This particular restaurant is way above my price range. I can only eat at places like this when Cynthia is footing the bill. Bailey always jokes that this is the one perk of this job. I get to eat like a rich bitch. "But Cynthia chose it," I continue. "So it's definitely good. She's got great taste."

"Where would you have chosen?"

The question catches me off guard, and when I look over at him, he's got an intense look in his eyes. Like he's genuinely interested in my answer. "This part of London is full of great restaurants," I tell him diplomatically. "If you need any recommendations, I'm sure your hotel concierge could help."

He shakes his head. "I want *your* recommendation. If you and your friend, the one from last week, were meeting up after to work to grab a bite to eat — where would you go?"

"Why?" I ask. "Planning on taking that from me too?"

His lips twitch. "I didn't take anything from you. You left. And like I said, you're more than welcome to come back up to the office."

"And like *I* said, I'm fine where I am."

I hear Bailey's voice echoing in my mind. *Do you always have to be so relentlessly stubborn?*

Yes. Yes I do. Especially when it makes Hawthorne grin like that. Like he's actually *enjoying* this little verbal sparring match we've started.

"Sure you are."

We reach the restaurant and I'm spared from having to think up a retort. I spot Cynthia immediately. She's sat at the back of the restaurant, wearing a turquoise blazer that's so bright, it would have been impossible to miss her.

"Finn Hawthorne," she cries, standing up to give Hawthorne two cheek kisses. "It's so lovely to finally meet you and put such a handsome face to that name, *darling*."

I fight the urge to roll my eyes. I know for a fact that they've spoken on video calls before, but Cynthia has always been one for dramatics.

She barely acknowledges me outside of a perfunctory nod. I take the opportunity to slide into my seat and let them get on with the introductions.

"The pleasure's all mine," Hawthorne says with an admittedly charming smile. He drops into the empty seat next to me. "The board also sends their regards. They were all very excited when I showed them the design concepts."

Cynthia beams. "Yes, well, nothing but the best for The August Room. I know you're on a tight deadline, so I worked overnight to get those concepts ready for you."

I reach for the glass of water in front of me and chug it down before I do something stupid like laugh in Cynthia's face. *I* worked overnight to get those designs done. But what does the truth matter?

I wonder if he buys it or if Cynthia's lie is only obvious to me because I know the truth.

"We really appreciate it," Hawthorne says easily, and he immediately drops down a notch in my already low estimation of him. "Your designs were stunning."

Cynthia's smile falters ever so slightly. "Oh, don't flatter me, Finn. I'm sure there are things you wanted to change."

"Just a few small things," Hawthorne admits with a contrite nod. "Amber's been extremely helpful ironing out a few details to get everything just right."

Cynthia turns and looks at me for the first time since I sat down. There's a glint in her eye that tells me she's pleased that Hawthorne has admitted to picking apart *my* designs. "I'm glad Amber's been helpful bringing the concepts to life," she drawls. "She's really a *rising* star."

It's meant to *sound* like a compliment — and I'm sure Hawthorne thinks it is — but I know it's meant truly as a stab in the gut. I know what she's trying to tell me.

You're still learning.

You're not perfect.

You're not better than me.

Is this Cynthia's idea of some kind of twisted punishment for me daring to ask for a promotion? I think so.

"We've decided to use this as an opportunity to give Amber a little more project managing experience," Cynthia tells Hawthorne. "So, I've been more hands-off than usual, barring the initial designs. But please feel free to come straight to me if you need any help or have any questions."

God. She's making me sound incompetent. Like I can't do my job properly without her hovering over me. I half expect Hawthorne to wheel out the laundry list of things he's been bothering me about all week, but he doesn't.

"I'm sure Amber can handle it," he says through a smile that doesn't quite reach his eyes. "But I'll keep that in mind."

Cynthia nods, and I wonder if she can hear the sudden coldness in his tone too. "How are things going, *darling?*" she asks me. "Still on schedule?"

"Yes," I say through a forced smile. "All the contractors are booked. They'll start coming in next week. I've ordered all the wallpaper and paint needed, and I'm working on sourcing the furniture and fixtures now. I've briefed Simon in the warehouse, and he's making space to hold everything while we do the messy work on the property."

"Excellent," Cynthia says. Am I imagining the disappointment I can hear lacing her tone? "Keep me in the loop." She turns away from me, already bored, and smiles at Hawthorne. "Ready to order?"

In my periphery, I see Hawthorne's gaze slide over to me. It hovers there for a beat too long before he turns back to Cynthia and offers her a bright smile. "Let's go."

I order a Greek salad and fade into the background as Cynthia dominates the conversation with discussion that's clearly geared to trying to figure out if Hawthorne has any rich contacts in need of interior design work.

It's weird, but I can't get a read on him. He answers her questions politely, laughs at her bad jokes when appropriate, and happily promises to dig out the email addresses of people he thinks Cynthia should be in touch with. But he doesn't *look* like he's enjoying their conversation. In fact, he looks a little pissed off.

I'll be the first one to put my hands up and admit I'm not an expert on all the intricacies of Hawthorne's facial expressions, but he doesn't look like he's having a good time.

That makes two of us.

Although Hawthorne keeps trying to include me in the conversation, Cynthia never lets the focus linger on me for more than a few seconds before she pulls it back to her. At one point I catch his eye and he gives me a sympathetic grimace. It's refreshing to know that I'm not the only one who can see past Cynthia's bullshit.

When the bill comes, he immediately snatches it up and pulls out a black credit card.

"Don't be silly," Cynthia titters, pretending to reach out for the bill. "This is on us."

"No, don't worry," Hawthorne says firmly. "It's been my pleasure. And besides, I wouldn't want to give anyone any reason to call Finn Hawthorne cheap, would I?"

I snort at that and try to turn it into a cough when Cynthia shoots me a puzzled look.

"I'm sure no one would ever call *you* that," Cynthia says.

Hawthorne smiles, clearly amused. "You'd be surprised."

Once he's paid, we file out of the restaurant. There's a black cab waiting outside for Cynthia.

"Finn, it's been a delight to finally meet." She stands up on her tiptoes and stains both his cheeks with bright red lipstick marks. "And you'll let me know if you have any problems?"

"Will do. Have a safe journey home."

Aside from a flippant wave as she climbs into the cab, she barely acknowledges me.

We wave her off and the second her car disappears round a corner, Hawthorne exhales a deep breath. He stuffs his hands into the pockets of his trousers and rocks back onto the balls of his feet. "That boss of yours is definitely a character, huh?"

"God," I say, huffing an equally loud sigh. "You don't know the half of it."

"I think I do." He looks over at me, his brows pinching together slightly in the middle. "I've known people like Cynthia all my life. People who expect others to do all the hard work while they take all the credit."

I shrug, feeling secretly pleased. "Cynthia's the boss. It's her name on the company."

"But it's *your* hard work. She shouldn't be palming it off as her own." He takes a step closer to me, invading my personal space again. "Those were your design concepts, weren't they, Amber?"

Yes, I want to scream. *Yes. Yes. Yes. They were mine.*

But I can't say that. Cynthia would never forgive me if word got out that she'd stopped designing for high-profile clients. The company might never recover from it and that would effectively mean the end of my career. So instead I ask, "Why does it matter?"

"Because you deserve the credit for them. Those concepts are amazing."

"You've done nothing but complain about them," I say, eyebrow raised. "Every day there's something else you want to change. That doesn't sound amazing to me."

His cheeks colour slightly and he raises his hands in defeat. "They're not complaints. Just a few tweaks. I just need this to be perfect."

"And you think I don't?"

"No, of c—"

"Maybe Cynthia takes credit for things she shouldn't. But she also *lets me do my job*." For the most part anyway. "You could learn something from that."

He opens his mouth, then seems to think better of whatever it is he was going to say, and closes it. He swallows and then gives me a sharp nod. "Noted. And since we're giving each other constructive criticism?"

"I didn't say that."

"It's only fair."

I cross my arms over my chest, bracing myself for whatever insult is sure to come.

"Don't stay with someone that makes you feel small. Eventually, you'll start to believe it. I learned that the hard way, and I hope you don't have to."

That is...That is *not* what I expected him to say. He doesn't give me any time to try to think of a response before he steps away and makes a start down the road.

"I think I'm going to head back to my hotel for a while," he says with a grimace. "Have a lovely weekend, Amber."

I don't know what makes me do it — maybe it's the weird warmth blooming in my chest or maybe my Greek salad was kind of funky — but I yell out his name and make him stop in his tracks. "You asked earlier what restaurant I would've chosen for today." I point down the road in the opposite direction. "There's an amazing pizza place about ten minutes that way. Little hole in the wall kind of place called *Rosa's*. The best pizza in London, hands down, or I owe you a beer."

He grins brightly, and it's so infectious I think I start to smile too.

"I'll hold you to that."

9

FINN

I feel like a dick. Hell, I *am* a dick.

I'm sure Cynthia thought she was hiding it well, but her barely concealed jabs at Amber didn't go unnoticed by me. The way she took credit for Amber's hard work and then not so subtly tried to put her down ignited a strange fury in me. But it was less about what she was saying and more about how Amber reacted to it.

Or how she *didn't* react.

In the short time I've known her, *docile* is one word I'd never considered using to describe Amber. She seems to take pleasure in the quick-witted barbs she throws back at me, and she's certainly never had any problem with showing how she really feels about *me*. So it was strange to see her almost crumble in on herself in front of Cynthia. The way she let the older woman fling spiteful attack after attack at her without even an attempt to defend herself.

I didn't like it.

Not one bit.

But worst of all, it's no surprise that Amber doesn't like me if what she says is true. That I've been hovering over her, picking at her work, and tearing it apart all under the guise of soothing my anxiety about this project.

I'm no better than her boss — *or* my uncle — and the thought makes my skin crawl.

I need to do better. Learn how to balance my need for perfection without being an overbearing asshole. Have I always been like this? Do all my employees back in New York secretly hate me and Amber's just the only person with the courage to say it to my face?

Fuck. I think they might.

"Oh no, somebody's spiralling."

My sister's frowning face fills the screen on my phone. In the background I can hear my four-year-old niece, Maya, making a truly unholy amount of noise.

I ignore Nel's statement and ask, "What's she doing?"

"Making music!" Maya screams in the background. Nel tilts the camera over her shoulder until Maya's in frame and I can see that she's got a cooking pot in one hand and a lid in the other. "You wanna hear my song, Uncle Finn?"

"Nope!" Nel says quickly. "He doesn't want to hear. *In fact,* Uncle Finn wants you to go to your room and find that new toy he sent you last week."

Maya's eyes light up. She immediately drops the pot and lid and quickly scampers away to complete this new mission.

"That'll buy us maybe five minutes," Nel says once Maya has disappeared. "So be quick. What's wrong?"

"Nothing's wrong," I say. "Can't I just check in?"

I don't know why I bother lying to Nel. There's no one else

on this planet who knows me as well as she does. We're only ten months apart and we've been stuck to each other from the day she was born. I don't have to pretend like everything's all right with Nel, like I'm not constantly struggling to stay afloat in a sea of my insecurities, only seconds away from drowning.

I don't *have* to pretend, but I still do. Not that it ever works out in my favour.

"I wasn't joking when I said we've only got five minutes, Finn. She *will* be back with more things to make even more noise. So spill."

I run a hand down my face and bite back the groan I feel building in the very depths of my chest. There's so much I want to say, but I lead with the easiest thing. "Ernest won't get off my back."

Nel snorts. Neither of us are very fond of our dear old Uncle Ernest. "Since when is that news?"

She's right of course, but it feels different this time. I tell her everything that happened with the call earlier this week and the check-in emails he's started sending every other day. By the time I'm finished, the frown on her face mirrors mine.

"What a dick." She says the last word quietly, just in case Maya is in earshot. "You'd think he'd be over this weird feud with Dad by now, wouldn't you? And remember how he didn't even want to give you the managing director job in the first place? Sounds like he's looking for any reason to get proved right."

"I'm not going to give it to him."

Nel grins. "Damn right you're not. How're things going with the launch?"

"Things are on track," I tell her. I've officially settled on food and drink suppliers, I've started the process to hire a property manager, and Amber has everything in control on her side of things. Her face flashes suddenly in my mind. She's wearing her signature unimpressed look — the one it seems she's reserved solely for me — her pretty face twisted into a frown. I shake my head and dispel the image in my mind.

This would be the right moment to tell Nel about everything that happened today. With Cynthia. With Amber. With me apparently being as much of a controlling dick as my uncle. But the words won't come. Instead I say, "Do you think I'm nice to work with?"

Nel's eyes widen a fraction and then she barks out a laugh. "Do I think you're *nice* to work with?"

I glare at my sister. "Just answer the question."

"I think *you're* a nice guy, yes. But would I want to work under you?" She wrinkles her nose. "Absolutely not."

"I'm being serious, Nel."

Her expression softens slightly. "What happened?"

"It's been brought to my attention that maybe I'm not the easiest person to work with," I tell her. Her lip twitches slightly, but she doesn't say anything. "That maybe I'm a bit of a micromanager."

"A bit?"

I scowl at her. "Yes. Just a bit."

"You're under a lot of pressure," she says slowly, and I can tell she's carefully considering her words. "Nobody can blame you for being a bit *hands-on*."

Hands-on. Isn't that the phrase I always use to describe myself? Hiding behind it like it's a good thing.

"And it's never bothered you before," Nel continues. "Why now?"

"It's not that it hasn't bothered me," I say, ignoring the second half of her question. "I just never realised until now."

"Yeah, but what's made you—"

Maya comes running back into the room holding a giant shark plush. It's about three times bigger than she is and her face is a mask of concentration as she drags it into the room.

"I got it, Mama!" Maya declares, looking ridiculously proud of herself as she drops the plush to the ground.

"Thank you, sweet pea," Nel says. "What do you say to Uncle Finn?"

"Thank you!" she declares as she beams. "Miss you, Uncle Finn."

I have no qualms about spending three months in London for this project, but that right there might be what eventually does me in. I've worked hard to get where I need to be in my career, but being an uncle might actually be my favourite job. Ever since Nel broke up with Maya's father two years ago and they moved back to New York, my niece has been a constant in my life.

Whatever free time I have between work and more work goes entirely to them. Spoiling her comes second nature to me, although Nel keeps trying to discourage it. Hence the look on her face that lands somewhere between irritated and amused as she eyes the giant shark.

"I miss you too, princess," I tell her. "I'll send you something from London soon."

"Something *small* please," Nel says pointedly.

"I make no promises."

"Are you coming home soon?" Maya asks, her big brown eyes wide and hopeful.

"Two months and three weeks."

Maya holds up three stubby little fingers. "This many?"

I can't help the smile that overtakes my face. "Something like that, princess. I'll be back before you know it."

"And you'll still be back before Mom and Dad's anniversary?" Nel asks. "We also need to figure out what present we're getting them. 35 years is a big one."

I nod. Their anniversary falls about two weeks after the launch of the club. If all goes well I should have handed the reigns over to my new property manager and be back in New York. "I'll be there."

"Great." Nel leans back slightly and bites her bottom lip. "Maya, sweet pea, why don't you go and see if Toast wants to play."

Toast is their grumpy, one-eyed cat who only seems to like Maya. I still have a scar on my leg from the first time I met the little gremlin, and I've made sure to keep a safe distance ever since.

Maya jumps up, so easily distracted, and runs off to find the cat. Once it's just us, Nel gives me a strange look. "Are you all right?"

My brows furrow in confusion. "Do I not seem all right?"

"No. Not really." Nel doesn't pull punches with me. She doesn't pull them with anyone, to be fair. "When I picked up the call you looked like you were five seconds away from entering full-blown panic attack territory. What's going on?"

"Nothing. I just—" I shake my head, trying to make sense of the words in my brain before they come spewing out. "There's a lot riding on this project. I need to get it right. I just...Maybe I don't like the person I'm becoming to do that."

Or is it just the person I've always been? I push that thought away. Don't need to think about that right now.

"Do you think about anything other than work? I mean outside of me and Maya," she adds quickly, accurately preempting my response. "What're your hobbies? Who are your friends?"

"I have friends, Nel."

"You have people that you send a Christmas card to every year because *I* remind you to do it. Work isn't everything, Finn."

This isn't new ground for us. Nel and I haven't had a real argument since we were teenagers, but if there's one thing that gets us close to one, it's discussing my work-life balance.

Despite us having the same upbringing, Nel has never shared the same anxieties as I do when it comes to proving myself. She's more than happy to take the connections our last name has given us, using them to propel her forward in her career as a realtor. If there are ever any whispers about her getting to where she is in her career simply because her father is Henry Hawthorne, pharmaceutical tycoon, she shuts them down immediately by showing them her track record.

I envy it. The confidence she has in herself to stand tall and proud among a sea of naysayers. I've tried to mimic it, but it never seems to work for me. Maybe because I'm still under my uncle's thumb and Nel has long since branched out to create something for herself.

"Listen," Nel says seriously. "You're in London for three months. *Enjoy it.* Yes, the project is important, but so is having a life. Get out there. See the sights. Make some friends. Go on a few dates. Live a little. No one is expecting you to be working 24/7."

I sense that I'm fighting a losing battle, so I force out a laugh and say, "Sure."

———

IF NEL COULD SEE me now, I think she'd try to put me in a headlock. It was always her favourite attack of choice growing up and, to be fair, I think I deserve it right now.

Because it's an uncharacteristically warm and sunny Saturday in London and I'm sitting on my beanbag, in an empty office, tapping away on my laptop.

I try to tell myself that this can't wait until Monday. That it's imperative I scan through these contracts and make notes right now even though our legal team back in New York won't even glance at it for another 48 hours. That I'm actually *helping* future me by getting a jumpstart on this all now.

It doesn't work.

I can practically hear the sound of Nel's eyeballs rolling into the back of her head as I settle in for another day of nothing but work.

It's a sickness at this point. But the call with Ernest on Monday rattled me more than I'd like to admit. He's an ocean away, but it's like I can feel him breathing down my neck, finding flaws in every single thing I do. So I pore through these contracts until my eyes start to water and my stomach starts to angrily protest, reminding me that, once again, all I've eaten today is a croissant.

I head out for lunch, intending this to be a quick one

because I still need to go through the contract with the catering company we're hiring. And it *is* a quick one.

Until I'm standing outside the building, fumbling around in my pockets for the keys. And then it hits me.

It's an uncharacteristically warm and sunny Saturday in London and because of that, I'm not wearing my sweatshirt. The sweatshirt with my keys in the front pocket.

I've locked myself out.

Shit.

I rattle the door handle a few times, half-heartedly hoping it'll develop sentience, feel some kind of sympathy toward me and swing open. No luck.

This is probably a sign that I should walk away and actually enjoy my weekend. I know if Nel were here, that's what she'd be saying.

Get out there. See the sights. Make some friends. Go on a few dates. Live a little.

I take a step back from the door, fully intending to turn around and head back to my hotel. But then I remember I'm only halfway through the contract I was looking over and I still have a to-do list as long as my arm to get through. I *need* my laptop.

For a few truly deranged seconds I consider trying to scale the walls up to the open window on the third floor, but then the rational side of my brain kicks in.

There's another key.

Before I can really give much thought to it, I pull out my phone and scroll through my inbox until I find an email from Amber. It doesn't take me long to find one — most of our correspondence happens through email despite being only a flight of stairs away from each other during the week.

I find what I'm looking for at the bottom of the last email to me. A phone number in her signature along with a curt *"If your enquiry is __urgent__ and I am unresponsive on email, please contact me on…"*.

Does this count as urgent?

I don't wait to talk myself out of it and quickly hit Call. It rings and rings and rings and I'm just about starting to realise that it *is* a bad idea and I absolutely *shouldn't* be bothering her on a weekend when she's already made her thoughts about me perfectly clear, when she finally picks up.

"Hello?"

"Hi, Amber. It's Finn."

Silence.

I clear my throat. "From The August Room?"

More silence, then something that sounds strangely like a suppressed snort. "I know who you are, Hawthorne. Why are you calling me on a Saturday? Is the building on fire?"

Now that…*that* would be an emergency worthy of calling my designer at 4 p.m. on a Saturday. Locking myself out? Not so much.

"I've locked myself out," I tell her, wincing slightly. The words sound so ridiculous now that I've said them out loud. "And I really need to get my laptop. I can't wait until Monday. Is there any chance you're in the area and have your key? I'll come to you."

Another round of silence.

"Amber?"

"I heard you."

And yeah. I don't think I'm imagining the blatant annoyance in her tone. I can't blame her, though.

"Sorry—" I begin, ready to take it all back and tell her to go and enjoy her weekend.

"I'm about a 20-minute tube ride from the club," she says, cutting me off. "Meet me here and I'll give you my key."

She relays her address, confirms I know how to get there without getting lost, and then hangs up without saying goodbye.

10

AMBER

IN THIS MOMENT, THERE'S NOBODY IN THE WORLD I LOVE more than Finn Hawthorne. Because it turns out that Mark from the event last week *is* younger than me. Quite a bit younger.

He's 21.

As in, still at university, currently prepping for his final year exams, 21. A baby really. So I've decided that I can't really blame him when it turns out that his idea of a date is *Nando's*, "chilling" at his place, and then heading to a student bar later tonight for cheap drinks. I'm dressed like he's about to take me out for a five-star meal — I'm even wearing *heels* — but *no*. We're in a *Nando's* and he made me order water so we wouldn't have to pay for the refillable sodas.

What the fuck is my life right now?

So when my phone lights up and it's Hawthorne on the other end sheepishly telling me he's locked himself out of the club and needs my key, I don't feel any anger or irritation toward him for daring to interrupt my weekend.

I only feel *gratitude*.

"Sorry, Mark," I say, hoping I've injected enough faux sympathy into my tone that he won't realise how secretly relieved I feel right now. "I've got an urgent work thing."

He frowns. "But it's Saturday."

Poor kid. He genuinely looks crushed. "I know, but it can't be helped. Demanding bosses and all that. I'm sure you know how it is." Or maybe he doesn't? Has he ever even had a job?

"I can come with you and hang around," he says, and *goddamnit*, he is quite literally pulling puppy dog eyes on me right now. "And then we can head to the bar after. It's two for one on cocktails tonight."

I fight the urge to wince. "No, no. You go and enjoy the rest of your evening. I don't know how long I'll be."

He looks like he wants to say something else, but maybe he can finally tell that I'm just not into this — convenient getaway excuse or not — because he gives me a sad nod. "I'll message you?"

"Sure."

He gives me a stiff hug that I return with just one arm and then walks out. As soon as I can't see him anymore, I exhale a deep breath and lean against the wall, rocking onto my heels to give my toes some reprieve.

I can't believe I wore heels to *Nando's*.

This is all Bailey's fault. She's the one who convinced me to give Mark a go.

AMBER

He is 21. I repeat. Baby Face is 21.

A shadow looms over me and I shriek, nearly dropping my phone in the process.

"Sorry, sorry," a familiar voice says hastily.

I watch as Hawthorne takes three very deliberate steps away from me, hands held up apologetically in front of him.

"Didn't mean to startle you," he says. "I called your name, but you didn't hear."

I'm still not really hearing him if I'm being honest. This is the first time I've seen him not wearing a suit and, I won't lie, I'm into it.

He's not wearing a coat or even a jumper — something only someone unfamiliar with this country's temperamental climate would dare do — and his thin, long-sleeved T-shirt clings to him like a second skin, showing off wide shoulders and lean, corded muscle hiding under the fabric. My gaze dips a little lower and I can't help but say a silent prayer of thanks to whoever invented grey sweatpants.

Hawthorne may be a neurotic asshole, but he's definitely an attractive one.

"Thanks for agreeing to this, by the way," he says. "I know I'm probably the last person you want to hear from on the weekend."

Honestly, with his constant amends and nit-picking, he's probably the last person I want to hear from on weekdays too, but I don't say that out loud. He seems like he's embarrassed enough. His cheeks are redder than usual and he's desperately avoiding making any eye contact with me. As much as I like getting one over on Hawthorne, I've never been one to kick a man while he's down.

"It's fine," I tell him. "I wasn't up to much."

He arches a brow and I watch as he slowly, *deliberately*, looks me up and down. His jaw ticks slightly as his dark green eyes take in my outfit, stopping for a brief moment at the hem of my leather skirt before darting lower.

For a second, I think his breath hitches slightly in his throat as his gaze travels the length of my legs, roving over the thigh-high heeled boots I'm wearing. But then he coughs and I tell my ego to calm all the way down.

He's not checking me out. In fact, he's probably wondering why I would bother lie about not being up to anything when I'm clearly dressed for a night out.

"Well, thanks anyway," he says, his voice a little gruffer than usual. "I appreciate it."

I nod and rifle through my bag to find my keys. "What were you doing in there on a Saturday anyway? Do you secretly live there and this hotel thing has been a ruse the entire time?" I'm joking but honestly, it wouldn't surprise me.

And it would explain how he's always there so early every morning and never leaves before me. The alternative, that he's such a workaholic he comes into an empty building on Saturdays to get some work done, is a tiny bit depressing. I work late most days, but Hawthorne puts even me to shame.

"Ha, ha," he deadpans. "Just let me have the key and I'll let you get on with..." He gestures vaguely toward me. "With whatever you were doing before I interrupted."

"It was nothing," I lie, and I'm not sure why. I tell myself that it's the lingering shame from this disastrous date and hand over the key. "Don't lose that."

He gives me a mock salute and slips the key into the pocket of his sweatpants. "Thanks again, Amber. I'll, uh, I'll see you on Monday?"

"Sure."

He moves to turn away, but then he swivels back to me, his cheeks still an odd shade of pink. "Are you heading to the station as well?"

I shake my head. "My friend is coming to pick me up in a little while." I don't know if I'm imagining his gaze flitting over my outfit again *or* why it bothers me that he might be coming to his own conclusion, so I quickly add, "Bailey. The one I was with the other week."

His brows furrow slightly in the middle. "So you're just going to wait here? Alone?"

"I'll probably wait inside a coffee shop or something," I tell him. Bailey's still a little while away and I don't feel like hanging out on the street until she gets here. "I'll be fine, Hawthorne. I'm a big girl, I can take care of myself."

"I know, I just—" He swallows, and for a brief second, a look of pure panic flits across his features. "I'll wait with you."

"I told you, I'm fine. You go and enjoy the rest of your Saturday doing whatever it is you do to have fun."

Probably making spreadsheets or something like that.

"I want something to drink." He shrugs nonchalantly and then shoots me a grin. "And it just so happens that someone I know is heading to a coffee shop right now."

I peer at him suspiciously, trying to figure out what his ulterior motive is here. He stares back at me, his gaze oddly earnest, and a soft smile tugs at his lips. "Fine. But no work talk or I'm charging the hours to your account."

He huffs out an almost laugh, nothing more than a soft puff of air that slips from between his pursed lips. "Fair enough. Is there a café close by?"

"There *should* be. But I don't really know this area very well."

"What about over there?" He points to an old building just across the road and I raise a brow.

"That's a pub."

"Pubs have drinks, don't they?"

"They don't have *coffee*. And I wouldn't really go into a pub by myself," I tell him.

"Good thing you're not by yourself then, isn't it?"

Before I have the chance to retort, he reaches for my arm and gently starts tugging me in the direction of the pub. I quite like the feel of his hand on my arm — strong, confident, gently possessive in a weird kind of way that makes my stomach do a tiny somersault — and I don't make any move to pull away until we're across the road.

The pub is crowded, already filled with Saturday night regulars sipping beer, laughing, and roaring at the football game plastered across the TV at the end of the room. Hawthorne goes first, carving a handy pathway through the throng of pubgoers for me. He glances back a few times, probably to check I haven't abandoned him and run off.

Why *haven't* I done that yet?

I've had plenty of opportunities. It would've been easy enough to shake him off when he grabbed my arm and walk off in the opposite direction. But here I am instead. With Finn Hawthorne, the current bane of my life (bar Cynthia) in a crowded and definitely too expensive pub in the middle of London.

I can't help but wrinkle my nose as I take in the exorbitant prices on the sticky menu once we reach the bar. I'm not a big beer drinker, but even I can tell the people in here are being robbed blind.

A bartender slides over to me and offers me a grin. "What'll you have, darling?"

I glance over the menu again and reluctantly settle for an equally overpriced cocktail. I reach for my purse, but Hawthorne suddenly sticks his hand over mine. The touch lasts for maybe half a second, but a warmth blooms almost immediately as his skin presses against mine. I almost miss it when he lifts his hand to point at the menu.

"And I'll have a pint of whatever you recommend,"

Hawthorne says to the bartender before looking over at me. "I'll get it."

I shake my head. No. Absolutely not. "I can pay for my own drinks."

"I know you can. It's my way of saying thank you."

"For what?"

"For the key."

Oh. Yes. The key. I'd already forgotten about that. Like it's perfectly normal for me and Hawthorne to be together in a crowded pub on a Saturday night.

"And I can't give you another reason to call me cheap, can I?"

I laugh. "You're buying me *one* drink, Hawthorne. You're gonna need to do better than that to beat the cheap allegations."

He drops his elbow onto the bar and leans in slightly, a teasing grin on his lips. "Like buy you a very comfortable and not at all cheap beanbag?"

The lunches too. But I don't say that out loud.

"That doesn't count," I tell him. "You only got that to make me come back upstairs. Ulterior motives don't negate cheapness."

Hawthorne's smile dips slightly. "I didn't mean to drive you away." He pulls away and rubs a hand around the back of his neck. That pink tinge to his cheeks is back. "I meant what I said on Friday. Your designs are good. *Great* even." He nods, to himself or me, I can't quite tell. "They're great. Honestly. And I'm sorry that I've said some things to make you think otherwise."

The warmth from when he briefly held my hand has somehow spread to my chest. I can feel his praise spreading from within, slowly crawling over every inch of me until I feel like I'm buzzing off it. The bartender places our drinks in front of us and Hawthorne wordlessly hands his black card over.

"Thank you," I murmur. And I'm not sure what I'm thanking him for. The drinks or his words?

He shrugs like it's no big deal, picks up both our drinks, and nods to a corner of the pub. "Want to see if we can find somewhere to sit?"

I should say no. Tell him that we can just stand at the bar because as soon as Bailey messages me, I'll be leaving. But I don't. I nod and follow him again as he carves another path through the crowd for me.

Despite the area being marginally quieter than the rest of the pub, we still can't find an empty table, so we end up tucked away in a corner holding our drinks. It's...It's *intimate*. My back is flush against the wall and Hawthorne is hovering over me, one hand cradling his drink, the other pressed against the wall, bracketing me in slightly.

He takes a sip from his beer and when he pulls the glass away from his lips, he's got a slight foam moustache. I force down the giggle I can feel threatening to erupt and keep my face as neutral as I can.

"This is pretty good," he says, going in for another sip.

"Sure looks it." My chest is practically vibrating from the threat of laughter, and I take a big gulp from my drink to disguise it.

Hawthorne throws me a suspicious look and it's *so hard* to take him seriously with that foam moustache still going strong. "What're you and your friend up to tonight? Anything fun?"

I shrug and glance down at my drink. "Not much." It's not

like I can tell him that we're heading back to her place to commiserate my truly awful and embarrassing love life, starting with my date earlier tonight. "Probably just catching up. Nothing special."

"Oh." He looks me up and down again with hooded eyes and the action almost makes me shiver. His gaze is intense, and I can feel it on me as he methodically inches down my body. "I thought you'd be going out or something. Because that skirt is... because you look so..."

He swallows and leans in some more. We're so close now, I would barely need to reach up to splay my hand against his chest. I can't say that it's not tempting. I'm eyeline with his upper body and the thin T-shirt he's wearing does so little to mask the quiet muscles rippling underneath.

"You look really nice," he finishes, his voice barely more than a whisper.

My breath gets caught in my throat.

"Not that you don't look nice every day," he says quickly, misinterpreting my stunned silence as something else entirely. "Because you do."

"You been checking me out, Hawthorne?"

I think watching the tips of his ears turn pink might just be my new favourite thing. It's remarkable how quickly the blush spreads to his cheeks, and I wonder if he knows this about himself. How easy he is to read. To tease.

"In a strictly professional sense," he says, and I'll do him this favour and pretend like I don't notice how his voice is slightly gruffer than before.

"You've been checking me out in a *strictly professional sense*?" I bring my drink back to my lips and take a slow sip, enjoying the way I can plainly see panic and regret spasming across his face. Am I evil? Maybe a little bit. "That sounds like something HR should be all over."

"Or." His tongue darts out for a brief second to run along his bottom lip as he leans in even farther. We're so close now, his short blond locks fall forward and brush against my forehead. "Or we could keep it between us."

What is happening here?

This is not how I expected my Saturday night to go. Tucked away in a dark corner of an expensive pub with Finn Hawthorne dangerously close to me. *Flirting* with me. Because he is flirting, isn't he? Toeing the line between professional and most definitely not.

My phone vibrates in my pocket, drawing my attention away from him. I pluck it out and look at the screen.

BAILEY

I'm outside

Lol…are you in a pub?

"Amber?"

I glance back up at Hawthorne. He looks uncertain, like he's not sure if he's crossed a line. It's flattering in a way and if this were anyone else, I'd be all over it. But this is *Finn Hawthorne*, and our working relationship is tenuous as it is. There's no need to make things more complicated.

But that doesn't mean I can't have some fun with it.

I reach up and ghost my thumb along his top lip, wiping away the foam moustache in one clean sweep. I pull my thumb back to *my* mouth and give it a little lick clean. It tastes like shit, but I'm enjoying the way his mouth falls open slack and his wide eyes follow my tongue as it runs along the flat of my thumb.

"*Amber*." His voice is a rough keen. An almost moan.

I like it. Maybe too much.

I slide out from beneath him and drop my half-empty glass onto a nearby table as I walk away. "Got to run, Hawthorne. I'll see you on Monday."

He doesn't say anything, but I can feel his eyes on me all the way until I reach the exit and step out into the cool night air.

11

FINN

I'M GOING TO BLAME IT ON JET LAG FOR THAT MOMENTARY lapse in judgement.

It doesn't matter that I've been in this country for nearly two weeks and that my body has definitely adjusted to the time difference. Still blaming it on jet lag. Because that's the only explanation I have for whatever the hell that just was.

It takes me a full minute to muster up the strength to even move after she saunters away. I can still feel the phantom touch of her thumb against my lip, and the image of her hips swaying as she walked out of the pub is playing on a loop in my mind.

I don't know what's worse: the fact that she was clearly toying with me — so obviously enjoying the way I immediately crumbled with just one fleeting touch — or the fact that I want more. The last half an hour or so with Amber might just be the highlight of my year so far. Which is incredibly pathetic, and I don't even need Nel to tell me that.

When I eventually remember how to move my legs, I entertain the thought that she might still be outside. Maybe I'll catch her before she climbs into her friend's car and I can say... Say *what* exactly? I'm not sure if I want to apologise or ask her out on a date. From what I know about her, I'm not sure either will go down well. But it doesn't matter either way because when I step out onto the street, there's no sign of her.

Even though I now have the key to the townhouse, I don't head back to the club. All thoughts of rescuing my laptop and spending the rest of the evening going through the contract I'd started earlier are the furthest thing on my mind. Instead, I take my time heading back to my hotel and do my best to shove Amber's grinning face out of my mind.

It doesn't work.

I spend the walk back wondering what she's doing with her friend. If she's told her about me. If they're both laughing hysterically at my misguided attempt at flirting. If on Monday morning I'm going to have an email at the top of my inbox from Amber, removing herself from this project because I definitely got too close back in the pub.

It's that thought that spurs me on to make my second stupidest decision of the day.

When I drop back into my bed at the hotel, I pull out my phone, and before the rational side of my brain can kick in, I do it.

FINN

Thanks again for meeting me today.

And sorry about the pub.

If it made you uncomfortable in any way.

She doesn't respond immediately. She doesn't respond for

hours, in fact, and I'm almost certain she's ignoring my messages. But then my phone vibrates and it's truly embarrassing how quickly I reach for it.

AMBER
Nothing to apologise for, Hawthorne.

For the first time in a long while, I feel incredibly grateful that I'm alone and I don't have to explain the ridiculously wide grin on my face to anyone.

DESPITE MY BEST ATTEMPTS, Amber stays firmly on my mind for the rest of the weekend. I wonder what she's up to as I'm sitting on my beanbag Sunday morning going through my inbox and triple checking my spreadsheets. I tell myself that old lie, that I'm helping future me out by coming in on a weekend, but that's even starting to sound like nothing more than a weak excuse to me now too.

I leave the front door unlocked for Amber when I get in on Monday. This might be one of our last days working in the club alone. Amber has scheduled the contractors to start coming in and working from next week. Soon this building will be filled with painters, decorators, carpet fitters, and more. The list is seemingly endless, and it's beyond impressive that Amber's managed to wrangle it all together in just over a week. There are so many moving parts, even I feel overwhelmed with each confirmation email that comes in, but Amber takes it in stride and soon enough every task is accounted for.

Knowing this should fill me with joy. We're inching closer

and closer to the launch date and the fact that the club will soon start to resemble Amber's concepts should make me excited. And it does...for a while. But that excitement is miniscule compared to the knot of anxiety growing beside it.

So much can go wrong from here.

Everything can go wrong. And it'll all be on me.

Concepts are one thing, but what happens if it doesn't translate to real life?

You're going to need to trust me on that.

Amber's voice echoes in my mind.

Trust me on that.

I want to trust her. I truly do. Logically I know she's phenomenal at what she does. There's an entire *testimonials* page on the *Zensi Designs* website filled with Amber's praises specifically, and I've seen firsthand just how quick, resourceful, and dedicated to the job she is. But it's funny how quickly anxiety can eat away at logic. Soon enough, the only thing I can think about is that if this all goes wrong, it's not on Amber's head. It's on mine.

It's me who'll have to step back into the New York office and hear everyone whispering about how they knew I wasn't up for the task. How they can't believe I got the job in the first place. How my uncle must have pulled some strings for me.

It's not Amber who'll have to face my uncle and the rest of the board.

No. Just me.

"Should I be worried?"

I jump. Amber is standing in the entrance to the office. She looks concerned. I realise that my fingers are wrapped around my tie, tugging it tightly away from my neck.

It's an irritating reflex I've developed over the years. When I'm anxious or nervous or worried about something, I start to feel like I can't breathe. Like I'm only seconds away from choking on all my fears. So I tug on my tie as a way to ground me, to remind me that I'm not actually choking, that the fears are in my head.

I drop my hand and smooth out my tie. "Not at all."

She nods, looking decidedly unconvinced, and steps into the office. I must look as surprised as I feel because she laughs as she strides across the room and drops into her empty beanbag with a flourish.

She bounces on it a few times and then leans back with a small, satisfied smile. "This is pretty comfy." She crosses one leg over the other and my throat goes dry.

Her skirt is short enough that it would probably make someone from HR run off to double check the employee hand-book. It's only an inch or two longer than the one she was wearing on Saturday night, and she looks just as good in it. I'm suddenly overcome with the urge to lean over and run a finger down one of her long legs so I can feel for myself if they're as soft as they look.

She glances over at me. "Lost for words, Hawthorne?"

The way my face heats up, you'd think I was sitting directly under the sun. Am I really that easy to read? She's been in here for all of thirty seconds and I've spent twenty-nine of them unashamedly ogling her. I open my mouth to apologise — seems like I'm doing that a lot lately — but she continues on.

"I know, I know. I'm back up here. Go on." She rolls her eyes dramatically. "Get it over with."

I frown. "Get what over with?"

"The gloating?" She shoots me a look that's halfway between teasing and genuine. "You win. I'm back in the office. Aren't you going to do a little victory dance or something?"

I huff out a relieved laugh. Maybe I'm not as easy to read as I thought. "I don't gloat, Amber."

She gives me a look that tells me she doesn't believe that at all.

"But it's good to have you back up here," I tell her earnestly. The space already feels brighter with her in it. "What made you change your mind?"

Visions of Saturday evening — us in a dark corner, her thumb swiping over my lip, her hips swaying as she walked away — flash in my mind. Is she remembering it too? Or was it barely a blip in her memory? Something as inconsequential as washing the dishes?

She shrugs and the mask of indifference she's wearing slips for a brief moment. Just long enough for me to register that maybe, *maybe*, she's thinking about it too. "My back was starting to hurt."

"Your back?"

She hums, her lips twitching as she fights back a smile. "My back."

I don't bother to hold my grin back. "I'm glad I could help."

She gives me a small nod and then turns to her laptop, fingers moving at lightning speed as she tackles an inbox I can only assume is as lawless a place as my own. She's got a magnetic quality to her, something that keeps dragging my gaze away from my laptop and back to her before long.

I could watch her all day. Every time I glance up, I notice something new. Like the way she bites her bottom lip when she's really concentrating, that makes *me* want to lean in and bite her lips, to discover if they're as luscious as they look. Or the soft sigh she huffs out every now and then. And before long I'm wondering what I'd need to do to coax those kinds of sounds out of her.

She looks up at me and frowns. "Did you need something?"

You.

The thought comes out of nowhere and plants itself front and centre in my mind. I shake my head and turn my attention back to my laptop, forcing it to stay there even when I can feel her curious gaze on me.

———

THE CLUB IS FILLED with strangers. It's odd going from the pleasant quiet that Amber and I have cultivated over the last few weeks to hearing the constant thrum of conversation and movement from the workers shuffling in and out.

Amber spends less time in the office these days and I miss her presence. She's busy overseeing the never-ending list of tasks assigned to her small army of contractors. If it's not checking that they're using the right wallpaper on the second floor, she's printing off floor plans and pasting them on the walls or rushing between the warehouse and the club, occasionally bringing smaller pieces of furniture or decorations with her to see how they'll look in the space.

I'm so busy organising the launch event and conducting online interviews for the property manager position that we've barely spoken or seen each other this week. So it brings me more than a little bit of joy when she steps into the office and plops down onto her beanbag with a soft groan.

She threads her hands through her hair and rubs at her temples. "I swear it's like everyone wants a piece of me today."

"Everything all right?" I ask, although I know the answer is no. The stress is evident on her face.

She nods, then shakes her head, and then groans loudly again. "Tiny scheduling mix-up. I've got the chandelier for the reception area being delivered now, but the electricians aren't coming 'till Friday to work their magic and hook it up. So we're going to have a chandelier that costs three thousand pounds just lying around for two days, which only makes me nervous."

"You think someone will take it?"

She snorts. "No. I think someone will *break* it. But I've asked Ric to clear a small corner downstairs, so at least it should be out of the way."

"It's a giant chandelier," I say. "It's not like someone's going to accidentally step on it."

"You'd be surprised." She shifts a little on her beanbag so she's facing me. She's wearing a skirt again — I think she's worn one every day since that Saturday in the pub — and the sight of her long legs makes my throat close up just tiny bit. Is she doing this on purpose? Teasing me? Or should that be taunting?

"I once had a guy break a sofa in two."

"How'd he manage that?" I ask with a laugh, happy for the distraction.

"No idea. I just came downstairs and the sofa was cut clean in two." She rolls her shoulders and cocks her head to the side. "How's your day going? Put out many fires?"

"I think I've settled on a property manager. She'll be coming in next week to check things out."

"Nice." She grins at me like she's genuinely happy I've been able to tick this off my to-do list. "And the planning for the launch? All going well?"

"For now," I say with a shrug. "Invites are going out this week. I've got entertainment lined up. Just need to sort out the menu."

"Well." She clears her throat and looks away. "Let me know if you need any help. Event planning isn't really my thing, but there's definitely some crossover there, so..."

I think this might be the first time she's ever offered to help me with something. "Thanks. We've got an events team back in New York who are helping me out as much as they can, but—"

A thundering crash makes us jump. There's dead silence for a second or two, and then somebody downstairs starts shouting.

"Shit." Amber leaps up from her beanbag and scrambles for the door. "The chandelier. Shit. Shit. Shit."

I follow her as she races downstairs, a stream of frustrated curses flowing from her mouth.

"No, no, no!" Amber groans as we reach the ground floor. It's covered in tiny, shattered pieces of glass, and the skeleton of what I assume was once my very expensive chandelier lies in a crumpled heap in the middle of the floor. "What happened?"

Ric, Amber's main contractor, is standing to the side with a look of pure dread etched onto his face. Next to him are three men and one of them has a long cut running down his arm with a thin trail of blood slowly oozing out of it.

"Shit," Amber says again as soon as she catches sight of the injury. "Where's the first aid kit? Do you need to go to the hospital? Are you okay?"

"I'm fine," the man mumbles. Someone comes running back into the room with a little green box with the first aid sign on it. "It's not a deep cut."

"I'm so sorry, Amber," Ric says, shaking his head. "I didn't check that they loaded it up properly and—"

"It's fine," Amber says, even as her jaw twitches. She closes her eyes for a few seconds, inhales deeply, and then opens them again. "Just...just sort him out, get him bandaged, and fill out an accident report form. Then make sure the glass is all cleaned up so nobody else hurts themselves."

Before anyone can say anything, she whirls around and dashes up the stairs. I hover awkwardly for a few seconds, not sure what else to say, and then follow Amber. When I get to the office, she's pacing the room. She's on the phone, and she's using her free hand to wind her fingers around the few strands of hair that frame her face.

"...You're sure there's no way?" She sounds desperate in a way I've never heard from her before. Like her voice is only one more piece of bad news away from cracking. "We can pay double your fee. Triple if you can guarantee it." A pause. Her brows are so tightly knit together, I'm afraid it's going to leave a permanent mark in the middle of her face. "All right. No, no, I understand. Thank you anyway." She hangs up the phone and sinks against the nearest wall with her eyes closed. "*Fucking hell.*"

"What's going on?"

She cracks open one eye. "Nothing. It's fine. I'll get it sorted. Don't worry."

There's a bite to her tone that almost makes me flinch. She sounds like the Amber from the first day we met. The one who had no time for me whatsoever. Not the Amber of today, who I seem to have struck up a tentatively pleasant working relationship with.

"That doesn't sound like nothing to me." I stride across the room until I'm standing right in front of her. She's closed her eyes again and she's still twisting that lock of hair around her finger. She's pulling on it so tightly, I worry she might yank it from the roots. "Amber."

She keeps her eyes closed. "Hawthorne."

I reach up and cradle my hand against her cheek. She stops twisting her hair and her eyes fly open. We stare at each other for a long moment that I never want to end. Then she lifts her hand up and holds it against the one I'm cradling her cheek with. She leans into my touch and breathes out a deep, deep sigh. After a few seconds, she pulls my hand away from her cheek and gives me a small nod. "Thanks."

I take a step back, letting my arm swing down to my side. Is she missing the warmth of my hand on her cheek as much as I'm missing the feel of her skin under my palm?

"Sorry about that," she murmurs. "I just needed a minute to breathe."

I'd give her every last one of my minutes on Earth if it meant I'd never have to see or hear her like that again.

"You going to tell me what's wrong now?"

"It's truly not a problem," she says quietly. "I'll figure it out. I always do."

"I could help."

She looks up at me and quirks a brow almost in challenge.

"The studio I bought the chandelier from has one more in stock, but the courier we usually use doesn't have any availability to go and collect it in time for Friday. That means I'll have to push the electricians back and hope they'll be able to come another time. It's not the end of the world, but—"

"It makes our very tight schedule even tighter," I finish for her.

"Exactly."

"What if you picked it up yourself?"

"The studio is about two hours from London, and I don't have a car."

"Rent one and do the drive yourself."

Her laugh is almost hysterical, but at least she's laughing again. "My license is currently expired and, anyway, it's also not in the budget. Cynthia would never approve it, especially since we're going to pay out of pocket for the replacement until I can file an insurance claim for the shattered chandelier."

"I'll pay for it and a driver too."

The expression on her face is somewhere between suspicious and confused. "It's not in *your* budget either, Hawthorne."

She's right. It's not. But I'm not planning to pay for this with the company credit card. "You don't know what my budget is."

She waves a dismissive hand in front of me. "Honestly, I'll figure it out."

"I'm going to pay for the car," I say firmly.

"Why?" Her voice is barely a whisper and there's a hopeful look in her eyes. "Why would you do that?"

I could tell her that it's because I never want to see her look so frustrated and vulnerable ever again if I can help it. Or that it's because maybe I want to be her hero right now so she can shine that beautiful smile on me even for just a few seconds.

But I don't.

I take another step back, increasing the distance between us, and say, "You'll drive there tomorrow, pick up the chandelier, and everything will stay on schedule. Simple."

The hopeful look in her eyes disappears without a trace. "Right." She swallows and finally pushes away from the wall. "Got it."

"Send me your address and I'll book the car to come for you tomorrow."

Her voice is so quiet — not even a whisper — but I don't miss the soft, "Thank you, Finn," she utters as she brushes past me.

12

AMBER

THE CAR HAWTHORNE IS SENDING FOR ME IS DUE TO arrive at 11 a.m., so I get a rare lie in. I earn some brownie points from my mother and Patrick by taking Noah to school. Afterward, I head back home and eat a proper breakfast for the first time in months.

I feel good. Really good. This is the first time in a long while that I've actually been able to slow down and enjoy something as simple as having the time to eat a breakfast that isn't a crumbly cereal bar. I needed this, particularly after yesterday. Seeing the chandelier in thousands of tiny pieces on the floor was bad enough, but getting denied by our courier very nearly tipped me over the edge.

If it hadn't been for Hawthorne and his surprisingly calming presence in that office, I don't know what I would've done. I want to tell Bailey, but I hover uncertainly over our chat history. Her entire world has imploded around her over the last few days, and she's going through a lot right now — a very horrible and public breakup and a potentially messy move back into her parents' home — and I doubt she has the headspace right now to listen to my ramblings about work and Finn Hawthorne. So instead of messaging my best friend, I pull up the property website I spend far too much time on and scroll through the listings while I eat my breakfast.

Almost all of them aren't right for me. The majority are too expensive and the ones that are in my budget are either so dilapidated it'll take tens of thousands of pounds to renovate them, or they're so far away they might as well be in a different country. But one listing stands out among all the others. It's a little farther away from the city than I would like, but it's within my budget and doesn't need any major renovations that'll prevent it from being liveable immediately.

It feels like I've found the holy grail, and I immediately contact the estate agent to organise a viewing. Could this be it? Have I finally found my home? The thought makes me giddy and then sad. Again, this is something I want to share with Bailey, but it doesn't feel right rubbing in my potential wins when she's going through something so awful.

Sitting in this kitchen, in a house that's definitely not a home for me, I suddenly feel very alone.

A car honks loudly outside, making me jump. I glance at my phone. Eleven a.m. on the dot. Impressive. I drop my plate into the sink and then make my way outside before the driver can get too impatient. There's a sleek black Range Rover parked outside the house, and I hurry over to the passenger side door.

"Thanks so much for this," I say as I haul myself into the car. "Hopefully we won't hit much traffic and we can—"

I freeze.

Hawthorne is sitting in the driver's seat with a wide grin plastered across his face. "Morning."

I blink at him. "What the hell are you doing here?"

He gives me a look like I've asked something incredibly stupid and then says slowly, "We're going to pick up the chandelier."

"No, *I'm* going to pick up the chandelier." I get myself fully into the car and pull the door shut. "What're *you* doing here?"

He shrugs, that big grin still going strong. "You said you don't drive."

"And you said you'd pay for a driver."

"Blame it on my cheapness," he says cheerfully, like it doesn't bother him at all if I actually think he's cheap.

Despite myself, I can't help but match his smile. "You know I always do."

I lean back into the comfortable leather seat as Hawthorne pulls out and begins to drive away. He's got his phone on a stand on the dashboard in front of us, a Google Maps route splayed across his screen. His phone *pings* every few seconds and a notification — usually an email — pops up in a banner on the top half of the screen.

It's incessant.

Ping.

Ping.

Ping.

Ping.

"Do you never turn that off?" I ask. "Or at least put it on vibrate?"

We're only about fifteen minutes into the journey, and I'm already getting a headache from the constant sound. We've got the radio on, but the *ping* cuts through the pop music, and it feels like it gets louder every time.

He gives me a rueful smile and when we hit a red light, he leans over and switches his phone to silent, but that doesn't stop the screen from lighting up every few seconds with more email notifications. I'm not trying to snoop, but I can't help but peek at the snippet of email that comes through on the banner.

RE: MEMBERSHIP FEES QUERY

RE: RE: SUMMER OPENING HOURS

LINDA'S BIRTHDAY COLLECTION

"Monday morning milk delivery?" I murmur, frowning at the latest email to pop up on the screen. "Is that something you really need to be involved with?"

His gaze flits from the road to his phone for a brief second, his brows furrowing slightly as he catches sight of the email notification. "We get a lot of deliveries every day back at the New York location," he explains. "It's helpful to keep track of what's coming in and when."

"I know that. Keeping track of deliveries is about eighty percent of my job right now. But that's what *I'm* paid to do. I didn't think keeping track of deliveries was in a *managing director's* job description."

He cracks a small, sad smile. "Fair point. I suppose it's not."

"Then why are you doing it?"

His phone vibrates.

It's another email notification. This one seems to be yet another mundane email from someone on his team. There's nothing urgent in the subject title, nothing that suggests this is something he specifically needs to be on top of.

"Isn't that one of the perks of being so high up?" I ask him. "That you've got a whole team of people at your disposal that can handle things like..." I squint at the phone as yet another email comes in. "Approving the social media schedule for the week? Surely you have a social media manager for that."

"We do. And he'll be copied into that thread too." His tone is uncharacteristically terse, and I know I'm toeing a line here.

Everything about his demeanour — the way he's gripping the wheel and how he's staring determinedly ahead barely blinking — tells me he doesn't want to talk about this. But what else do we have to talk about? We've still got just under two hours left of this drive and I can't pretend like I don't see the stream of emails flooding in.

"But why do *you* need to be copied into it too?" I ask, and I'm genuinely curious. As soon as Cynthia realised she could palm work off on me, she did. Not saying that she's the kind of manager anyone should be looking to emulate, but I think she'd fire me on principle if I copied her into every single email I sent each day.

Hawthorne looks like he's wrestling with something, and he doesn't answer right away. We pull up to another red light and he turns to look at me with hooded, tired eyes. "If something goes wrong, then I can jump in and fix it quickly." His voice is so low, I have to strain to hear him over the quiet vibrations of our idling car. "I don't have to ask people to bring me up to speed, I can just deal with it."

"And how often does something go wrong?"

I can tell that's not the response he was expecting. His

frown deepens as he purses his lips and squints into the distance, like he's looking for the answer out on the long road stretching in front of us.

"Not often," he says quietly, after a long beat of silence. He says it like it's a revelation even to him.

"I'm going to teach you a new word today, Hawthorne. And you better remember it because there's going to be a surprise quiz next week."

I can tell he's biting back a smile.

"Go on..."

"The word is *delegate*."

The hint of his smile drops, and he scowls at me. "Ha, ha. You're hilarious."

"I'm serious. *Delegate*. You're going to drive yourself mad trying to stay on top of everything like this." His phone buzzes in its holder again with another email notification, kindly helping to illustrate my point. "It won't kill you to trust the people you've hired to do their jobs without you breathing down their necks, you know?"

"It won't kill me, but—"

"But what?"

He takes one hand off the wheel and reaches for his tie — only he's not wearing one today, and his hand drops limply into his lap. My mind flashes back to that day I found him on the floor of the office, a pained look etched onto his face as he pulled on the already loose tie around his neck. He looks like he's in pain right now, and before I can talk myself out of it, I reach over and squeeze his dropped hand.

He looks down at our hands — mine resting gently over his, my fingers tracing gentle circles on his skin. He blinks a few times and then swallows thickly. I keep my hand there for a full minute until he starts to look more like himself again and less like he's on the brink of something catastrophic.

When I pull away, he clears his throat. "Thanks. I just needed—" The car rolls to a slow crawl as we hit some traffic and he turns to look at me properly. "I needed a minute."

"I get it. And you don't have to answer my question. I'm just being pushy."

"I know it won't kill me," he says, completely ignoring the out I've just given him. "But sometimes failing feels like an even worse alternative. So I stay on top of them to make sure I can't fail."

"That seems exhausting."

"It is."

And that horrible, sad little smile is back. I want to wipe it off his face. It doesn't suit him. Not one bit.

"Trust the team you've put together," I tell him. "Just for a week. Tell them not to copy you into anything that doesn't genuinely need your immediate attention. No more emails about milk deliveries or social media schedules or..." Another email notification pops up. "Or...approving the final press release for the launch of the London location. Okay, *that* one can stay, but everything else needs to go. You can't keep working like this, Finn."

His first name slips out without me thinking and I suppose I should be happy about it because as soon as it falls from my lips, his wide, bright smile is back and he looks like *him* again.

"Finn, huh?"

"Don't make it a big deal."

He looks like he's on the verge of absolutely making it a big deal, but I suppose I must've earned some goodwill with him because he settles for just giving me a small shrug.

The next time we grind to a slow halt behind some unmoving traffic, Hawthorne reaches over and plucks his phone from the stand.

"What're you doing?" I ask as he taps the screen a few times.

"I think you'd call it *delegating*." He puts the phone back onto its stand, and for the rest of the journey, not a single email comes through.

13

FINN

"Can I get you anything else, dear?"

Amber shakes her head and moves to reach for her purse. I inch forward and drop my card onto the counter, ignoring the half-hearted look of protest she flashes me.

The woman behind the counter giggles as she scoops up my card. "What a gentleman you've got there, dear. And quite the handsome one too. You make sure you hold onto him."

Amber rolls her eyes. "I'm trying to get rid of him, actually."

The woman — the name badge on her shirt reads Eileen — laughs fondly. "That's what they all say, love. Next thing you know, twenty years have passed and your first born is expecting your first grandchild." She hands me back my card and gives me a little wink. "You make sure to take care of her now."

I let my grin take over my face. "Will do, ma'am."

Amber looks like she wants the floor to open up and swallow her whole. She mumbles a polite goodbye to Eileen and then hurries out with me hot on her heels.

We're refuelling at a gas station about halfway between

London and the studio from where we've just picked up the chandelier. It's safely strapped in the back of the car, surrounded in so much protective wrap I'm pretty sure we could bounce it all the way back to the city and it wouldn't get so much as a scratch. But Amber isn't taking any chances, and after what happened yesterday, I can't say I blame her.

When I get back into the car, Amber is already strapped into her seat. There's a slightly darker tinge to her cheeks and she purposefully doesn't look at me as I slide in, her gaze focused firmly ahead.

I add "*seeing her blush*" to my rapidly growing list of my favourite things about her. It sits right there between "*the sound of her laugh*" and "*that look she gives me when I've annoyed her.*"

"If we leave right now, we should miss the rush hour traffic," she says, still looking stubbornly ahead.

I glance at my watch. She's right. We've got about an hour before the roads fill with commuters heading back to their homes. If we leave right now, we'll definitely be able to beat the worst of it and get back to our respective homes relatively quickly. But I don't want that.

"Should we get something to eat first?" I ask. "I'm pretty hungry, and I saw a few places on the way here that looked good."

It's an entirely selfish ask, born out of a desire to stretch out this increasingly rare one-on-one time we have together. Judging by the way she's still determinedly staring ahead, I'm certain she's going to say no.

"Sure."

"Really?"

She glances over at me for the first time since I got in the car.

The blush on her cheeks has dulled slightly, but I can still see a shadow of it lingering. "Why do you sound so surprised?"

"What was it you said back there? '*I'm trying to get rid of him, actually*'?"

She laughs and I'm reminded why that sound is number one on my list. "Trying and failing it seems." She gives me a funny look, like she's trying to figure something out but can't quite get there. After a few seconds, she shakes her head in defeat and shoots me a resigned smile. "Let's go get something to eat, Hawthorne."

Back to Hawthorne again, but she's smiling at me, so I'll take it.

"Okay, dear."

She jerks in her seat like she's been slapped. "*What?*"

I don't think I've ever seen her look so flustered before, and I bite the inside of my cheek to stop myself from laughing. "I said 'okay'."

"No. You said 'okay, *dear*'." She squints at me suspiciously. "Don't say that."

"Why not? You didn't mind when Eileen said it back inside the store."

"That's because she didn't mean it– She didn't mean it like that."

"Like what?"

She's glaring at me, but there's no bite in it. Not really. She can tell I'm teasing her, and for the first time, I feel like I understand the rules of this game she started all those weeks ago.

"You know what you're doing."

I hold up my hands. "I'm just doing what everyone else does around here."

It's something interesting I've learned about the English during my time here so far. People often end their sentences with surprisingly intimate terms of endearment to complete strangers. The woman behind the check-in counter at my hotel calls me "darling" every time I walk past; the elderly doorman calls me "son"; and I've been called "pet," "love," and even "sweetie" more times than I can count by people I've never met before and will never see again.

"Well, you're not doing it right."

"Okay, darling."

She rolls her eyes. "No."

"Why not, pet?"

"Gross."

"What about hon, hon?"

"Stop it."

"No, sweetheart."

"I—" Her voice catches in her throat and I smile. That's the one.

Sweetheart.

"You ready to get something to eat before we head back, *sweetheart*?"

"You're not going to stop, are you?"

"Maybe, sweetheart."

"You don't have to say it after *everything*, you know?"

"I like it," I say with a shrug. "Sounds nice."

Suits you.

"Just...just don't overdo it," she mumbles as she glances down at her lap, tucking a strand of hair behind her ear.

"I make no promises, sweetheart."

It doesn't escape me that, this time, she doesn't protest the name.

WE FIND a small restaurant about twenty minutes away from the gas station. Despite being tucked away down a heavily wooded and bumpy side road, there's only one space in the small parking lot outside when we pull up.

"I feel like we're underdressed," Amber mutters as we wait at the entrance for the waiter to see if he can find us a table. She's standing so close to me, I think we could probably pass as a couple right now. It wouldn't take anything for me to drape an arm over her shoulder and pull her into me. My fingers twitch by my side, daring me to do it.

"You look beautiful," I tell her as I stuff my hands into the pockets of my pants. And she does. I think this is the most casual I've ever seen her — dressed for nothing but spending the day in a car organising the transportation of an expensive chandelier, but she still looks amazing.

She opens her mouth, then closes it and swallows. Her tongue darts out to run over her lips, and I can practically hear the gears in her head working overtime as she figures out what she wants to say.

A woman in a fitted black dress saunters past us, followed by a man in a tailored suit. Amber laughs quietly under her breath and shakes her head. "We're definitely underdressed."

The waiter doesn't seem to mind. He re-emerges after a few minutes and happily informs us that he's found a table. As we walk farther into the restaurant, it's easy to see why the other guests are dressed the way they are.

"Wow." Amber's voice is a breathy whisper as we step into an atrium with high ceilings and a mixture of earthy wooden decor and gold accents. Despite the large room, there are only a few tables in the space, each covered in a white tablecloth. They're so far away from the others that they might as well all be their own little islands.

The waiter leads us to an empty table right next to a row of large French windows that overlook the lake beneath us. He moves to pull out Amber's seat for her, but I step forward first and enjoy the small smile she gives me as she drops into it.

"This place is just...wow." She turns her head in every direction, soaking up every inch of the decor around us. "It's a real hidden gem. I can't believe I've never heard of it before. I wonder who the designer was. Did you see that detailing on the walls near the entrance? And these chairs?" She grips the hand rest of her seat and looks at me with wide, excited eyes. "They're stunning! I've had them on my design wish list for years. I've just been waiting for a project they'd work for."

I lean forward, enthralled, as she launches into a five-minute ramble about the furniture and decor choices and *the truly genius way the designer has combined natural and modern.* I don't recognize any of the names of the designers and artists she throws out, and I can barely keep up as she starts reeling off various techniques and tricks the designer of this restaurant has apparently utilised, but I love it.

I love the way she lights up and comes alive as she goes through everything she likes about the way this restaurant has been designed.

"Sorry," she says sheepishly once she finally stops to take a breath. She dips her head and I hate how she suddenly looks uncertain and afraid that I'm going to suddenly dismiss her. "You probably didn't care about any of that."

I don't know how she could possibly think that. I've got my elbow propped up on the table, my chin resting in the palm of my hand, my gaze focused solely on her. Can she really not tell how enamoured I am with her? How I could easily sit here for years listening to her talk about colour schemes and something called "*modern organic*" design and never, ever get bored?

"I cared about it because you care about it," I say with an easy shrug. "And it was interesting. Really interesting, sweetheart."

She doesn't complain about the use of *sweetheart*. Instead, she beams at me like I've just told her she's won the lottery. "Thank you."

"Have you always wanted to be a designer?" I ask her.

She nods as our waiter comes back with our drinks and cutlery. Once he's gone again, she says, "It's the only thing I've ever really wanted to do."

A tiny pang of jealousy ripples through me, but I push it away.

"How come?"

She shrugs and the light in her eyes dims a little bit. "I've always been a bit obsessed with creating a space for me." She leans back in her seat and frowns. Any trace of the happiness she had just a few seconds ago is long gone.

"You don't have to tell me," I say quickly. "It's personal. I get it."

"It's not that," she says softly. "I just haven't thought about why I chose this career in a long time." She taps her fingers against the table, and I know she's itching to twist them around her hair.

"My parents had me when they were really young. I think my mother had just turned sixteen, and my father wasn't much older. They were just kids having a kid and, surprise, surprise, they didn't last. I think they made it about three years before they called it quits. Which was probably for the best." She snorts out a laugh void of any actual humour or warmth. "They weren't good together. At *all*. My father got a new girlfriend pretty quickly after and they didn't have any room for me in their flat. Whenever I had to spend the night at his place, I slept on the sofa. I didn't even have anywhere to put my clothes." She winces slightly like she's remembering something particularly unpleasant.

"Things were better at my mother's house, but she was a young, single mother, and we couldn't afford very much. We shared a bedroom until she met Patrick, her husband, and he moved us into his house. I had my own room there finally, but it wasn't really mine. I wasn't allowed to decorate or put any posters on the walls or even choose my own bedsheets. It always felt like I was just a guest in their home, even though it was supposed to be my home too."

She blinks quickly and when she looks up at me again, her eyes are watery.

"Amber—"

"It's fine. *I'm* fine," she says, even as her voice cracks slightly. She reaches for the strands of hair falling in front of her face, but then she catches my eye and brings her hand back to the table. "That's all I've ever wanted really. A home of my own. Some place I can decorate how *I* want to. Somewhere I actually belong. I guess that's where interior design came in. I love designing and decorating spaces and making them come to life. Until I can do it in a home of my own, I'll do it for my clients." She shakes her head and then laughs like she hasn't just split my heart in two. "God, that was bleak."

"I'm sorry, sweetheart."

She wrinkles her nose, and I feel a tiny bit of relief to see a glimmer of the Amber I'm used to coming back. "Don't *you* apologise. There's nothing to apologise for. It is what it is."

"Are things better at home now at least?" I ask. "With your parents?"

She reaches for her glass and takes a long sip before answering. "I see my father *maybe* twice a year at best, and we don't really talk outside of that. I don't even know where he is right now. And I wouldn't say I'm close with my mother. Don't get me wrong, I know she loves me and she tried her best, but sometimes I just feel like there's this lingering resentment between us. Like every time she looks at me, she just sees a reminder of how much she missed out on growing up because she had to raise me."

"That's—" I swallow down the lump of anger rising in my throat. "That's awful."

She shrugs like it barely bothers her, even though it's so painfully clear that it does. "I've got a little brother — Noah. He's my angel." Her face lights up when she says his name. "But it's like night and day seeing how she treats him compared to how she treated me growing up and even the way she treats me now. I know that people can change and that I should be grateful that Noah only knows happiness with her. But sometimes I wonder what was so wrong with *me* that she couldn't be this kind of mother back when I needed her."

If her words earlier cleaved my heart in two, that right there just smashed the remains into millions of tiny pieces.

"But enough of this extremely depressing deep dive into my life," she says, cracking a weak smile. "Your turn. Did you always want to be a managing director?"

I feel like I should say something. No— What I *want* to do is leap over the table and pull her into my arms. I want to cradle her face in my hands and tell her over and over again that there's absolutely nothing wrong with her and that anyone who can't see that isn't worth her time. Family or not. But it's clear that she desperately wants to change the topic, so I follow her lead and force out a strained laugh. "No. I can't imagine many little kids dream of being a managing director some day."

"Fair. What did you want to be then?"

Successful? I think that's the only thing I've ever wanted to be. Successful in my own right, without it being attached to my last name. But I don't think that's the answer she's looking for, and *I* don't want to get into all of that right now. "G.I. Joe."

"I can see that." She looks me up and down slowly, deliberately. "You've got the whole blond, muscled hero thing going on."

"Is that your type?" I ask, leaning in. "Blond, muscled heroes?"

"I don't have a type," she says with a smirk. "Treat me nice, and we'll see where it goes."

Is that a challenge? It feels like a challenge and one I'd happily rise to.

"Really?" I ask. "That's it? No big, romantic gestures or anything like that?"

Because I could definitely do that.

She shrugs and gives me a wry smile. "When I get one, I'll let you know how it lands."

I find it hard to believe that Amber isn't swimming in romantic affection, that men aren't lining up in the streets daily to profess their love to her.

The waiter comes back with our food, but we don't break eye contact with each other. We sit in a charged silence as he places our dishes in front of us and tells us to enjoy our meal. When he's gone, she asks, "What about you? Do you have a type?"

I don't even have to think about it. "Beautiful, passionate, *stubborn* women who don't have a problem telling me what they really think about me."

She lifts a brow and hums. "That's very specific."

"I know what I like."

She tries to hide her smile by spearing some chicken onto her fork and taking a bite. "Well, I hope you find her one of these days."

I wonder how long we're going to pretend like I haven't already.

14

FINN

I've developed an annoying new habit. Staring.

Specifically, staring at Amber.

It's as if there's a magnet between us and it keeps tugging on my gaze, twisting my head in whichever direction she happens to be in. Like right now, for instance. She's lounging on her bean bag, slowly making her way through the lunch I bought her today while she scrolls through her phone.

And I can't look away.

The light from the nearby window spills across her face, highlighting things I've never noticed before. Like the streaks of slightly lighter brown that sporadically appear throughout her chin length hair. Or how there's a tiny constellation of little brown freckles dotted along the apples of her cheeks. A ray of sunlight scatters across her chest and draws my attention lower.

The first few buttons of the fitted blouse she's wearing are open, offering up a tantalising peek at the swell of her breasts.

I shake my head and force my attention back to my own lunch. We've sparked up something nice after our trip to collect the chandelier, and I don't need to ruin it by ogling her while we're supposed to be working.

But then I feel that magnetic pull again and, before I know it, I'm watching as a slow but bright smile starts to spread across her face. Her eyes widen slightly and she makes a noise that's halfway between a squeal and a happy sigh.

"Good news?" I ask through a mouthful of bánh mì.

Her gaze flits over to me and her smile seems to widen a fraction. "The best news."

She spins her phone around and points excitedly at the screen. An artsy looking Instagram page is open. Photos of carefully placed furniture, colourful fabric prints, and dainty looking ceramics dominate the screen.

I squint at it. "Not entirely sure what I'm supposed to be looking at, sweetheart."

She gives me a tiny roll of her eyes at the name, but otherwise doesn't protest. "This is the Instagram page for *The Interiors Fair*. It only happens once a year and it's basically a giant indoor market but everything has been curated by famous designers, editors, and collectors. You can get some really amazing finds there. I'm talking like one of a kind antiques." She leans forward on her bean bag and I have to fight to keep my gaze from dipping down her neck and into the popped buttons of her blouse. "A girl I follow on Instagram found a pair of hand painted and upholstered French Louis drawing room chairs last year for £200!"

I have no idea what '*French Louis drawing room chairs*' are, but I could sit here for hours and listen to her tell me about them. The excitement in her voice is infectious and I can't help but match her smile as she launches into a mini speech about how jealous she was when the girl posted about them.

It must be nice to be so passionate about something that it brings you to life like this.

"I had to miss the fair last year because Cynthia had me running errands for her." She pulls a face, but then the smile is back. "But it's coming back again this year on Saturday, and I'm going to go."

"Sounds like it'll be a good time." A thought pops into my head and I frown. "You're not going for work, are you?"

She shrugs. "Not explicitly. But if I see anything that might work for the club while I'm there and it's within the remaining budget, I might pick it up."

"So you're going for fun?"

It's an innocent question but there must be something in my tone that rubs her the wrong way, because she suddenly sits up a little straighter and her smile disappears as her lips turn downwards. She looks a lot more like the Amber I first met than the cautiously friendly woman I've come to know.

"Yes." Her tone is clipped, curt, and guarded.

"Well, it sounds like it'll be fun," I say slowly, trying to figure out where exactly this conversation went off the rails. "Hope you have a good time."

She watches me for a long moment, beautiful brown eyes narrowed suspiciously. But whatever it is she sees reflected on my face must satisfy her, because her expression soon softens. "Sorry, sorry. I'm just– I guess I'm just defensive. If I tell my mother or Patrick where I'm going, they'll just…" She trails off and huffs out a clearly frustrated breath. "Let's just say, they don't support my career and they definitely don't support me doing it for fun in my free time. Why waste my time doing something that doesn't make me any money, when I could spend it studying and retraining in something else, you know?"

The more I learn about her mother and her husband, the less I want to know.

"Have you ever thought about moving out?"

Amber blinks at me, once, twice, and then barks out a sharp laugh. "Yes, I've thought about moving out. It's just not that simple for all of us."

There's an underlying implication in her words when she says '*all of us*' and I immediately feel like an ass.

"Was that a little tone deaf?" I ask sheepishly.

"Incredibly. But..." she says, with a little wink. "I'll forgive you this time since the lunch you bought us today was truly phenomenal."

A sense of relief washes over me.

"And I am moving out, by the way," she adds, almost defensively. "I'm in the process anyway. I've found a place and I think–" Her expression turns almost shy. "I think I'm going to put an offer on it?"

It's a statement, but it comes out sounding more like a question – like she can't quite believe she's even considering it.

I'm pretty sure the level of pride I can feel for her that's blooming in my chest right now isn't normal, but I let myself feel it all the same.

"It's nothing special," she says quickly, and my heart immediately sinks. Here she is, telling me about a huge achievement in her life, and the first thing she does is try and minimise it. I can't tell if she's just trying to get ahead of whatever she thinks her mother might say, or if her mother has just managed to chip

down her sense of worth over the years, that negatively quali-
fying something like this is just second nature to her now.

"And it's quite small, and–"

"Don't do that."

Her brows furrow. "Don't do what?"

"Make yourself small."

Her lips part and, even with the distant sound of the
contractors working below us, I swear I can hear the way her
breath catches in her throat.

"You don't have to do that around me, sweetheart."

*I'm not going to dismiss you. I'm not going to make you feel
like your wins don't matter.*

The realisation that her life is apparently filled with people
who do make her feel like this is a sobering one, and I refuse to
be one of them.

The beginnings of a soft smile starts to form as she gives me
a small nod. "Okay." She dips her head for a moment and when
she looks back at me, there's a new fire behind her eyes. "I'm
going to look for some things to add to my mood board for my
house while I'm at the fair."

I grin. *That's my girl.*

"Are you going with anyone?"

She shakes her head. "Usually I'd ask Bailey if she wants to
come. She's not into design like I am, but I'm sure we could
make a day of it."

"What would '*making a day of it*' entail?" I ask, genuinely
curiously. I know very little of what Amber does during her free
time. A streak of jealously shoots through me as I consider that
Amber has a whole life outside of these walls that I'm not
part of.

"We'd probably go for lunch somewhere after," she says. "Or maybe we'd have a picnic. The weather's supposed to be good this weekend, and there's a beautiful park not far from the fair." She sighs and seems to deflate slightly into her bean bag. "But Bailey is– She's going through some things right now."

She doesn't elaborate and I don't ask, sensing it's not a topic she's willing to share on.

"As much as I'd love to drag her out of the house, she probably wouldn't be down for it. So, I'll just go by myself," she says with a little shrug. "It'll still be a fun day. Might take myself out for lunch after."

"Haven't we set a lunch precedent?" I ask, my mouth moving before my brain can really comprehend what I'm about to say. I hold up my half eaten bánh mì and raise a pointed brow. "I buy the lunches around here."

"At work," she says, sounding at least a little amused. "When we're in the same building all day. It doesn't count on a weekend when I'm at a fair and you're..." She trails off and frowns. "Doing whatever it is you do on the weekend."

Work, mostly.

I've explored embarrassingly little of London during my time here, something Nel is sure to scold me about when I get back home.

"Then I'll come to the fair with you," I say. "That'll solve the whole not being in the same building thing."

She blinks at me slowly. "Why would you do that?"

I shrug. "Sounds like it'll be a fun afternoon."

She narrows her eyes, clearly not buying it. "It'll be fun for *me*. Less so for someone like you."

And there it is again. An underlying bite that colours her

tone. It feels like she's trying to say something – something she feels she can't voice out loud – but I can't figure out what it is. She doesn't give me the chance to ask.

"The weather is going to be nice, though," she says quickly. The redirect is obvious. "You should head out, see the sights. The London Eye is usually a good one in the sun."

The only thing I want to see in the sun is her.

"Nah, you've sold me on the fair," I say, ignoring the scowl she shoots me. She's really quite an expressive woman. "And besides, if you do happen to see something you think might be a good fit for the club, I should probably be there to approve it."

It's a flimsy excuse.

I know it.

She knows it.

"I don't need your approval, Hawthorne."

"I know you don't," I tell her honestly, because she's right. Amber doesn't need or *want* my approval when it comes to anything. It's a strange feeling going from being the person who has to sign off on everything from milk deliveries to important press releases, to being around someone who clearly couldn't care less about my opinions on the intricacies of their job.

I don't think I mind it though.

"But humour me," I continue. "Let me still act like I'm the one in charge around here."

"As long as we both know it's just an act."

"I'm well aware, sweetheart."

She laughs, and the sound vibrates along my bones. Such a beautiful laugh.

"So I'll come then?" I ask. "To the fair, with you?"

"Yes, Hawthorne," she says with a dramatic, long-suffering sigh. "You can come."

———

IT'S the first genuinely warm and sunny day I've had since landing in the UK. The sky is blue, the few sparse clouds in the sky are a blinding white, and the sun is shining high above us.

It's not hot exactly – probably no higher than 68F – but everyone is dressed like we're in Spain or Greece.

Amber included.

My throat goes dry as I spot her in the queue for the fair. She's wearing a short yellow summer dress. I think there's some kind of pattern to it – maybe spirals or clouds – but I barely register it. I can only focus on the way it hugs at her waist, accentuating her subtle curves, or the way the soft breeze makes the hem flutter around her thighs and full hips.

She looks gorgeous. Like she was made to be in the sun. Her warm brown skin is practically glowing and when she looks up and sees me staring at her, I swear her smile could rival the sun.

"I was just starting to wonder if you'd bailed on me," she teases as I push through the small crowd to join her in the queue.

Never.

"Sorry, got a bit turned around on the tube." My hotel is within walking distance from the club and, aside from that one evening when I locked myself out, I've not had much use for London's expansive underground network yet.

"I thought New Yorkers were supposed to be good on the underground. Don't you have a subway there?"

"We do," I concede. "But I rarely use it. I like walking. New York's an interesting city, when I walk it's almost a guarantee I'll stumble on something new every time I leave my apartment."

"Yeah, London's a bit like that too," she says. "That's actually how I first found out about this fair a few years back. They don't really advertise it properly – it's more of a '*if you know, you know*' kind of situation, and I accidentally came across it doing the walk of shame one Saturday morning."

My eyes widen a fraction. It's clear that she immediately regrets divulging that to me, but she quickly schools her expression into a mask of casual indifference. "Don't pretend like *you've* never done the walk of shame before, Hawthorne."

"Nothing shameful about it," I say with a shrug. "But no, I haven't."

The queue shuffles forward and I use the opportunity to step a little closer and bridge the distance between us. "And anyone who spends the night with me isn't *walking* home either."

"Why? Because you're *so* good, they can't walk once you're finished with them? Disappointing, Hawthorne." She shakes her head and gives me a blank stare. "If that's the kind of line you're using on women, I find that very hard to believe."

"That wasn't a line," I say with a smirk. "I meant that I always pay for a cab home for them as a bare minimum, as any gentleman should. But." I lean in and bump my arm against hers. "Interesting that your mind went there."

A blush creeps up her neck. "My mind didn't go anywhere."

"Sure sounds like it did."

She runs a hand through her hair, doing her best to hide the way her lips are desperately trying to curve into a smile. "You must have misheard."

I didn't mishear and she knows it. Still, she gives me a look that tells me she's not going to budge on this, so I shrug. "Guess I must have."

We only have to wait for ten minutes or so more before it's our turn to enter the fair. Strangely, it's being hosted inside a church. We walk into the large chapel and, as beautiful as they are, the high stone ceilings and colourful mosaic windows pale in comparison to the rows and rows of stalls that fill the space. They're covered in bright artwork, furniture, ornaments, fabrics, and there's even a stall that's been crushed under the weight of a large, comfortable looking armchair.

Amber is practically vibrating with excitement. Her deep brown eyes flit this way and that as she takes in everything around us. I follow close behind as she leads me through the fair, stopping every now and then to admire something on a stall and take a photo.

"Is this for your moodboard?" I ask as she stops in front of a stall and immediately begins taking photos of a pair of lamp bases.

Her eyes are bright as she drags her gaze away from the bases to me. "These are *vintage Fornasetti*'s."

I nod like I know what she's talking about.

"He was an Italian designer," she says with a little laugh, clearly seeing through my act. "An icon, really."

I glance at the price tag the vendor has scrawled on a piece of paper in front of the bases. My brows shoot into my hairline. "That much for two lamp bases?"

Amber rolls her eyes. "Good design costs money,

Hawthorne. Everything from *Fornasetti* is made by hand in Milan." She points at the base nearest her. "You see the design on that? All hand-drawn and hand-painted. Someone's put their heart and soul into learning this craft and creating this and I think that's beautiful. So yes, it's *this much* for two lamp bases."

She's scolding me and is most definitely on the verge of calling me cheap again, but I can't bring myself to care.

"Why're you smiling like that?" she asks, instantly suspicious.

"Am I smiling?" I say, even as I can feel my grin stretching further. "I didn't notice."

"Don't ruin this for me, Hawthorne. If you're here just to make fun of me, you can leave now."

"I'm not making fun," I say. "I just– I feel like I understand you a little better now."

Her initial reason for getting into interior design might be tinged with sadness, but it's clear that she's truly found something she loves. I'm somehow both jealous and incredibly happy for her at the same time.

"What do you mean?" she asks, eyes still narrowed with suspicion.

We've meandered away from the *Fornasetti* lamp bases and now we're slowly walking up and down the busy aisles.

"I mean exactly what I'm saying, sweetheart. I like listening to you explain these things to me. I like knowing why *you* like this kind of stuff."

We stop in front a large ornate mirror. It's in need of a good clean, and about as wide as I am if I hold my arms out to my side, with a thick decorative gold border around its edge. Amber practically purrs in appreciation as she runs a gentle hand down it.

"Now *this* is a dream. A holy grail type item."

"You going to get it for your new place?"

"No, it's way too big for the house I've got my eye on. It would look silly in the space." She snaps a photo of the mirror and I watch as she sorts it into a folder on her phone named *'DREAM HOME'*. "One day though."

"Tell me about it," I say, nodding to the mirror. Our reflections are distorted amidst the grime and dust, but I can make out her smiling face next to mine. "Tell me all about this mirror."

"You don't want to hear about that."

"Yes, I do. Tell me about who designed it and what techniques they used and anything else you can think of."

She catches my eye in the mirror. "You sure?"

I nod. "Go wild, sweetheart."

She does, and the five minutes I spend listening to her passionately tell me all about the history of Parisian mirror making might just be five of the best minutes I've ever had in my life.

Later, when she's distracted by a soft green rug with intricate silver threading woven throughout it, I make my way back to the mirror. The woman stood beside it gives me a knowing smile when I hand over my business card and let her know I'll be in touch soon.

15

AMBER

I think this might just be one of the best days I've had in a very long while, and I'm spending it with Finn Hawthorne of all people.

"What's next, sweetheart?"

Truth be told, I thought he'd tire of the whole *sweetheart* thing by now, but he shows no signs of giving it up. Another truth? I definitely don't mind as much as I probably should.

Every time he says it, a little frisson of pleasure shoots through me. I like the way it rolls off his tongue, the way his eyes always find mine, how it feels like more than just a silly little game. Like he really means it.

Sweetheart.

"I think you promised me lunch?" I say, not quite ready for this day to end yet.

Although, it *is* long past an acceptable time for lunch. We spent close to four hours in the fair with Hawthorne taking a surprising interest in all the items being showcased. It was nice actually – *really* nice – sharing with him my thoughts about everything we looked at. He took everything in his stride, listened, asked questions, pointed at things that caught his interest and, by the end of it, was even pointing out things that he thought I'd like.

And it doesn't escape me that he was right in most of his choices. Or how it made my heart skip a beat every time he pointed something out.

Maybe that's why I don't mind how close we are right now as we walk down the street. Our arms brush against each other with every step, and my fingers twitch against his, itching to reach out and link our hands together.

I fumble through my bag and find my phone as a way to give my traitorous hands something to do. "There's a supermarket just around the corner. We can grab some food and then, if you want, we could head to Primrose Hill?"

"What's Primrose Hill?"

"It's a park on a hill not too far from here." I nod in the direction we'll be going. "If we start making our way there now, we should be able to camp out and get a good spot for sunset. It's a bit of a trek, but the views once you reach the top on a clear day are second to none. Definitely the most beautiful thing you'll see in the city today."

Hawthorne gives me a slow, deliberate once over. "I doubt that."

I feel my cheeks begin to warm, but I've never been one to back down and I force myself to hold his gaze. "Something else caught your eye?"

His Adam's apple bobs up and down, and I don't think he can blame the pink tinge slowly spreading over his cheeks on the sun.

"Something." He shrugs. "Someone."

We're teetering on the edge of something new here, and I think we both know it. There's a sweet tension in the air and the temptation to lean into it and see where this could go is overwhelming. It brings me back to that evening in the pub, but there are no dark corners here. Just bright skies and the sun beaming down on us.

Nowhere to hide.

I'm not sure I want to.

If you told me six weeks ago that I'd be spending my weekend with Hawthorne *and* enjoying it, I would've laughed in your face. But the man I first met – the one I overheard dismissing my career, time, and energy – isn't the man standing in front of me today.

I wonder if I was too quick to pass judgement on him, because the Hawthorne grinning down on me, his eyes shining with the promise of something fun, feels like a different person entirely.

"That was very smooth."

His grin widens. "Is this you finally admitting that you're charmed by me now?"

Yes.

"Nope," I lie. "Gonna have to work harder than that."

He gives me a mock salute. "Mission accepted."

"Really leaning into the whole G.I. Joe thing, huh?"

"Is it doing it for you?"

Also yes.

I roll my eyes and shove him gently in the direction of the supermarket. "Keep it moving, Hawthorne."

He could easily wiggle out of my touch, but he doesn't. He

lets me shove him through the doors and I wonder if he's enjoying the feel of my skin on his as much as I am.

———

"YOU KNOW, I don't think your phone has pinged once today."

We've taken the long route towards Primrose Hill, chewing on our sandwiches and talking as we slowly meander through the streets. The conversation flows easily, like we've been good friends for years, and this doesn't surprise me as much as it probably should.

Hawthorne looks at me sideways. "Is that a problem?"

"Definitely not," I say. "How're you finding the whole *delegating* thing?"

He exhales a long breath and runs a hand through his hair. "Good."

I poke him with my elbow. "Doesn't sound good."

"It *is* good," he insists with a wry smile. "But also difficult. For me anyway. I'm sure everyone else back in New York is relieved not to have to report into me every hour of the day."

"What's so difficult about it?"

We come to a crossing and wait for the steady flow of traffic to halt for us. Hawthorne turns to face me, his expression thoughtful, maybe even a little sad. "It's not in my nature to be so hands off. I'm doing it, because you're right, I needed to for my own sanity. But that doesn't mean there's not a voice in the back of my mind, constantly telling me that everything's always on the brink of going wrong. I have to actively stop myself from checking my phone every five minutes."

I reach out and give his arm a little squeeze. His gaze drops down and he swallows thickly. I should snatch my hand back and apologise for being too familiar, but I don't. I let my fingers trail down the length of his arm. "You're doing a good job. I don't think I've seen you even look at your phone all day."

His dark green eyes lift up from his arm and sweep across my face, searching for something. I suddenly feel very exposed. My tongue darts out to run along my lips and his eyes move from left to right, following the action with perfect precision.

Whatever he's looking for, I think he finds it.

"I've had a good distraction." His voice is so low, I have to fight to hear it over the sound of traffic.

"Yeah?" I ask and, *goddamnit*, my voice is basically a whisper too.

He nods and takes a step closer to me. The movement makes my hand drop from his arm, but he reaches out and grabs it before it can swing back to my side. His touch is like fire, but in the best kind of way. "Do *you* need a distraction, sweetheart?"

I open my mouth, but no words come out. My throat is dry and the only thing I can focus on right now are the soft, gentle movements of his fingers as they dance up my arm, over my shoulders, across my collarbone, and up my neck.

"No," I whisper.

A lie.

A stupid, obvious lie.

Hawthorne raises a brow but doesn't break our eye-contact as he brings his hand up higher, fingers ghosting over my jaw to cradle my face.

I think I've stopped breathing.

He leans in and my eyelids flutter shut of their own accord.

But the next thing I feel *isn't* his lips caressing mine. It's the scratch from the slight stubble around his jaw brushing against my cheek as he leans in and whispers in my ear.

"When you're ready for a distraction, you know where to find me."

My eyes snap open in time to see him pull back, a smug grin on his face.

"I already told you," I say, my voice too shaky to believable. "I don't need a distraction."

"Whatever you say, sweetheart," he says with a shrug before he laces his fingers with mine and pulls me across the road. "We're heading this way, right?"

I nod, not sure I can trust my voice to say anything, and let him guide me towards the entrance to Primrose Hill.

By the time we reach the top, the sky has already begun to turn pink and Hawthorne still hasn't let go of my hand.

Not that I'm in any kind of rush for him to do so.

I like the feel of his hand in mine. We fit together nicely and each small caress of his thumb against my skin sends a new wave of heat flowing through me.

"You weren't kidding about the view," Hawthorne says with an appreciative nod once we come to a still. The lush green grass rolls out beneath us and the London skyline stretches across the horizon in front of us. It's the perfect blend of nature and architecture, and one of my favourite spots in the city.

With his free hand, Hawthorne digs around in his pocket and pulls out his phone for the first time all day.

"What're you doing?"

He lines his camera up with the skyline and snaps a few

photos. "Getting some evidence for my sister that I actually left my hotel room and had some fun while I was here."

"Might be a bit more believable if you're actually in the photo," I say. "You could easily have just grabbed those from the internet."

"You think I'd go that far just to avoid a lecture from my sister?" He pretends to look offended but then breaks out into a sheepish grin. "Because I absolutely would."

That gets a laugh out of me. I reluctantly drop his hand and reach for his phone. "Give it here and you go and stand over there."

He does what I say with only a hint of resignation. "Is here good?"

I take a step backwards so he's centred in the middle of the frame and the full skyline is in the backdrop. "All good. Now smile."

He gives me a blank stare.

"Come on, Hawthorne. I've seen your smile before. It's not half bad."

The corners of his lips lift ever so slightly. "You think I've got a nice smile?"

"I *said* it's not half bad. Take from that what you will." He's got a wonderful smile, actually. The kind of smile that lights up a room and lifts your mood when he turns it on you. "Don't tell me you're the kind of guy who sees a camera and immediately wheels out the thousand yard stare."

"I'm going for more of a handsome *smoulder* actually."

"And how's that going for you?"

"Judging by the look on your face right now?" He smirks and shoots me a playful wink. "I'd say pretty good."

I force my features into a scowl, idly wondering what emotion had been painted across my face seconds prior. "No idea what you're talking about."

"You sure about that, sweetheart? Because you look—"

"I can take that for you, hon." Someone taps my shoulder and I whirl around. A jogger stands in front of me, bouncing on the spot. She nods to Hawthorne and then back at me. "So you can get in the photo with your boyfriend?"

"Oh. No. He's not—"

"Thank you! That's so kind of you," Hawthorne yells across the short distance between us. He crooks a finger towards me. "Get over here, *sweetheart*."

He says *sweetheart* with more emphasis than usual, making the word sound sickly sweet.

"It's no problem," the jogger says as she snatches Hawthorne's phone out of my hands and then waves me off in his direction.

I march almost robotically over to him. It figures, but *now* he's beaming. I arch a brow. "So you *can* smile, then?"

"Now I have a reason to."

As soon as I'm within touching distance he pulls me flush against him, so my back is pressed up against his chest. His arms move to wrap around my middle and I feel him drop his chin gently to rest on my head.

"Alright," the jogger calls. "Three. Two. One. Say cheese!"

His arms tighten around me and I don't need to force the soft smile that lifts my lips as I bring up a hand to rest on his forearm and relax into his touch.

I think that I could get used to being in Finn Hawthorne's arms.

"Nice!" She jogs over to us and, despite the warm temperature, I immediately feel cold when Hawthorne unravels himself from me and reaches for his phone.

He glances at the photo and then shoves his phone back into his pocket without letting me see. "Thanks."

"No problem." She gives us both a wink before she quickly jogs away.

I watch as she disappears down the hill, and when I turn back to Hawthorne he's got his eyes firmly planted on me.

"What?"

"Nothing," he says. "Just admiring the view."

My heart does a little flip, but I roll my eyes anyway as I plop down onto the grass. "How incredibly corny of you."

"Couldn't waste the opportunity." He joins me on the grass but doesn't come to sit by my side. Instead he sits directly behind me, spreading his legs wide so I'm nestled between his thighs. "It *is* a beautiful view though."

"Which one are you talking about now?"

I feel, rather than hear, the quiet laugh that rumbles through his chest. "Assume I'm always talking about you, sweetheart." He brings his arms around me again and I waste no time melting into his touch.

We stay like this – me, leaning against him, his arms wrapped loosely around my waist – until the sun sets and the sky turns dark. If it wasn't for the sudden chill that descends upon us once the last orange rays disappear beyond the horizon, I would've gladly stayed for longer.

It feels good being in Hawthorne's arms.

It feels *right*.

Like this is where I'm supposed to be.

But the wind is surprisingly cold and when I shiver for the third time in a row, Hawthorne suggests we start making our way home. He insists on calling me a taxi despite my protests.

"I told you," he says as we wait for it to arrive. "Anyone who spends the night with me isn't walking home."

I force out a snort. "In your dreams, Hawthorne."

And mine too it seems. Because when I'm home later that evening, tucked under my blankets, and my traitorous hands dip under the band of my pyjama shorts to find myself wet and wanting, it's Hawthorne's face that swims in my vision.

It's his voice I hear coaxing me on as my fingers slip inside and take up a slow but steady rhythm.

And it's *Finn* that spills from my lips when my thumb brushes against my clit one too many times and I see stars.

16

AMBER

THE OFFICE HAS BEEN FINISHED FOR WEEKS. THE WALLS have been plastered and painted, the fixtures and rugs have been fitted, the furniture is all in place — including a large wooden desk and several comfortable armchairs. But Hawthorne and I are still sitting on our beanbags.

There's been a shift, and I'm not sure when it happened. It's difficult to tell if it's been a gradual thing slowly building since he started buying me lunch all those weeks ago, or if there was one moment — maybe that fancy riverside meal we had or our day at the fair and Primrose Hill — that sparked it. Maybe we've been building towards it for longer than I realised. All I know is that when Hawthorne's leg bumps against mine as he fidgets on his beanbag, I barely register the touch because it's become so familiar.

I want to say that it was Hawthorne who brought our beanbags closer together one day, but I'm not entirely certain. We no longer sit on opposite sides of the office sneaking curious glances at each other as we work. Both our beanbags are pulled up against the same wall, barely a couple centimetres apart, and these little touches between us have become commonplace. Sometimes it's a leg, other times he'll lean into me, strong arms brushing against mine. I find that I don't mind the intimacy that comes with each fleeting touch.

One day, after a particularly irritating call with his uncle — a perpetually irritable man who I've come to dislike almost as much as Hawthorne does — he closed his laptop and snuggled up to me, resting his head gently on mine. I didn't make any move to shake him off, and I didn't want to either.

I liked it.

Liked the feel of him leaning on me, using me as a safe space to quietly breathe as he got back some of his strength after another stressful call.

We've become pretty open with each other too.

When my offer gets accepted on the property I first saw that day we went to collect the chandelier, Hawthorne is the first person I tell. Even before Bailey.

We're in the office and I can't stop my shriek of delight from coming out when I get the confirmation email. I wave my phone excitedly in his face so he can see the email, and from the way he matches my energy, you'd think *he* was the one who'd just bought his first house.

He tells me he's proud of me — makes sure to drop a casual *sweetheart* in there too — and makes me promise to invite him over for a housewarming party when I'm ready.

And you know what's weird? I agree to it. *Happily* even. Like Finn Hawthorne and I are good, good friends and inviting him to visit my new home is one of the most natural things in the world.

He shares with me too. Like when he tells me it's been a full month since someone last copied him on a pointless email, and he feels like he's breathing easier these days. Or when his sister FaceTimes him when we're in the office together and he doesn't think twice about tilting the camera toward me and introducing us like that's a perfectly normal thing to do. And when I help him find a souvenir for his niece that *won't* drive his sister mad — a cute *Build-A-Bear* wearing a special edition London jumper — he thanks me and orders one for Noah too without even hesitating.

The lunches keep coming — even on days when I'm barely in the office, too busy running around the property making sure everything is still on track. He always comes to find me and hands me whatever it is he bought that day. I start trying to make time for him at lunch at least once a week and those, secretly, have become some of my favourite days. We'll sit on our beanbags, legs bumping, arms brushing, quietly enjoying each other's company as we eat our lunch.

It's annoying to admit, but I'm starting to wish this project's end date wasn't rapidly approaching. If everything goes to schedule, the property should be finished in just over three weeks, and then Hawthorne is planning the official launch of The August Room in London shortly after. I've not asked him how long he plans to stay in London after the launch, but I don't imagine he'll linger for long.

In a month, this will all be gone; the little routine we've developed each day, the lunches, the quiet moments we steal when it's just us, the strange sense of calm I feel when he drops his head onto my shoulder, the teasing look in his eyes when he calls me *sweetheart,* and the funny little *thud* my heart does every time he says it.

I'm going to miss it, but I take a little bit of comfort in the fact that we've still got a few weeks left to enjoy this new friendship we've developed.

And so, of course, Cynthia has to ruin everything.

***

CYNTHIA IS SMILING, which should actually be my first sign that something is about to go horribly wrong. I don't think Cynthia has ever directed a genuine smile at me in the seven years I've been working for her. At best, I'll get an upturned grimace that doesn't extend to her eyes. But right now, she's smiling wide and bright, looking like a cat who's just found an unguarded bird's nest.

"Amber, darling," she purrs. "Do have a seat."

It's the first time I've visited the Zensi Designs office since I started working on The August Room project, and it takes me all of five seconds to remember why I've avoided coming here. I can't believe I've never noticed it before, but working with Hawthorne in the club office has really made the difference clear. It's silent in the main pen, but it's not a comfortable, easy silence like the one Hawthorne and I have cultivated. It's like the people in the office are scared of making a noise or doing anything to garner Cynthia's attention from her glass-walled throne room.

It's stifling.

How can anyone be creative in a place like this? How have *I* managed to survive in a place like this for as long as I have?

I drop into the seat. "Is everything okay?"

"Everything is just divine, darling." She pours herself a small cup of tea without offering me any. Back when I was her assistant, it was my job to fetch tea or water for Cynthia's guests. Either Kirsty hasn't been forced to take on that particular job, or Cynthia hasn't deemed me worthy of a polite beverage. I don't know which one annoys me more.

"How are things going with The August Room?"

"Great," I tell her, relaxing into my seat. She just wants a status update. A bit unorthodox to call me all the way into the office for that, but Cynthia has always been one for dramatics. "We're nearly finished, and the launch is still on schedule."

"Yes. I received an invitation from Hawthorne a few days ago."

"You should come down and see it before the party," I say reluctantly. I don't want her in the space really, but it seems like the polite thing to say. "I think you'll be happy with what I've done. Hawthorne seems very pleased with it all."

More than pleased, actually. The annoying emails nit-picking and changing everything have long since stopped darkening my inbox. I can tell it doesn't come easily to him, stepping back and letting me do what I do best. But he's trying.

"Glad to hear it," Cynthia says through pursed lips. Only she doesn't sound very glad at all. "I'll see if I have some space in my schedule to inspect your work. But really, dear, I shouldn't have to hover over you like this."

"I didn't mean—"

"I worry your lack of confidence in your own work means you're not ready for this promotion."

I stare at her unblinking. "Excuse me?"

"I expect my senior designers to have a certain level of independence and autonomy, and I'm not quite sure you're there yet, darling."

She's joking. Surely she's got to be joking. "Cynthia, I just thought you might like to see the property before the launch party. I wasn't suggesting that I need you to—"

"But don't worry." She raises her voice slightly to cut me off. "I know we've agreed that you'll receive a promotion following the completion of this project with Hawthorne, and I don't intend to go back on my word."

Relief floods through me. "Thank—"

"But you'll need to convince me that you have what it takes."

I frown. How much more can I possibly do?

"The Pevensey is opening up a new branch in Brighton and they'd like us to put in a design bid."

I sit up a little straighter in my seat. The Pevensey is a luxury boutique hotel brand and would definitely be a major get for my portfolio. "That sounds amazing. As soon as I finish up with The August Room, I can start working on concepts to pitch to them."

Cynthia shakes her head. "The bid is due in a week. We're on a tight time frame here. I'll need you to have the concepts over to me by Wednesday so I can go over them, make any changes, and send them on."

My throat goes dry. "Cynthia, when am I supposed to find the time to do that? We're in the final stages of The August Room project and that's the busiest time for us."

"Being a senior designer means being able to multitask."

I know that. Of course I fucking know that. Day in, day out, all I do is multitask. I take a deep, steadying breath and try to remind myself how close I am to the finish line.

The house. The promotion. The pay rise. So, so close.

"I'm not sure I'll have time to go to Brighton, check out the location, design the concepts, and source items all while working on The August Room."

Cynthia's lips curl back up into that not-a-smile again. "Well, as I said, this is the kind of workload my senior designers should expect. If that's not something you can handle, then perhaps we should revisit whether you're truly ready for this step up."

I think Cynthia may be the worst person I've ever had the displeasure of meeting. I grip the fabric of my skirt tightly, balling it up into my fists to stop myself from doing something stupid like leaping across the table and throttling her. "No," I say through teeth so gritted I'm surprised I haven't ground them down to little nubs yet. "I can handle it. I'll make time."

"Excellent." Cynthia claps her hands. "This is a truly brilliant opportunity for you, Amber, darling. Work on those concepts and get them over to me as soon as you can."

"Fine, but—"

Her phone rings and she picks it up without so much as a glance in my direction. "Genevieve, darling, so good to hear from you..." She waves a hand toward the door, dismissively ushering me away.

I sit there simmering in my fury for a second or two and then grab my bag and leave. The only reason I don't let the door slam on the way out is because I'm afraid the glass might shatter.

17

AMBER

I don't think I've ever been so exhausted. Every single part of me aches, from my muscles to my brain. My vision is blurry, I don't remember what the last real meal I ate was, and I'm pretty sure I'm running on less than four hours of sleep a night at this point.

Definitely running on fumes right now.

My phone *pings* and my already dark mood darkens even further.

FROM: Finn Hawthorne <fhawthorne@theaugustroom.com>
SUBJECT: RE: RE: RE: Ground floor toilets
BODY: No, I'm not sure the lighting is working. Looks too seedy. Can you come and give your thoughts?

Another ping.

FROM: Cynthia Zensi <cynthia@zensidesigns.com>
SUBJECT: RE: The Pevensey concepts

BODY: Pevensey have accepted the bid. Work begins shortly – will organise a schedule for you.

Another.

FROM: Caleb Burrows <caleb.burrows@grovehomes.com>
SUBJECT: Congratulations!
BODY: Dear Amber, I hope all is well. I'm pleased to let you know that the payment has cleared and the contract has been signed on both ends. The house is officially yours! Give me a call and we'll discuss the hand over of keys and anything else. Best, Caleb.

Although that last email fills me with nothing but joy, I pick up my phone and do something I haven't done in years: I turn it off. The screen goes black and I feel the first sense of peace I've felt in almost two weeks.

How did I get here again? Ah, yes. Cynthia.

All roads to my personal hell seem to lead back to Cynthia.

In just one annoying conversation, she single-handedly undid everything Hawthorne and I had been working toward with this new friendship of ours. With my new workload for The Pevensey, my time at The August Room has dwindled down to a few hours a week. Hawthorne and I barely see each other now, and he's reverted back to sending me nit-picking emails every couple of hours.

As annoying as it is, I can't even say that I blame him entirely. We're less than two weeks out from the launch party and there's still so much to do. I should be there coordinating the finishing touches, making sure the furniture is in the right places, and ensuring the rooms are dressed properly. It doesn't help that every day something new seems to go wrong.

Yesterday, it was the cushions. Apparently, there'd been a mix-up and Simon from the warehouse accidentally sent the wrong pattern covers. Cue about twelve missed calls and a slew of increasingly panicky emails from Hawthorne.

The day before that, it was the tiling in the bar area on the second floor. One of the contractors had done a sloppy job with a small patch of tiling and it needed to be fixed. It wasn't a big deal and I would've been *all* over it if I'd been there. But I wasn't, and so Hawthorne had been left to spiral.

Allegedly.

Today it's the lighting. I have no idea what he means by it looking "seedy," and I'm half-heartedly considering that maybe — *maybe* — he's making these problems seem bigger than they are in a misguided attempt to bring me back to The August Room.

But I don't have the time or the energy to figure out if he's playing games. The team at The Pevensey are almost as demanding as Hawthorne is and don't even have the decency to be charming or attractive when they're sending me demanding emails at all hours of the day. I've just spent the entire day in Brighton with them, taking photos and documenting every inch of the huge manor house they've purchased for their next location.

This project is a designer's dream, and I hate how disinterested I am in it.

Bailey says I have burn out.

We've barely spoken over the last few weeks, an unfortunate consequence of me drowning in an increasingly impossible workload and Bailey desperately trying to stay afloat after a horrible breakup. She's been slow to respond to my messages — not that I can blame her given the situation — but I think she's finally starting to come out of the worst of it. When she's ready, maybe we'll talk about how I never thought her ex was good enough for her anyway, but right now all she needs is a friend and a sympathetic shoulder to cry on.

So I haven't told her much about what's really going on. She doesn't know about Cynthia's mind games or how truly drained I am, how I'm barely eating, or how my days start before the sun rises and end well after it sets. I stick to petty complaints about Hawthorne's emails and hope she can't see through it.

She does, though, of course.

She's my best friend in the world, the closest thing I have to a sister, and even through a haze of heartbreak, Bailey can see that there's something wrong.

"You're burnt out, babe," she told me when we last spoke. Her eyes were red and puffy from crying, but she still found the space to worry about me. "You need a break."

And *yes*. God is she right. But I can't really afford to take any time off right now. Because, as my estate agent Caleb has so helpfully informed me, I've just purchased a house. While I can afford it on my current salary, living any kind of comfortably depends on this promotion. I can't give Cynthia any reason to snatch it from me — not that she needs one.

The thought of having to move back into my parents' house if this all falls through is maybe the only thing keeping me going. And I'm truly hanging on by a thread right now.

I dig through my bag and find my phone as my train pulls into London Victoria station. The silence has been a welcome reprieve on my journey back from Brighton, but I should really turn it back on and try to put out some fires before I crawl into bed.

As soon as the screen sparks to life, about twenty email notifications come through at once. A couple are from Cynthia, one is from my bank about my new mortgage, but the rest are all from Hawthorne. Alongside the emails, there are notifications for sixteen missed calls– all from him.

Sixteen.

I don't know if he's playing games or if he has genuinely reverted back to the neurotic asshole I first met nearly three months ago, but enough is enough.

It's late and the sky is only getting darker as I stomp toward the underground entrance. I know he'll still be at the club. Powered by nothing but fury and exhaustion, I quickly fire off a quick response to his latest email.

FROM: Amber Wyatt <amber@zensidesigns.com>
SUBJECT: RE: URGENT
BODY: Give me 20 mins. I'm on my way.

18

FINN

YOU'RE GOING TO NEED TO TRUST ME ON THAT.

Trust me on that.

Okay, I've trusted her, and look what's happened.

It's been three days since I last saw Amber in person, and even that was only for a few minutes before she rushed out again. She's become a ghost in this building and without her, what was once a well-maintained ship has suddenly started leaking. Aside from Ric, her contractors don't listen to me, and when things go wrong, there's nobody here to steer them in the right direction.

I have Amber's concepts and her floor plans, but it's a whole different beast trying to bring them to life. I can't tell if something is a genuine mistake or if it's just because a certain colour or design choice just translates differently in real life. Amber's also been making changes as she goes along — some at my request and others because she realises something else might work better in person. Her initial concepts are only about eighty percent accurate at this point, and it's difficult to keep track of what's supposed to be different and what's not.

How she keeps it all in her head is beyond me, but I've done what she asked.

I've delegated.

I've *trusted*.

And now I'm less than two weeks away from the launch party and the walls in the second floor lounge look like vomit.

Literal vomit.

They've been painted a horrific shade of yellow mixed with green, and staring at it almost makes *me* want to puke. I don't know who would willingly paint a room this colour, but I know that I need it changed now. But Ric isn't here, and the guy he's put in charge seems unbothered by the vomit-coloured walls.

"That's the colour we were told to use," he says with an indifferent shrug. "Our job here is done. If you want it repainted, you'll need to talk to the boss man about booking in some more hours."

"You can't be serious." I gesture wildly at the wall. "Why would I willingly choose this colour?"

The guy laughs. "I did wonder. 'Cause, you know, it looks like—"

"I know what it looks like."

He grins like this is all a big joke. "Like I said, talk to the boss man and let him know. It's 5 p.m. and my boys are done for the day."

So, *he's* useless, and it doesn't help that my emails to Amber are going unanswered and every time I call her it just goes straight to voicemail.

That noxious feeling of anxiety hasn't been bothering me so

much over the last month or so, but I can feel it looming over me again.

I trusted Amber, and she's left me in the lurch.

We've got a photographer coming in a few days to take some promotional photos for the website, and vomit-stained walls are the last thing I need right now. Adding to my frustration, Ernest is demanding to review the photos, and I know he'll be looking for anything to pick out and critique.

I try Amber's phone again, and for the sixteenth time in a row, it goes straight to voicemail.

I'm not even entirely sure what happened between us. One minute, we'd been getting along just fine. I might've even called us friends — *good* friends. I'd begun to look forward to the little pockets of alone time we'd steal every day and the feel of her arm brushing against mine as we sat on our beanbags and worked. Knowing that she was beginning to seek me out for lunch brought a smile to my face every day. She'd opened up to me, sharing her journey to home ownership with me and telling me about her rocky relationship with her parents. I'd even introduced her to Nel and ignored my sister's smug smirk when Amber waved at her through the screen.

When she told me that Cynthia had assigned her a new project, I'd been irritated but not worried. I'd worked with Amber long enough to trust her, to believe that she could juggle both projects with relative ease. And outside of the job, I guess I'd naively hoped that the foundations of the friendship we'd started to build would be enough to keep this going. But here we are with ten days until the launch and I don't think we've said a word to each other in person in days.

I grab my phone to give her another call, and as I do so, it buzzes with an email notification.

FROM: Amber Wyatt <amber@zensidesigns.com>
SUBJECT: RE: URGENT
BODY: Give me 20 mins. I'm on my way.

I wait impatiently for her in the reception area. This part of the club looks amazing, but I can't even force myself to admire the results of her hard work because of that damn wall.

I try to convince myself that it's illogical, childish even, for me to be so riled up about one thing when the rest of the property is nearly perfect. I tell myself that I need to take a deep breath, step back, and trust that Amber will sort this all out. The same way she dealt with the wrong cushions and the poor tiling job. The same way she will probably deal with the seedy lighting in the bathroom whenever she's next in.

Amber will handle it.

The thought lands in my mind with surprising clarity, and I know it to be true. I reach for my phone again, intending to send her an email apologising for being so high-strung, but then the door flies open and Amber comes storming in.

Her face is like thunder, an almost identical look she wore on the day we met. She scans the room and finds me sitting on the foot of the stairs. I give her a weak smile, but it isn't returned.

"What's wrong?" she asks, her tone brisk and clipped. As she steps farther into the room, the entrance door swinging shut as she goes, I notice a few things. Like how tired she looks. There are big, purplish bags under her bloodshot eyes, and her hair holds all the signs of having had a hand run through it anxiously for hours on end. She walks with a slight slouch, like she doesn't currently possess the energy to stand tall.

She looks like a woman on the edge, and I'm worried that I may have helped push her there.

"Amber, I—"

"Just tell me what the *urgent* problem is." Her voice is more of a sigh than anything else. "I'm tired. I'm hungry. I just want to sleep. So hurry up."

There's no room for argument there, so I mumble, "Second floor lounge."

She nods and strides past me. I follow her up the two flights of stairs and brace myself as we enter the lounge. The vile shade of yellow jumps out at me as soon as we walk in. The paint has clearly had time to fester and seep into the walls, and I think it may have gotten uglier since I last saw it.

Amber steps into the room and her whole body stills for several seconds. She suddenly doubles over and I lurch forward, thinking she's about to faint. The only thing that stops me from grabbing her and keeping her upright is the hysterical and incredibly high-pitched laugh that comes out of her mouth.

She throws her head back, shoulders shaking, tears forming, and laughs. "Oh my *god.*" She manages to get the words out between cackles. "What...what the hell is this?"

Despite the absurdity of the situation and my confusion, I crack a smile too. "My thoughts exactly."

She wipes at her eyes and gives me a watery smile. "Okay, yes. *This* was urgent. But only this one. The rest of your emails were just annoying."

"So you *have* been getting them?"

She ignores my question and instead reaches out and

gingerly touches the wall. "This is obviously the wrong colour. There must've been a mix-up at the warehouse and they've sent the wrong colour. Wish they would've used their common sense, but..." She trails off and shakes her head before turning to me. "It's *supposed* to be more of a saffron yellow — warm and inviting. This is—"

"It looks like puke."

"Exactly." She makes a face and runs a hand through her hair. "What did Ric say?"

"He hasn't been around. I think he's out for a few days. I flagged it with the guy he put in charge, but he said this was the colour they were told to use."

"Definitely not." She pauses for a moment and bites the inside of her cheek. "I'll get in touch with Ric and sort this out. Don't worry," she adds quickly. "It'll be done in time for the launch. I promise."

"Thank you."

She gives me a little nod and I'm suddenly struck by how frail she looks.

"Have you been eating?" I ask. She's told me before that when she throws herself into her work she often forgets to eat. "Real food, I mean. Since I haven't been feeding you for lunch lately?"

"Not really," she admits with a small sigh, and even that tiny action looks like it takes so much out of her. "I've been so busy. This new project Cynthia's given me is so time consuming, I feel like all I'm doing is catching trains to Brighton or staring at my tablet working on these new designs. Food is an afterthought at this point."

"You need to eat, sweetheart."

I haven't called her that in a while — haven't had the chance to — but the name slips from my lips easily, like it's second nature.

A shadow of a smile flits over her face at the endearment. "I know. I'll get something when I get—" Her eyes roll back for a second and she sways slightly on the spot. This time, I think she really is about to faint. I close the small gap between us and let her collapse in my arms.

"*Finn.*"

I don't even have time to revel at the use of my first name because she renders me speechless as she takes in a shuddery breath and wraps her arms tightly around me.

We stand there for a full minute, just breathing each other in. I can feel her slow, heavy heartbeat against my chest, and I time my breathing to match hers. When she leans back, arms still wrapped around my middle, she looks a little more like herself. I can tell she's dangerously tired, but there's a soft spark in her eyes that I hadn't realised I'd been missing.

She blinks up at me and smiles. "Thank you."

That smile of hers...I've missed it.

She lets go of me, and although I miss her touch, I'm glad because it's taking everything in my power not to lean down and kiss her right now.

"I'm going to head home now, but don't worry. First thing in the morning I'll get this sorted." She moves to take a step back, but I pull my arms up and hold her in place.

It's ridiculous that she thinks *that's* what I'm worried about right now. "Let's get something to eat."

She scrunches her face. "I'm so tired, Finn. I'm barely going to make it to the station at this point. Another time?"

"I can grab us something and we can eat here." I can tell that she's about to protest, so I put my hands on her shoulders and guide her to the staircase. "Go on up to the office. *Relax*. I'll get us something to eat and bring it right up."

"Are you sure?" she asks, and I hate how uncertain she sounds. "Really, I can get something at home. My mother usually cooks, so there's probably leftovers."

"I'm sure," I say firmly. I keep my hands on her until she puts a foot on the stairs. "I'll be twenty minutes. Go on, sweetheart."

"Twenty minutes?"

"Twenty minutes."

"Okay." She gives me a little nod and then starts slowly making her way up the stairs. I keep an eye on her until she disappears from view, and I don't leave until I hear the sound of the office door open and close.

WHEN I GET BACK to the club, Amber is curled up on her beanbag, legs tucked underneath her, heels kicked off and banished to the side. She gives me a reproachful look when I enter the office.

"That was much longer than twenty minutes."

"Were you worried?"

She smirks. "Nope. Just hungry."

I match her grin and hold up the two large white boxes in my hands, enjoying the way her eyes light up as she spies the red lettering on the lid.

"Is that from *Rosa's*?"

172

"The one and only."

Her eyes light up as I join her on my beanbag, placing the boxes between us. "Wasn't sure what toppings you like, so I went for the two safest bets."

Amber gingerly lifts the lid on the boxes. "Cheese and... pepperoni. So daring of you, Finn."

That's the third time she's used my name now. I don't think she's even realised.

"What's your usual topping of choice?" I ask as I unearth the pile of napkins I'd shoved into my pocket and hand half of them to her. "For future reference."

"Mushrooms and sausage. Oh, and it's got to be covered in hot sauce."

I pretend to gag. "Mushrooms and sausage covered in hot sauce? Sweetheart, that's disgusting. A waste of perfectly good pizza, even."

She laughs as she tugs a slice free and brings it to her lips. "Don't knock it until you try it." She bites into the slice and closes her eyes, humming contentedly as she chews. "So. Damn. Good."

I grab a slice from the pepperoni box and quickly discover that she's not exaggerating. "This *is* pretty good. For a non-New York pizza, I mean."

She rolls her eyes. "Ah yes, that old stereotype."

"It's not a stereotype if it's true."

"Well, if I ever make it over there you'll have to take me to your favourite pizza place and *then* I'll make my final decision."

"Sure. It's a date."

She hums and I can't tell if she's blushing or if she's just finally getting some more life back into her after eating. "Do you take a lot of your dates out to get pizza then?"

I know she's trying to sound indifferent, but there's a slight edge to her tone that betrays her.

"I don't go on many dates," I tell her honestly.

She snorts. "Sure you don't."

"Why is that so difficult to believe?" I ask, brow raised.

"Because *look at you*," she says, sounding somewhere between amused and exasperated. She waves a pizza-laden hand in my direction, the greasy slice flopping up and down as she moves. "I don't know if you're fishing for a compliment or what, but I'm pretty sure you're not lacking for romantic attention."

"Is that the closest you're going to get to calling me hot?"

Her cheeks flush unmistakably, but she holds her ground and stares back at me with defiant eyes. "Absolutely."

I laugh. "Then I'll take it. But seriously, I really don't date often." There have been a few random flings over the years, but nothing serious and they all end the same way. "Too busy with work."

"That—" She cuts herself off and shakes her head. "Never mind."

"No, go on." I scootch my beanbag even closer to hers and bump her leg with mine. "Say it."

The look she shoots me is slightly bashful. "I was just going to say...That it's sad. That you don't date because of work. You're a good guy, Finn and I know this is going to sound incredibly hypocritical coming from me of all people, but work isn't everything."

"You and Nel would get along very well."

She gives me a sad smile. "I'm glad you have someone in your corner back home. Even if you don't listen to her."

We eat in silence for a few minutes. I don't know if there's something on her mind or if she's just giving me the space to stew in my thoughts before I say something else.

"How'd you start working with Cynthia?" I ask.

Amber frowns, looking confused at the sudden change in topic. "I applied for an assistant role with her not long after I graduated university. I was so happy the day I got the email saying that she'd chosen me for the role." She chuckles quietly under her breath. "Little did I know. Why're you asking? Looking for a change in career?"

"My aunt Marion got me my first job," I tell her. "I was an intern in the IT department for *The August Room*. I didn't really do anything apart from the coffee rounds for the higher-ups and I'd sometimes respond to the occasional misplaced query in the contact box."

She nods, still looking confused.

"Aunt Marion is married to my uncle Ernest. The CEO of *The August Room*."

Realisation dawns on her face and she grins. "Finn, are you telling me that you're a nepotism hire?"

I shrug. "Depending on who you ask, yes."

"What's that supposed to mean?"

"I'm good at my job, Amber," I say, and there's more frustration in my tone than I'd like. "Yes, my aunt got me in the door, but I worked my way up. Every promotion that I got, I deserved it. But a lot of people don't see it that way. They just see my last name and know that I'm technically related to the CEO—"

"Who is a major dick, by the way."

"Agreed. But dick or not, he *is* legally my uncle and people just assume that anything I get is because of him. Especially this role. The other serious candidate was a senior manager in another area of the business. He actually ended up quitting when it was announced that I got the job over him, but not before telling everyone that I only got it because my uncle pulled some strings for me."

"And did he?"

"Fuck no," I say as I snort. "My uncle can't stand me. I'm not entirely sure why, but there's some bad blood between him and my dad. If I had to guess, I'd say it's because of that. Anyway. That's why I don't really have time to date."

Her brows furrow. "Because your uncle's a dick?"

"No," I say with a laugh. "Because I'm too busy trying to show everyone that I deserve to be where I am right now. That's why I'm so involved in everything. I don't have any room to fail, not if I want people to believe that I'm not here because my uncle called in a favour or is secretly looking out for me."

"And how's that going for you?"

"Not great," I admit. "As hard as I work, people still just see my last name and assume I got here through nepotism."

She wrinkles her nose. "But you did. And I know, *I know* that you work hard," she says quickly. "Believe me, Finn. You've been a pain in my ass for the last three months, and I know just how hard you work. But do me a favour and humour me for a second."

I nod and she continues on.

"Imagine you're still you, nothing has changed except your last name isn't Hawthorne and you don't have an Aunt Marion to get you in at her husband's company. You're just a normal 22-

year-old fresh from university, and you're frantically applying for jobs like the rest of us. What do you do?"

"I...I apply for an internship in the IT department."

"Okay, cool. So you apply and four weeks later you get a rejection. And it's not a nicely personalised one either. It's one of those *'Dear Candidate'* form type emails."

"What?" I scowl at her. "Why am I being rejected? Nepotism or not, I graduated with honours from an Ivy League."

"So did about ten thousand other students. And because there's a little rich boy whose aunt is married to the CEO, *he* got the internship that you applied for. And in ten years or so, he's going to become the managing director for the company and you're going to be...I don't know." She shrugs. "Burnt out, broke, and bitter. Just like the rest of us."

"That wasn't very fun."

"It wasn't supposed to be fun," she says with a dry laugh. "You're good at what you do, Finn. But I bet you rub a lot of people the wrong way back home by acting like you didn't have help getting where you are. That leg up in the beginning put you miles ahead of the rest of your peers. It's like winning a marathon you started at the halfway point and not understanding why everyone else is so tired. Do you know how many jobs I applied to before I got this one?"

I shake my head.

"Me either because I *lost count*. Did you even have to do an application for the internship?"

"No." I can feel warmth spreading to my cheeks. "I didn't want to work at my dad's company — pharmaceuticals wasn't for me — so he asked my aunt to help me out. I think I had the internship secured the next day."

She throws me a satisfied look. "Exactly."

"So what am I supposed to do? It feels like I can't win."

"You can't," she says simply. "But you can stop caring about it so much. It is what it is. Stop trying to change the minds of people who have already clearly decided they know what box to put you in. You're good at your job. Own that." She pauses and frowns. "Or there is one other alternative."

"And what's that?"

"Quit," she says like it's the simplest thing in the world. "Go and work somewhere that has absolutely nothing to do with your family name. Don't give anyone a chance to blame nepotism for everything you achieve."

It's not like I haven't thought about that before. But where would I go? What would I do? "I'm not like you," I tell her. "I don't have anything I'm passionate about. There's never been one career that always just made sense to me. That felt right. The only thing I've ever wanted to be is successful."

"So find it," she says, looking me square in the eye. "Find your passion."

Can a passion be a person? Because right now *she's* the only thing I feel strongly about. This beautiful, passionate, stubborn woman who doesn't think twice about telling me what I really need to hear. I'd happily dedicate my life to making *her* happy if she'd let me.

It's strange to think that we've come this far from that disastrous first meeting.

"Can I ask you something? It's been on my mind for a while."

She nods. "Shoot."

"When we first met, you didn't like me."

She arches a brow. "And who says I like you now?"

I feel emboldened by the smile toying at her lips, and I lean in close enough for our fingers to brush. When she doesn't jerk away, I thread my fingers through hers and marvel over how nicely her hand fits in mine. She doesn't move to pull away. In fact, she folds her fingers over mine and gives me a tentative squeeze. I squeeze back and gently tug her toward me, making room as she slides off her beanbag and onto mine. She drapes her long legs over mine and rests her head against my chest.

"Why didn't you like me?"

My voice is barely a whisper and she doesn't respond at first. I wonder if maybe the thudding of my heart is too loud for her to hear over, but then she shifts slightly and looks up at me. There's a sheepish expression on her face.

"I overheard you on the phone complaining about how much the design was going to cost," she says wryly. "I think you said something about us charging you too much for picking out a few paint colours and picking out some furniture at IKEA."

Shame pools inside me. I remember that conversation; I'd been talking to my property manager back in New York. "Amber, I—"

She smacks my chest gently with her free hand. "You've already apologised. It's *fine*."

"It's not fine. I didn't know how much went into your job before, but that's no excuse for talking down on you like that. I'm so sorry. I told you to leave Cynthia for making you feel small, but I've been doing the same thing."

Although she told me not to apologise, the smile she throws my way tells me she's glad to hear me say that. "Firstly, never compare yourself to Cynthia. And secondly, it really is fine. It was always less about you and more about me. My mother and Patrick aren't my biggest supporters and that's the kind of thing they always say. When I heard you say it, it just felt like another stab to the gut, you know? It was easy to take my frustrations about them out on you."

I lean back on my beanbag until I'm practically lying horizontal. I pull her body over mine and she swings a leg over my thigh, her head still resting on my chest. "I'm so sorry, sweetheart," I murmur as I absentmindedly run my hand up and down her back. "For what I said. For how I acted. For your parents—"

Another smack to my chest. "Definitely don't apologise for *them*."

"I don't understand them. Why wouldn't they be supportive of you?"

I feel her shrug against my chest.

"Cynthia doesn't pay me very well and they don't really understand what I do every day that has me gone for such long hours. They think it's just picking out paint and furniture too."

There's a bitterness to her voice and I understand now why my words cut her so deep.

"But it's fine—"

"Stop saying it's fine when it's clearly not."

She lifts her head and pokes my chin. "It *is* fine, because I'll be moving out soon." She looks down and then back up at me and grins shyly. "I bought the house."

"You bought the house?"

She nods and says, a little louder this time, "I bought the house!"

I don't even think as I wrap my arms tightly around her,

pulling her flush against my body as I squeeze. "Congratulations, sweetheart." I press a chaste kiss to her temple. "I'm so proud of you."

She beams up at me and winds her arms around my neck. "Thank you."

"When do you move in?"

"Soon. I think I can pick up the keys this week at some point."

"That's amazing. We'll have to do something to celebrate."

Her smile doesn't falter. "That would be nice."

My mind immediately begins to race with ideas. It'll have to be something special. Between having to deal with Cynthia, her parents, *and* me, Amber deserves this more than anyone I know. Maybe I'll take her out to a Michelin starred restaurant? Fly her to Paris for the weekend? Or a shopping spree for her new home? I think she'd like that.

I'm about to suggest it to her, when she shifts suddenly, and it feels like every ounce of blood in my body heads to my groin. It's an innocent enough move — I'm sure she's just making herself more comfortable — but as she wiggles on top of me, she hikes her leg up a little higher and the hem of her skirt bunches all the way up.

Several things happen at once. I desperately try not to look at her now exposed thigh and the curve of her ass but fail miserably. And Amber's knee brushes against my now embarrassingly hard cock.

"Oh."

I squeeze my eyes shut, not out of any sense of modesty toward her. But because she's wearing a pair of thin, pink panties, and a devious voice in the back of my mind won't stop telling me that it would take me almost no time at all to pull them down and slide inside her right now.

"Sorry. *Sorry.*" She tries to scramble off me, but that only makes it worse. I'm now acutely aware of her breasts bumping against my chest as she tries to shimmy away, and I can't stop thinking about how good her body feels moving on top of mine like this.

I wrap an arm around her waist and hold her firmly in place. "Don't apologise. Isn't that what you keep telling me?"

I can't see her face right now, but I can hear her swallow. "Yes, but—"

"I'm hard."

There's a beat of silence before her head lolls against my chest and she lets out a quiet giggle. "You're *very* hard."

I grin. Are we flirting? This feels like flirting. "Did you cop a feel?"

"Kind of hard not to, Finn." She pauses to splay her fingers against my chest, right over my heart. "You should reconsider that whole '*no dating*' thing. I think you'd make someone a very happy woman. As long as you know how to use it."

"I haven't had any complaints so far."

"Mhmm. I bet."

We lie there for a few minutes until I can get myself under control. When I open my eyes again, I expect her to be looking up at me with a teasing grin plastered across her face, but she's not. She's got her eyes closed, and it almost looks like she's sleeping. I give her shoulders a gentle shake and her eyes flutter open.

"You good?"

She nods. "Just enjoying the moment."

I'd like to lie here and continue to enjoy this moment too,

but it's getting late. I sit up, pulling her with me as I go. "Let me call you a cab."

"You don't have to do that," she says. "I think I can still get the last train."

"I'm calling you a cab, Amber."

She groans. "It makes it very hard to call you cheap when you insist on doing things like this."

"You know that *I'm* actually not cheap, right?" I ask as we stand up. I'm suddenly worried that this hasn't been a joke the entire time. "It's the company, not me."

"Yes, Finn," she says with a roll of the eyes. "I'm very aware that you yourself are not a cheap guy. I'm just messing with you."

"Good, because all you have to do is ask, and I'd buy it for you."

She raises a brow. "Anything?"

"Anything."

"I'll keep that in mind when I'm in the market for my second home. It'll be something on a lake and *very* expensive. So you better start saving now."

She's joking, but I'm not. If she's asking, I'm buying.

We clean up our pizza mess, and I call for her cab. It arrives in record time and I walk her out just to extend the time we have together.

I *really* don't want this night to end.

"You'll be back tomorrow?" I ask, and I don't care that I sound needy.

She nods. "The vomit wall is my number one priority for tomorrow."

"What about the other project?"

"It'll have to wait. Like I said..." She pokes me with her index finger. "Priority number one right here."

I grab her finger and hold it against my chest. "Appreciate it."

She smiles up at me. "It's a shame you don't date. This could've been a halfway decent one."

And she's right. It would've been. And if this had been a date, this would be the moment I lean in and kiss her. But it's not a date, and I can't kiss her. Can I?

My gaze darts to her lips – soft, plump, full – and then back up to her face.

No. I can't.

We're effectively co-workers, and I don't want to upset the tentative balance we've thankfully managed to restore tonight.

I drop her finger and she makes an irritated sound that comes from the very depths of her throat. "Stop looking at me like that."

"Like what?"

"Like you're trying to come up with more excuses not to kiss me right now."

"Okay." Disappointment flashes in her eyes and she takes a small step backward. I close the new space between us immediately. "Okay," I say again, my voice low. "I'll stop coming up with excuses."

19

AMBER

FINN'S HANDS COME UP TO GHOST OVER MY JAW, threading his fingers in the hair at the nape of my neck. I get precisely half a second of warning before his lips are on mine and I melt into his touch.

Finn kisses the same way he does everything — like he's got something to prove. His fingers tilt my head back as he slants over my mouth and peppers me with soft, insistent kisses. He's not forceful with it — in fact, he's surprisingly gentle. But there's a fiery intensity behind each kiss that sends shockwaves pooling in the pit of my stomach. It feels like he's claiming me. Like he's leaving marks on my lips that only he can see.

I don't mind.

I can't get enough of him. If kissing Finn is the only thing I do for the rest of my life, I'd die happy and content.

I step forward and press my body as close to his as I can, idly acknowledging how good the rigid plains of his muscles feel against my softer curves. I snake my arms around his neck and eagerly meet each and every kiss with just as much fervour.

Kissing Finn feels like coming home. It feels good. It feels *right*. Standing here, his arms tightly around me, his lips gently caressing mine, feels like something we've done a million times before and we'll do a million times more.

He groans, his lips parting just a little more, and I take the opportunity to slip inside. His entire body seems to vibrate with pleasure when our tongues meet, and I grin into the kiss. The fingers currently gripping the back of my hair skitter downward, and I shiver against him as his hands run down the length of my back to cup my ass. He pulls our lower bodies flush against each other and I'm greeted with a thick hardness straining against the confines of his trousers.

He pulls back for a second — to catch his breath, to say something, I'm not sure — and the brief absence of his lips on mine irritates me. I surge forward, recapturing them. He takes it in his stride, effortlessly flipping us around so my back is against the door. His hand drops from my ass and both arms come up to cage me in. I bring a leg up to wrap around his waist and—

The taxi driver honks impatiently and we both freeze.

I look up at him through my lashes. His eyes are dark and hooded, his cheeks are sporting an impressive red glow, and his lips are wet and swollen. I feel strangely proud that I'm the one responsible for this.

"*Amber.*" That's all he says, just my name through panted breaths. His chest heaves up and down for a few seconds before he takes his hand and runs a gentle finger along the side of my face. "What am I going to do with you?"

Invite me back to your hotel? Fuck me until I can't walk? Hold me in your arms as we drift off to sleep together? A wonderful combination of all three? Any of those options sound incredibly appealing right now.

He leans in and tries to give me another quick kiss, but I reach out and grab his tie, holding him in place so I can steal just a little more.

The taxi driver honks again and we both groan as we pull apart. All of a sudden, the fatigue I've been feeling over the last few days hits me all at once. I attempt to stifle a yawn and fail. A night with Finn is incredibly tempting right now, but it seems like my body has other ideas.

I think Finn is on the same page because he presses a chaste kiss to my forehead and then laces our fingers together. "Come on. Let's get you home, sweetheart." He tugs me toward the taxi and I semi-reluctantly follow.

"Let me know when you get home, all right?" he says softly once I'm safely inside the taxi.

"I will."

"Good." He leans in through the open window and kisses me one last time. It's not a quick kiss either, and I'm truly about one second away from pulling him into the taxi with me, when the driver clears his throat and pointedly taps the running meter.

Finn gives the driver an apologetic smile and pulls away. "I'll see you tomorrow?"

I nod. "Tomorrow."

He steps back onto the pavement and my driver wastes no time pulling off and hurtling down the street. I look out the window until we turn a corner and Finn disappears from view. My phone buzzes the second he does.

Goodnight, sweetheart. Sleep well.

I lean back against my seat and smile. For the first night in weeks, I think I'm going to.

MY HAND SHAKES as I push the key into the lock. There are a thousand places I'd like to be right now, but standing outside my new home with my mother and Patrick is definitely not one of them.

I've taken a rare day off work, which wasn't easy. Between The August Room and The Pevensey, I had to fight for this little nugget of free time and Cynthia only relented under the promise of me working overtime over the weekend to catch up. It puts a bit of a dampener on the whole thing and it doesn't help that I, against my better judgement, have taken this day to invite my mother and Patrick to come and see my new house.

I'm not entirely sure why I've done it. Maybe it's because I'm still on a high from that night with Finn a few days ago. Not just from the kiss or the way he held me in his arms like I was something particularly precious to him, but from how he reacted when I told him I'd bought the house. How proud and genuinely excited he'd been for me. I keep replaying that moment in my head, and I guess it lulls me into a false sense of security because I forget that not everyone is as excited for me as Finn is.

My mother and Patrick quickly remind me of that, though. Her face is a mask of disgust as she walks up the small pathway in front of my new home. The front garden needs some work. There are weeds everywhere and the hedges need trimming, but it's not that bad. Is it? I second-guess myself as I watch her nose wrinkle and her lips curl.

"Really, Amber?" she says bluntly. "Here?"

I frown. "What do you mean?"

"It's not a very nice neighbourhood, is it?" She jerks her chin toward a wall across the road where there's some creative graffiti sprayed across it. "Seems very rough."

"Couldn't you have chosen somewhere a little nicer?" Patrick asks, the look on his face mirroring the one on my mother's. He kicks away a stray Coke can that has somehow found its way into my front garden.

"It's a perfectly safe area," I tell them. "And it just needs a bit of a tidy up. That's all."

I reluctantly push open the front door and step aside for them to enter.

"It's very small, isn't it?" my mother comments as she walks inside. "Barely any space to swing around."

I grit my teeth and follow them in. "Good thing I won't be doing much swinging around."

They traipse through the house — *my* new home — making disparaging comments as they go.

"Terrible natural light."

"The kitchen is tiny."

"The carpet is disgusting. You'll have to tear it all out."

"Why you'd purchase somewhere so far away is beyond me."

"Is it too late to back out? This doesn't seem like a very sound investment."

My vision blurs, not with tears but with anger. I lean against the doorframe to steady me. "Most people — most *parents* — would just say congratulations, you know?"

My mother turns to face me and there's not even a hint of joy for me in her expression. "Why on earth would we congratulate you? This isn't an achievement, Amber."

A lump forms in my throat. It's so big, I think I'm going to choke on it. "Mum. I've just bought a house. By *myself*. Without any help from you two, or Dad, or anyone."

Patrick clears his throat. "I wouldn't say we haven't helped you. You stay in our home for well below market price rent. We've taken a big hit by letting you stay, and that's allowed you to save for this...home."

"I'm your *daughter*." The word comes out like venom on my tongue. *Daughter*. "Or, at the very least, I'm *supposed* to be. I shouldn't have to thank you for letting me live at home."

"You're 28-years-old for Christ's sake," my mother snaps. "You should've been out years ago. Honestly, Amber. It's like you're stunted somehow. You're in a dead-end job—"

"I am *not*."

"And you've purchased a filthy, tiny, run-down home, and you expect us to tell you that we're proud of you?" She huffs out a humourless laugh. "We shouldn't have to keep babying you like this."

"You've *never* babied me," I cry. Tears are flowing freely now, but I don't care and neither do they apparently. "Not even when I was a baby and actually needed it. You just act like I'm such a big inconvenience and that I should be grateful for you doing the bare minimum."

My mother presses a hand against her chest and gasps.

"How *dare you*. Do you know how much I've had to sacrifice for you?"

"You're my *mother*," I sob. "That's what you're supposed to do. I shouldn't have to thank you for it. And you." I whirl around and glare at Patrick. "You've been in my life for nearly two decades. You're the closest thing to a father figure that I have, and you act like I'm just getting in the way of what your perfect idea of family is. You both do."

Patrick flinches like I've slapped him, and my mother inhales sharply. "Don't you dare talk to him like that. Patrick's been so good to you — to us both. He took you in and stepped up when your father refused to."

Stepped up? Does she really think that *this* is stepping up? Treating me like an afterthought? Dismissing every little thing I do? *Really?*

"He doesn't even call me his stepdaughter." I tell her. "Not once in the entire time I've known him. And I'm tired. I'm so, so tired of not being enough for either of you. Or for being too much. I don't know. I just know that I'm done. I brought you here today because I wanted to share this amazing achievement with you. I *wanted* you to be excited for me. To hug me. To tell me that you're proud of me for the first time in my life."

"Amber—"

I shake my head and point to the door. "Like I said, I'm done. I'll come back to the house soon to collect my stuff, but that's it. Until something changes here, I'm not coming back. This is my safe space. This is my *home*. And if you can't respect that, I'm going to ask you both to please leave."

There's a small part of me that hopes maybe this will be the turning point. That maybe my mother will suddenly see the error of her ways and apologise. Maybe she'll pull me into a deep hug as she sobs and tells me how sorry she is.

But that doesn't happen.

My mother's jaw twitches, her eyes harden, and she gives Patrick a little nod. Neither of them say a word to me as they push past me and leave.

I wait for a little while, half-heartedly hoping that they'll come back and apologise, but they don't.

It's just me.

Alone in the home I was so excited about just twenty minutes ago, but now I can't stand it. Everywhere I look, I hear their complaints.

Maybe it *is* too small, and the natural lighting does suck, and yes, I really should get rid of this carpet shouldn't I?

I hate that they've done this. Taken something that I loved and turned it into something horrible.

I need to get out of here. But where? My parents' home isn't an option right now for obvious reasons. Bailey is at *her* parents' house and I don't particularly need Mr and Mrs Clarke to know about this — they're still on friendly terms with my parents, and while I don't think they'd do anything maliciously, I don't want them to know what's happened. So that leaves...

Finn.

His smiling face swims in my mind's eye and I immediately feel a strange sense of calm. When did this happen? When did Finn become the person I turn to in times of crisis? I'm not sure, but it doesn't bother me nearly as much as it should.

I pull out my phone and open up my chat history with Finn. I haven't responded to his last messages yet and the sight of them makes me smile.

FINN

Hope you're enjoying your day off.

Miss you.

I take a deep breath and wipe away the tears that are still falling.

AMBER

Are you at the club?

His response is immediate.

FINN

That's a silly question.

I snort.

AMBER

Fair.

I'll be there soon. Need to see you.

FINN

Is everything all right?

AMBER

It will be.

20

FINN

I TAP MY FINGERS AGAINST MY THIGH, EYES NARROWED ON the office door. It's been a full hour since Amber last messaged me, and I have no idea where she is.

I'm not sure what's happened since she refused to elaborate over text, but I know something definitely isn't right. She told me that she was going to bring her mother and her mother's husband to visit her new house today. Did something happen? I frown. From what she's told me about them, they're not my favourite people in the world and it wouldn't surprise me if they've said or done something to upset her today.

The more I think about it, the more I'm sure that's the case. Why else would she be coming into work on the only day off she's had over the last three months? It's only just midday and I know how much she was looking forward to having one day without having to worry about The August Room or the new hotel project Cynthia dumped on her.

I'm about to drive myself crazy wondering what could have happened, when the office door flies open. Amber kicks the door closed behind her, strides across the room, and without saying anything, wraps her arms around me and buries her face in my chest. I feel a wet patch forming on my shirt where her head currently is, and alarm bells immediately start ringing.

Is she crying?

"Hey, hey," I whisper as I run my hands down her arms and gently pry her off me. "What happened, sweetheart?"

She *is* crying, and by the looks of it, she's been doing it for a while. Her eyes are bloodshot and swollen, and her cheeks are stained with tears. My heart breaks, quickly repairs itself, and then shatters all over again when she takes a shaky breath.

"I could really use that distraction right now." She's trying to crack a joke, but the pain in her eyes makes it fall flat.

I wrap my arms around her and squeeze tightly, wanting so badly to undo whatever it is that's caused this. "What happened?" I ask her again, my mind racing with worst case scenarios. "Did someone hurt you?"

"No. Yes. It's stupid," she croaks out, her voice hoarse and low. "I just...I had a fight with my mother and her husband."

I knew it.

"They were really rude about my house." She laughs, but it comes out sounding more like a sob than anything else. "Which is such a *stupid* reason to be getting all worked up for."

"No, it's not," I say softly, still running my hands down her side. "What did they say?"

She leans into the touch, her eyelids fluttering shut for a moment. When she opens her eyes again, she gives me a weak smile and then tells me what happened.

By the time she's finished, my blood is boiling. The way they've treated her would be unacceptable for anyone, but to treat your own daughter like that? I think about my parents and how endlessly supportive they are of me and Nel. They weren't particularly strict with us growing up — we only had to maintain good grades and be polite, and they taught us the value of money from an early age. I don't imagine there's much we could do that would have them treating us how Amber's parents treat her.

"Do you know what's the worst thing?" she mumbles. "I don't even hate them. I want to. I want to hate them so badly, but I don't. I just want to know what I did wrong."

I cup her face in my hands and force her to look me in the eye. "You've done nothing wrong, sweetheart." We're so close, I can hear the tiny hitch of her breath when I call her sweetheart. "You're too good for them, and if they can't be a part of your life on your terms, then that's *their* loss. Not yours."

"I know. Logically, I know. It's just—"

"Sometimes the logical answer isn't always the easiest one to stomach."

She bites her lip and nods. "It made me realise something, though."

"What's that?"

"I'm tired of feeling like this. I'm tired of being around people who *make* me feel like this."

"Like what?"

"Bad," she mumbles. "Like there's something wrong with me. Like I'm always doing something wrong or I'm chasing after an impossible goal. My parents make me feel like this. Cynthia makes me feel like this. I look in the mirror and I make *myself* feel like this. And I'm tired, Finn. I'm so tired. I just want to feel good again."

"I want to make you feel good." I'd do anything if it meant she never felt like this again.

She looks up at me, eyes watery. "You already do."

My heart soars.

"That's why I'm here. I wanted to be with you instead of wallowing at home."

I hook a finger under her chin and lift it, leaning in until our lips are almost brushing. "Let me make you feel good now, sweetheart."

She drops her gaze, debate flashing across her face. When she looks up at me again, there's something else in her still watery eyes. Want? Trust? A beautiful mix of the two? "Please make me feel good, Finn."

I nod and press my lips over hers. She stands up on her tiptoes to meet me hungrily. I can taste the remnants of her salty tears on her, and I pepper her face with kisses determined to rid her cheeks of every last tear streak.

Her arms come to wrap around my neck, and I waste no time hoisting her up. Her skirt bunches up at the waist, giving me full access to her soft thighs. She immediately wraps her legs around my midsection and I groan into the kiss as I palm her ass.

It's truly a wonderful ass.

Soft and pliable under my hands, and it's got a nice bounce to it when I give it a tentative slap. I do it again and she lets out a pleased little hiss and arches farther into my touch. I don't think I'll ever tire of the sounds she makes, particularly her moans. They sound like they come from the very depths of her chest, low and needy — *so* needy. She wants more.

She *needs* more. And I'm more than happy to give it to her.

I walk us to the desk and drop her onto it. We've never used it, preferring the beanbags I bought that first week, but this seems as good a way as any to christen it. She doesn't question the choice and immediately opens up her legs so I can stand between them.

Her thighs press against mine, and I can feel an obsession building. I want her legs wrapped around my neck, her thighs on either side of my face, squeezing tightly as she comes undone. She could smother me to death with them for all I care and I'd thank her for it.

She scootches back slightly, taking her skirt with her as she goes, and I get a flash of purple panties. I lean forward and dip my thumb under the thin band of purple elastic below her belly button.

"Do you always wear such pretty panties, sweetheart?"

She flushes underneath me. "Yes. I have a collection."

I hum and drop my head to the crook of her neck. "You'll have to show me sometime."

"I could do that," she says coyly. "What's your favourite colour?"

"Right now? Purple."

She laughs and the tail end of it jumps up a pitch or two as I tug her panties down and slide a finger along her entrance. She's so fucking warm and slick, and the realisation sends a jolt straight to my already hard cock.

"God, Amber."

She shudders beneath me and bucks her hips forward, trying to coax my fingers inside. *"Finn."*

"All right, sweetheart," I say as I laugh. Right now, my focus is on making her feel good. My desires — to take it slow and take my time exploring every inch of her body, learning what makes her tick and moan — can take a back seat here. There will be plenty of time for that later.

I pull my hand back, ignoring the way she huffs in protest, and then bring two fingers up to her lips. "Suck these for me."

Her eyes widen a fraction, but she does exactly what I say. She doesn't break eye contact as she takes both fingers in her mouth and swirls her tongue around them. When I pull them out, they're slick with her saliva.

"Good?" she asks, a brow raised in challenge.

"You tell me."

I kiss her again and swallow her moan as I simultaneously slip two wet fingers inside her and begin to pump.

"God. Fuck. *Finn*."

My cock twitches every time she says my name.

Her head rolls back between her shoulders, mouth parted in a tiny 'o' as I bring my thumb to her clit and press down. I learn quickly that she likes long, slow strokes, and that when I want to hear that moan again — the low one that I can feel reverberating against my chest — I just have to curl my fingers inside her and grin as she shakes beneath me.

I want to learn more. Discover how she'll react if I play with her nipples or sink my teeth into her thighs or flip her over and pump my fingers into her from behind. I want to know what she tastes like and figure out what the ultimate combination is to drive her over the edge and have her lying across my chest spent, satisfied, and beaming.

But she's close and there's no time for any of that right now. I can tell by the erratic way her chest begins to rise and fall, and her moans are becoming more breathy, more desperate.

This time is supposed to be all about her, but I guess I'm a selfish man at heart because I do give into one of my urges.

I pull the elastic of her panties and let it snap back against her hips. "I need these off, sweetheart."

She lifts her hips without question, seemingly working on autopilot now that she's so close. I pull her panties down so they pool around her ankles and then crouch down and hook her legs over my shoulders. The sharp tips of her heels dig into my back as she locks her ankles, and I don't mind the small pinch of pain that shoots through me. In fact, it spurs me on. Definitely something to unpack later, but I like it.

"I just need you to do one thing for me."

"What's that?" she gasps out.

"Come." I lean in and run my tongue along her opening. She nearly bucks off the desk, but I hold her hips in place as I mimic the movements I'd been doing with my fingers as best I can with my tongue.

Her thighs are wrapped so tightly around my face, I can just about hear her moan my name.

"*Finn.*"

Her body stiffens beneath me as she rocks faster and faster into each stroke of my tongue. She squeezes her thighs even tighter still and I think this might be the way I go. I wouldn't even mind.

Death by the best pussy I've ever had the privilege of tasting. What an epitaph.

I can feel every pulsation against my tongue and when she finally gets there, when she finally reaches that peak and tips over the edge, her grip becomes almost vicelike.

I hear the muffled sound of my name again and pull myself

backward, gently spreading her thighs apart so I can free myself and sit upright again.

When I finally get back up, she's biting down on her palm, smothering her cry. The action irritates me more than it should. I want to hear her scream my name as she finishes, to hear her come completely undone because of me.

"You feeling better now?" I murmur.

"So good." Her chest heaves as she comes down from her high. "Fuck, Finn." She reaches for my tie and tugs my face down to meet hers. Her lips slant over mine without hesitation, tongue slipping into my mouth like she's desperate to taste herself on me.

She doesn't break the kiss as she reaches for my belt and just about manages to unbuckle it before an annoying sense of clarity washes over me.

The little bubble we've been in pops and I'm suddenly acutely aware that we're not alone. There's a tiny army of contractors just a few floors below and the fact that nobody's walked in on us yet is nothing short of a miracle.

I place my hand over the one fumbling with my belt.

She looks up at me with confusion in her eyes.

"If we don't stop now, we're never going to," I say.

The confusion makes way for something else entirely. Rejection? Hurt? "Right." She glances away and I use my free hand to tilt her chin upward.

"Sweetheart," I say, holding her gaze so she knows just how serious I am and that this isn't a rejection. "There are too many people in this building right now, and the first time I fuck you, it's going to be somewhere you can scream my name."

Her eyes widen, her chest heaves slightly, and her tongue

darts out to run along her full lips. I want to lean in and bite them, see what kind of reaction I can coax out of her by doing that.

Slowly, torturously slow even, she lets her gaze drop to my crotch. My cock stirs in response and when she looks back up at me again, she's grinning. "I look forward to it."

21

AMBER

I LOOK FORWARD TO IT.

Who says that? I sound like bloody Danica in HR. There's no point in pretending, though. I *am* looking forward to it.

Every time I glance at him, I get flashbacks to that afternoon in the office. The electricity that surged through every inch of my body when he put his hands on me. The way I arched into his touch when he slipped his fingers inside. How I saw stars when his tongue ran along my lips and he sucked at my clit.

I don't think I've ever been touched like that before. Like the only thing that mattered to him was pleasing me and he would've done whatever it took to get me to that point.

I want more.

I need it, really.

I'm so close to pushing him into a supply closet and jumping his bones, it's getting ridiculous. If this were anyone else, I think I would've done it by now. But between me putting the finishing touches on the property and working on The Pevensey project, and Finn running around getting things ready for the launch party in two days, we've barely had a spare moment together.

So when I walk into the office and find him there, sprawled across both my beanbag and his, the giddy little jump my heart does doesn't surprise me at all.

He's on a call, and judging by the displeased frown on his face, it's with his uncle.

I slink into the room as quietly as I can and lean against the desk, not wanting to interrupt the call.

He mouths a silent apology and I shake my head, content to stand here and watch him. He's wearing headphones, so I can't hear whatever it is that prompts the fleeting look of irritation on his face, but I hear Finn's response loud and clear.

"Yes, I'll be back in New York on Sunday. Check in with my office and I'm sure we can find a time and day that suits us both."

Sunday.

He's leaving in *four days*.

Something unpleasant settles in the pit of my stomach.

I've always known that his presence here wasn't going to be permanent, but maybe I'd been naïve in thinking that we had more time together.

It's not even about the promise of sex — though I don't think I've ever wanted anyone so badly before. It's all the little things I know I'm going to miss. The lunches. His calming presence and uncanny ability to bring me down from a ledge with just a gentle touch or soft look in my direction. The quiet laugh he huffs out when he's trying to bite back a smile. How he effortlessly cheers me on and champions everything I do. How secure he makes me feel.

Just *Finn* in general.

And yes, all right, the sex too. If he can do that with his fingers and tongue, I can't wait to find out what he can do with the thick, long dick I felt rubbing against the fabric of his trousers.

At some point over the last three months, Finn has wormed his way into my life and become a staple. It feels strange to think that when this all started, I couldn't stand him and had been so eager for this project to end. There's not a lot I wouldn't give to get another three months with him right now.

Funny how things work out.

Without me realising, Finn has slowly chipped away at the walls I'd carefully put up around me and carved himself a place front and centre in my heart.

It figures that I finally meet a man who makes me feel all the things Finn does and in four days we'll be an ocean apart.

Bailey would think this is all hilarious. She's in Jamaica right now on a PR trip with her brother's best friend, Cash, and I know she's going to lose her mind when I update her on everything that's happened. Though, judging by the sporadic messages I've been getting from her and some of the photos she's posted, *she's* got a few updates for me as well.

Finn makes an irritated sound and I look over at him just as he pulls the headphones away. I slide off the desk and drop down into his lap without a second thought. It feels right, and when his arms come up to pull me in even closer, my heart flutters again.

"Bad call?" I ask as he closes his laptop lid and pushes it to the side.

"Nothing to worry about," he says. He rests his chin on my

head and I hear him take in a deep inhale before he threads his fingers through my hair. "I feel like I haven't see you in a while."

"You haven't," I say as I lean into his touch. "We've both been so busy, but everything's nearly finished on my end. How're things going with the launch?"

"Good. All the suppliers have confirmed they'll be here, and judging from the response to the invites we sent out, we should have a full house."

"How're you feeling about that?"

He shrugs. "Nervous, I think."

"Will your uncle be there?"

Finn rolls his eyes. "No. Despite getting on my ass every step of the way, he hasn't deemed this an important enough event to attend."

"But he's the CEO and this is a big deal. It's the first location outside of New York. Don't you think people would wonder where he is?"

"Probably," Finn says. "But I really don't care at this point. Besides, there's only one person I really want there." He runs a hand down my jaw, his thumb ghosting over my bottom lip. "You'll be there, right?"

"Of course." I smile up at him and mirror his movements, holding his face in my hands. "I wouldn't miss it for the world. But I'll probably have to leave a little early. Now that I've moved even further out of London, I have to pay attention to things like last trains."

"I'll get you a cab," he says with a shrug. "Or a hotel room. Your choice. You've got to celebrate the right way after all your hard work."

"We're celebrating *your* hard work," I remind him. "And you don't have to do that."

"I know I don't have to. I want to."

"If anything, Cynthia should be the one footing the bill for my taxi home. But she's so stingy about what goes on the company card these days."

"There's—" He clears his throat, and my favourite pink tinge dances over the tips of his ears. "There's another alternative, you know?"

"And what's that?"

"Stay with me."

I freeze and wonder if he's also having flashbacks to that afternoon, because I know what he's really asking. We *both* know what he's really asking.

The first time I fuck you, it's going to be somewhere you can scream my name.

Somewhere like a hotel room?

His hotel room?

"That could...that could work." My pussy quite literally throbs in anticipation. "And maybe we could finish what we started the other day?"

He leans down until his lips brush against my earlobe. "There's no *maybe* about it, sweetheart." His voice is low and husky and sends a shiver rippling through me. He pulls back and shoots me a wide and bright grin. "So you'll stay?"

"I'll stay."

I DON'T MEAN to toot my own horn, but the club looks stunning.

I step through the entrance for the first time as a guest and take it in through fresh eyes. It's like I've walked into a fantasy world. The walls are bright and busy, the decorations decadent and eccentric, but there's an air of class and sophistication to it all that elevates the space and brings everything together.

It's *beautiful* and I have to blink away a few tears as I walk through the growing crowd. I don't think I've ever been so proud of a finished project before.

"Cynthia, you've done an absolutely phenomenal job, as always!" A tall man wearing a brightly patterned shirt descends on us and gives Cynthia two quick kisses on the cheek. He ignores me, although I'm standing right by her side.

Cynthia happily laps up the praise from him and the four other people who come after him and tell her what a fantastic job she did with the design.

When the fifth person approaches, I reach my limit. We're only twenty minutes into the launch party for The August Room and already I'm drained. I don't think I can bear an entire evening standing next to Cynthia and listening to her claiming my work as her own without so much of a hint of guilt flashing across her face.

I excuse myself, not that anyone hears me, and venture upstairs to the fourth floor to take a breather. I've got my overnight bag with me, and I need to stow it somewhere anyway. The guests have been relegated to the first two floors, and I feel a bit of the tension that's been building within start to ebb away as the sounds of music and laughter disappear the higher up I go.

Finn's not in the office, which is to be expected. He's probably in one of the lounge areas schmoozing the hundreds of high-profile guests currently packed into the building. I stuff my overnight bag under the desk and then lean against it, taking several deep breaths. It's going to be a long night, but there's a Finn-shaped light at the end of the tunnel and knowing that is enough to keep me going.

I head back downstairs and join the throng of partygoers. It's easy enough to find Cynthia again. She's always got to be the centre of attention, and I find her by the first floor bar. She's cackling and loudly taking credit for the plant pot statues embedded in the walls that I spent hours sourcing from a particularly tricky overseas supplier. Filling out the customs forms had been a nightmare but, of course, Cynthia doesn't know that.

I quietly join the back of the group huddled around her and tune out Cynthia's drawl.

"Now, you know, it was a bit of a rush job, but when The August Room comes calling, you don't hesitate..."

Well, I *try* to tune her out. Her voice has an irritating way of permeating my senses, like my brain is perfectly attuned to it and has some morbid sort of fascination with her lies.

I scan the room to try to distract myself, keeping an eye out for a familiar head of sandy blond hair. When I eventually spot him, he's got a jovial grin on his face, and one hand is gesturing wildly as he says something to the group of fully enraptured people surrounding him. Whatever he just said, it's apparently hilarious because they all break out into loud laughter. Including him.

They're like moths to a flame, hanging onto his every word, and I can't blame them. Even from across the room I can feel his magnetic pull, desperately trying to draw me in. I force myself to stay where I am and admire him from afar.

He looks divine in a midnight blue suit that's been cut perfectly, accentuating his broad shoulders and subtle muscles. It fits him like a dream.

My dream specifically, because it's going to take me a while to get this image of him — smiling, laughing, the light from the overhead lamps bathing him in a warm, inviting glow — out of my mind.

As if he can sense me watching him, his head suddenly snaps up in my direction. For a moment, it's like everyone else in the room disappears. Green eyes lock onto mine and my heart stutters. His gaze roves over me slowly. Does he like what he sees — the fitted red satin dress I'm wearing with a long slit that goes all the way up my left thigh? Judging by the way he swallows, his gaze stopping on the small peek of skin he can see on my exposed thigh, and the flash of unmistakable *want* in his eyes when they come back up to meet mine, I'm pretty sure he does.

My fingers twitch by my side in anticipation for what's to come later.

He gives me a tiny nod, barely imperceptible if you weren't looking for it, and I know that we're both thinking the same thing.

The first time I fuck you, it's going to be somewhere you can scream my name.

Those words have been running on a loop in my mind ever since he said them.

He says something to the group he's with and then seconds later he's striding across the floor and making a beeline toward me.

"Finn, darling!" Cynthia cries as she spots him. She grabs onto his arm and pulls him into a hug like they're lifelong friends. "I was just telling everyone what a delight you've been to work with."

I'm going to have to get him to teach me the art of keeping your face neutral, because his smile doesn't falter for even a second. It's only because I know him so well and I've become accustomed to seeing that bright spark in his eyes whenever he looks at me, that I notice when it dims slightly as he listens to Cynthia's lies.

"Yes, well, the team at Zensi Designs are truly phenomenal," he says. It makes my heart swell when I realise he's choosing his words carefully, refusing to directly give Cynthia any credit but being vague enough that she doesn't seem to notice. "It was a pleasure working with them."

Cynthia beams, completely oblivious.

Finn makes his way around the group, politely introducing himself and sharing business cards as he goes.

"You're quite the schmoozer, Mr. Hawthorne," I say quietly when he gets to me. Cynthia has pulled the attention of the group back to her and it grants us a brief reprieve.

"Mr. Hawthorne?" He raises a brow and takes a step forward, caging me in just a little. "I thought we were past that."

I shrug. "Just keeping up appearances."

He makes an irritated sound and dips his head so he can brush his lips against my ear. "Nope. Don't like that."

I choke on my breath as he splays his hand against my exposed thigh and gives it a squeeze. "But as long as it's *Finn* that comes out of those pretty lips later on tonight, I'll let it slide."

"*Finn—*"

"There we go." He drops his hand, takes a step backward, and gives me an appreciative once over. "You look beautiful, sweetheart."

"You don't look too bad yourself."

He grins. "Seems like we make a pretty good couple then."

My heart twists. "Seems like it."

He's about to say something else but someone calls his name from across the room. He glances at the sleek watch on his wrist and mutters out a quiet curse. "It's time for my speech."

"Go," I tell him, waving him away. "Come and find me once this is all over?"

"The *second* it's over."

He disappears into the crowd and I lean against the bar. Finn appears again after a few minutes at the top end of the room on a makeshift stage. The music quiets down and a polite hush spreads over the crowd as people start to notice him.

"Good evening, everyone, and thank you so much for coming." Finn launches into his speech, going over the long history of The August Room. He's even graceful enough to briefly mention his uncle and tell everyone how the club has been thriving since Ernest took over as CEO fifteen years ago. The praise is undeserved in my opinion, but I suppose it might earn Finn some brownie points with the miserable man.

He follows that with a little bit about how special this London location is. He talks about how this is the first in the series of planned expansions across the globe and how London will always have a special place in his heart because of it.

I think he glances over at me when he says that, but he's so far away I can't be sure.

He introduces his new property manager, Viola, to the crowd and earns himself a roar of laughter across the board when he puts on a truly awful British accent to do so. And then he brings up Zensi Designs.

"This London expansion has been a long time in the making," he says. "But I have to admit something. Not once in my wildest dreams did I ever think that I'd be able to find a designer to accurately depict my vision for the club. What Zensi Designs has done here—"

Cynthia clears her throat and stands tall. She's practically glowing.

"What they've done here is nothing short of a miracle. I've had the pleasure of working closely with the design team. Though..." He gives a bashful pause. "Maybe it wasn't always a pleasure for them."

A good-natured chuckle ripples across the room, and I can't help but join in.

"But they took my vision, all my admittedly unreasonable demands and gave me this. The most exquisitely designed members club in the city — and I can say that because I'm incredibly biased."

Everyone laughs again and it's truly remarkable how easily he works the crowd.

"I was painfully ignorant about what goes into designing a space when I first arrived, but my eyes have been opened."

There's no denying it this time. He *does* scan the room looking for me when he says that.

"I encourage you all, when you have a moment, to spend some time walking around the club and really appreciate all the unique design choices made by the team. It's truly phenomenal and I can't thank them enough for everything they've done."

Everyone around us is clapping Cynthia on the shoulder and heaping her with congratulations. I can tell she's trying to look pleased, but it doesn't quite reach her eyes. Her narrowed gaze finds me and her lips thin into a displeased frown.

"It seems you've made quite the impression on Hawthorne," she says quietly, voice too low for anyone else to hear but me.

I nod, trying to keep my expression as neutral as possible. "It's been a long three months."

"Hm. Well, let's see if you can keep this up with The Pevensey."

Irritation flares through me. Is it really so hard to just give me a compliment? To tell me I've done a good job and let *me* reap the praise just this once?

She turns away from me as Finn raises a glass.

"Now, if you'd all join me in a toast as we officially celebrate the launch of the London location of The August Room."

I don't have a glass, but I tip my head in his direction as everyone else cheers or yells some form of congratulation.

"To The August Room!"

"Congratulations!"

But not Finn.

Even from across the room, I can see the way his lips move as he tilts his glass toward me and mouths, *"To Amber."*

22

AMBER

It's long gone midnight by the time the party starts to fizzle out. I don't get the chance to talk to Finn again; he's too busy being swarmed by hordes of people all eager for him to know their names. He's been talking about this launch for months, making it seem like an actual party, but really it's just an overdressed networking event and it's *exhausting*.

I know Cynthia would like me to be working the crowd, handing out my business card to anyone who seems like they might have a need for some design services, but I can't bring myself to do it.

I sneak back up to the fourth floor and spend the rest of the evening alone as I wait for Finn. I don't mind it; the time alone gives me the chance to think about what I'm doing here and my future with Cynthia.

I meant it when I told Finn that I was tired of feeling terrible. It's been two weeks since I last spoke to my mother and while not being able to see Noah hasn't been ideal, the lift in my mood has been unmistakable. I don't feel a sense of dread and anxiety when I stick my keys in the door to *my* home. I may have minimal furniture and my phone bill might be ridiculously high because I haven't had the chance to sort out my Wi-Fi yet, but it actually feels like a home should.

I want that feeling in my career too. I'm tired of feeling small. Tired of having to make myself invisible so Cynthia can shine. And for what? I can't claim any of the projects I've completed on my portfolio, and I don't trust that Cynthia is actually going to follow through and actually give me the promotion.

I need to quit.

I've had the thought before, but this is the first time it's floated into my mind with such clarity.

I'm *going* to quit.

On Monday morning, I'm going to walk into her office and slam my resignation down on her desk. She'll fight it of course. Maybe she'll promise to give me the promotion and pay rise on the spot in an attempt to get me to stay. Doubtful. It's more likely that she'll threaten to ruin me if I leave. And I have no doubt that she'll do it too. Before I've even left the office she'll have poisoned my name to everyone in her extensive contact book.

But that's okay.

It'll be slow at first, but I don't need her high-profile clients to get started. I've made hundreds of connections of my own over the last seven years, and I'm sure it won't take me long to drum up a steady stream of work.

The last part of Finn's speech echoes in my mind, giving me a little boost of confidence in this new decision I've just made.

I'm going to do it. I'm really going to do it.

"You ready to go, sweetheart?" Finn leans against the door frame to the office.

"Are you finished?" If I strain, I can just about hear faint music and laughter. "Still sounds like the party's going."

"*I'm* finished," he says as he steps into the office. He meets me at my beanbag and offers a hand to help me stand. "Made a few excuses about some early morning meetings tomorrow and slipped out."

"They're not going to miss you?"

"Maybe," he says with a shrug. "But I've spoken to everyone I absolutely needed to see today, and Viola's got things handled downstairs."

"Look at you delegating like a pro," I tease him as he pulls me to my feet. "Who are you and what have you done with Finn Hawthorne?"

He laughs and warmth floods through me. It's such a lovely sound. I'm going to miss hearing it every day. "Come on, sweetheart. Let's go."

I grab my overnight bag, which he immediately takes from me, and follow him downstairs, out of the building, and into the black cab waiting for us outside. His hotel is less than a ten-minute drive away, but the journey feels like it stretches on. The energy between us is electric, and I'm acutely aware of his body next to mine. Every time our legs bump or our arms brush against each other, a frisson of excitement and anticipation for what's to come shoots through me.

I'm sure he can feel it too. His jaw ticks as he stares determinedly, and I can practically see the conflict raging behind his eyes. I know the feeling. The only thing that's stopping me from lifting my dress and sliding onto his lap right now is the driver.

And if we don't get to the hotel soon, even that might not be enough.

I lean into him to try to steady myself, resting my head on his chest. I let the comforting beat of his heart act as a guide, and by the time we pull up outside his hotel, I'm marginally less horny.

But only marginally.

He takes my bag without a word and laces his fingers with mine so he can tug me into the elevator.

"Did you have a nice time tonight?" I ask as we walk down the corridor once we reach his floor. He's on the very top floor and the carpet here is thick and plush, masking the sounds of our footsteps as we walk to his door.

"It went well," he says, sounding distracted. Dark green eyes meet mine for a fraction of a second and the corners of his lips curl upward into a small smirk. "I think I'm going to enjoy the second half the evening a lot more, though."

I bite my lip to stop my smile from spreading. "I'm serious, Finn. Tonight was a really big deal for you. Did you get the chance to enjoy it properly?"

He sighs as he slides his key card against the little square by his door. It flashes green and he pushes the door open, gesturing for me to go inside. "It was pretty bittersweet, if I'm being honest."

"Why's that?"

His hotel room is about five times the size of my living room at home. It's cool, sleek and swanky, and painted with dark, moody colours. There's a king sized bed against the wall farthest from the door, several plush-looking armchairs dotted around, and an amazing view of the London skyline. There are two large, open suitcases scattered beside his mirrored wardrobe, and the sight of them makes my throat close up.

One of the suitcases is half open, and it's clear he's been haphazardly throwing clothes into it recently.

He tosses my overnight bag beside the bed and then falls down onto it, gesturing for me to follow. I let myself drop into his open arms, and I drape my legs over his as he pulls me onto his lap.

"Because this project has been my baby ever since I first started thinking about it. Even before I flew out. For the last six months, all I've wanted to do is launch this location."

"And now you've done it."

"And now I've done it," he parrots quietly.

"So what's next?" I ask.

He shrugs. "I'm not sure. I'll be leaving the day-to-day management of the property with Viola, but I'll be keeping an eye on things for at least a few months."

"From here?" I ask, my voice full of hope.

He shakes his head. "From New York."

I feel myself deflate in his arms. "You're leaving soon."

"Sunday."

I nod and he must see the sadness flashing across my face because he tilts my chin up with his finger. "When I booked my flights I didn't have a reason to stay much longer past the launch date."

I swallow, hating how wobbly and vulnerable I know I must sound. "And now?"

He presses a soft kiss against my forehead. "I'd definitely have a reason now."

I bury my face in the crook of his neck to stop myself from verbalising the thought that suddenly jumps into my mind.

So stay.

Stay with me.

"I'll be back," he says, like he can read my mind anyway and knows exactly what I'm desperately trying not to say. Maybe he's thinking it too. "I'll definitely be back. And—"

"And what?" I say. "I'll be your London booty call?" It's meant to be a joke, but it doesn't come out that way. I sound hurt, and I think I am.

"Amber—" He inhales sharply and guilt immediately washes over me. "*Sweetheart.* Look at me."

I do as he says and when I look up, I see honest, sad eyes. "Sorry," I mumble. "That wasn't fair. I know you don't—"

"I wish we had more time together."

I melt into his touch. "Me too. I'm sorry that I spent so much of it hating you."

He snorts. "It was definitely deserved. But we probably wouldn't be where we are now if we hadn't taken that route."

"And where are we now?"

"I'm hoping..." he says slowly as he drags a finger along my leg. "I'm hoping that we're about to have a very fun night together."

I laugh and some of the tension that had begun to build dissipates. "Let's have some fun, Finn."

The grin on his face is full of promise, and he wastes no time getting things started.

He kicks things off by planting soft, wet kisses along my collarbone and shoulders and then bites down when he meets the thin strip of fabric from my dress. The feel of his teeth on my skin sends shockwaves racing through me, and I'm surprised by how much I enjoy the sensation.

"This needs to go," he murmurs as he nips at my skin again.

"You don't like my dress?" I ask, pretending to be offended.

He can see right through me, but he plays along. "You look gorgeous, sweetheart. Stunning. Ethereal. Find a thesaurus and take your pick. I could go on all night. But that dress has had its time to shine, and it's just going to get in the way." He rolls us over, punctuating his point with a gentle thud as my head hits the soft pillows at the top of the bed. I wrap my legs around him and pull his crotch flush against mine. The imprint of his dick rubs against the thin fabric covering my pussy and I whimper in frustration.

There are far too many layers between us right now.

"Now you see what I mean?" he asks with a smirk.

"Fair point."

He finds my zipper and gently tugs it down, shifting slightly over me so I can slip out of the dress. As soon as it's out of the way, he pushes me back into the mattress and resumes this newfound love of leaving a fiery trail of kisses on my exposed skin.

I've never been touched like this before.

Finn is slow. Torturous. Revenant.

He treats every inch of my body like it's something to worship, and I'm more than happy to lie back for a minute and let him work his magic.

He kisses me all the way down my body, taking his sweet time when he gets to my breasts and slowly rolls his tongue over my nipples. I gasp when he bites down on one and gives it a gentle suck. The only thing that stops me from bucking up off the bed is his firm hand on my hip, keeping me pressed into the mattress.

"I love those sounds you make," he says as he continues his slow descent toward the part where I need him most.

It's almost embarrassing how wet I am for him. *Almost.* If I couldn't plainly see how hard his dick is currently fighting to free itself from his suit trousers, I might've been a little self-conscious. But he wants me as badly as I want him, so I don't mind when he reaches the waistband of my panties — black and lacy tonight — and quickly finds me soaking for him.

Our groans meet and mix together in the air as he slips a finger inside and slowly, so *fucking slowly*, starts to move.

"What's your record?" he asks, voice lower than I've ever heard it before. He keeps his eyes on me as he fucks me with his fingers, and I have to fight to keep mine open.

My thoughts are hazy and I can barely think straight. "My record?"

"How many times have you come in one night?"

I blink, trying to parse through increasingly fuzzy memories. "Twice? Maybe? I...I don't know. What—"

He presses his thumb against my clit and I fall apart beneath him.

"Fuck. *Finn—*" My moans come out as choked sobs.

"That's one."

"What?" I pant.

He brings himself up until his face is level with mine, fingers still slowly stroking my pussy. I wonder if he can feel each pulsation as I ride out the aftershocks of a surprisingly powerful orgasm.

"Two more to go, sweetheart." He kisses me and grins. "At least."

He gives me a minute to catch my breath and quickly discards his own clothing. I drink in the sight of him as he sheds his shirt and kicks away the tailored suit trousers into a dark corner of the room. His body is a work of art, and I'm very much enjoying the private viewing.

"Eyes up here, sweetheart," he says with a knowing smirk.

"No thanks," I say. He dips his thumb into the waistband of his boxers and tugs downward. "I'm good down here."

His dick springs free and I can't help but run my tongue along my lips at the sight of it. I could tell by the imprint and the feel of it rubbing against me that Finn's dick would be nothing to scoff at, but this is something else entirely. It's big and veiny — seven inches at a *conservative* guess — and my pussy twitches, already ready for round two, as I watch him lazily palm it.

I make a mental note of the way he touches himself, committing the speed and pressure he applies to memory.

"You good?" he asks, hand still pumping up his rock hard shaft.

I nod, my words sticking in my throat as he walks toward me and rubs the tip of his dick down my jaw. I turn my head and take him in my mouth before he even has the chance to ask. He groans low and deep, eyes rolling to the back of his head as he slides himself along my tongue.

"*Amber.*" He groans my name like it's a prayer, and I bring a hand up to squeeze the base of his dick experimentally. "*Shit.*"

That does it. He bucks into me, the tip of his dick hitting the back of my throat. "Shit. Sorry," he wheezes, trying to still the erratic motion of his moving hips. "Sorry, sweetheart."

I pull back a little bit and swirl my tongue around his head, lapping up the little droplets of pre-cum that have already begun to form. He hisses as my tongue slips into the slit on his head.

"Stop," he pants. "Stop, *stop.*"

I frown up at him. "You don't like that?"

He shakes his head, a sheepish smile twisting his lips. "I loved it. But I don't want to finish in your mouth. Not tonight."

"Oh." Not tonight. As if we've got more time together beyond this one evening. I glance back at his length and bite my lips, resisting the urge to take him in my mouth again. "You were close?"

He nods, and if *that's* not an ego boost, I don't know what is. I give his dick one last long stroke, enjoying the way he shudders, and then I pull back.

I expect him to climb into bed with me, but he doesn't. Instead, a playful look flashes over his face as he walks away.

"Finn?"

He rummages through his suitcase and pulls out a strip of condoms. He tears one open and slides it on, but he still doesn't come back to bed. I watch, confused, as he grabs one of the comfy looking armchairs and drags it across the room until he reaches the large, mirrored wardrobe. He gives me a wink and then drops down onto the armchair and spreads his legs. "Come sit, sweetheart." He slaps his thighs, making his dick bounce with each movement.

I slide off the bed and pad toward him. As soon as I'm close enough to touch, he reaches out and pulls me on top of him. My breasts bump against his bare chest as I straddle him and his dick slides impatiently against my opening. I wiggle around a bit, trying to find the right angle to sit on him and take him in, but Finn shakes his head.

"Not yet. Look." He uses two fingers to tilt my head toward the mirror. "Look how beautiful you are, sweetheart."

I catch a glimpse of us in the mirror, our bodies pressed together, our skin flushed, our chests heaving. I'm focused less on myself and more on how good we look together.

My pussy throbs again.

"Are you going to fuck me in front of this mirror?"

"Damn right I am." He lifts me like I weigh nothing and gives me half a second of warning before he slowly drops me down over his dick. My toes curl as I take in every inch of him. If I thought his fingers or tongue felt good, this is like a whole other world. He slowly slides himself inside me and just as I'm beginning to think that I won't be able to take any more, he bottoms out, and I have to marvel at how perfectly he fits inside me.

He gives me an experimental thrust. "How's that?"

My head hits his shoulder and I bite down on the soft skin there in an attempt to muffle my cry. How can it possibly feel so good already?

I hear him chuckle and then I feel his fingers come up to tug at the back of my hair. It's not painful; he uses just enough force for me to recognise that it's intentional and he's trying to catch my attention. I lift my head up and bite back another moan as the movement has me involuntarily grinding on him.

"As much as I liked that," he says, nodding to the patch on his shoulder where a small, purple bruise is surely going to form by the morning. "Don't hold back, sweetheart. I told you I want to hear you scream my name. Okay?"

I nod. "Okay."

"Make sure you keep watching," he murmurs as he grabs my hips and starts to bounce me up and down. "I want you to see everything your beautiful body does to me. I need you to see, first-hand, what I see – what I feel – every time I look at you. Can you do that for me, sweetheart? Can you keep your eyes on me? On us?"

I nod and he smiles. It's a soft smile, a sweet smile, one reserved just for me.

For us.

I keep my word and my gaze remains locked on our reflections. Even when he presses into me, his dick hitting that sweet spot that makes my vision blur, I force myself to keep my eyes open. I'm so glad that I do. Because I don't miss the way *his* eyes roll back, the way he bites his bottom lip as I roll my hips against his, the increasingly erratic rise and fall of his chest as he moans my name between grunted pants.

I think this may just be the hottest thing I've ever done.

I love watching the way Finn's hips roll into mine as he bucks upward, finding a steady pace that works well for us both. I stick to my word and don't muffle my moans and cries as he hits me in all the right spots.

"*Finn.*"

Every time I moan out his name he sinks himself deeper into me and I feel his body shudder. This might just be my super-power. The ability to make Finn Hawthorne lose his mind with just one word.

"*Finn.*"

"You feel so *good, Amber,*" he groans as I bounce, fingers digging tightly into my skin. "Fuck, baby, you feel so good."

Baby. I pause. That's a new one, and while I don't hate it, there's one I prefer more.

I tear my gaze away from the mirror and grip his chin tightly between my thumb and forefinger, forcing him to look into my eyes. "Sweetheart," I tell him between moans. "*You* call me *sweetheart.*"

I don't know what it is exactly that sends him over the edge — Is it the eye contact, the little order I give him, or the way I roll my hips to punctuate that last *sweetheart* — but it works.

His grip on my waist tightens, and the rhythmic thrusts turn almost feral as he jerks into me. "Sweetheart. Oh, *fuck,* I—"

I capture his lips in a kiss and swallow down the deep, loud groan that spills out as he finishes inside me. I bring my other hand down to my clit and rub just how I like it, taking me to that sweet, sweet spot in seconds. I arch my back and let my head roll between my shoulders as my vision blurs, and for the second time in less than an hour, I see stars.

I watch our reflections in the mirror as we pull ourselves back together. I like the way I look sitting in his arms, like this is where I belong. After a few minutes, our breathing returns to normal and he plants a lazy kiss on the corner of my mouth.

"That was number two," I remind him as he stands up, cradling me in his arms as he walks us toward the bathroom. "You promised me a least one more, or did you forget?"

He shoots me a tired grin. "I don't break promises, sweetheart. And tonight is just getting started."

23

AMBER

Finn sleeps like a log.

I've been up for at least an hour now, woken by the sunlight cracking through the slits in the curtains, but Finn is still peacefully snoring away. I don't wake him, though. He deserves as much sleep as he can get after last night, both the launch party and *our* evening together.

I watch him as he softly snores. There's a row of purplishpink bruises forming along his collarbone. I did that. I marked him. He might be leaving in less than 24 hours, but those marks will linger for a while, and I feel a strange sense of territorial pride as I look at them.

Mine.

For a few more hours at least.

My phone buzzes and I quickly scoop it up before the sound can wake him. I've been trying to contact Bailey since I woke up — she's due to land back in London from her trip to Jamaica today — and so it doesn't surprise me when her grinning and definitely tanned face fills my screen.

"You're home!" I say, my voice a half-whisper. "How was the flight?"

"Not too bad. Where *are* you?" I can see her eyes darting around the screen, trying to figure out where I am because I'm *clearly* not in my own room.

"Well—"

Finn groans beside me, rolls over, mumbles something sleepily, and drapes an arm over my waist. Bailey's eyes widen and I bite my lip to smother the giggle that's desperate to come out. "Yeah," I whisper. "I need to update you on some *developments*."

And then it's my turn to stare at *her* in shock, because a figure suddenly looms over her. He's tall and handsome, his shoulder length wavy hair pulled into a messy bun. Caspian "Cash" Reid. Bailey's older brother's best friend and her reluctant companion on this PR trip.

Or maybe not so reluctant anymore.

He drops his head onto her shoulder and she leans into the touch that's definitely too intimate for two people who supposedly dislike each other.

"Caspian," I say with a nod, my voice full of unasked questions.

Cash nods back, his lips twitching in obvious amusement. "Amber."

Before I can say anything else, Finn's arm tightens around my waist and he groans as he tries to pull me over to his side of the bed.

I shoot Bailey a wink. "We'll talk later."

She laughs as she hangs up the call.

"Mornin', sweetheart," Finn grumbles as he pulls me on top

of him. "Who was that?"

"Bailey," I tell him. "You remember my friend?"

His eyes are low and sleepy and it's interesting to learn that Finn is not a morning person. Given how early he arrived at the club every morning, I never would've guessed. "Yeah, I remember her. Everything all right?"

"Pretty sure everything is a lot more than all right."

His brows furrow in confusion before he shakes his head and apparently decides it's too early to try to get into this. He lifts his head just enough to give me a quick kiss before he flops down onto his pillow again. "What time is it?"

"Just gone eleven."

He hums and his eyes flutter shut again. I lie down on his chest and trace invisible patterns on his skin.

"I didn't tell you, but I made a big decision last night," I murmur.

"What was it?"

"I'm going to quit Zensi Designs."

He opens both eyes and beams down at me. "Really?"

I prop myself up onto my elbow and frown. "Why do you look so happy?"

"Because that place...because *Cynthia* makes you miserable. I'm glad you're getting out of there. Where are you going to go?"

I bite my lip. "I'm not sure yet. I was thinking that I'd maybe try to start something up of my own. It'll be hard," I say quickly, like I need to convince him. "But I think I can do it."

"I *know* you can do it."

There's no doubt in his voice, just pure, unwavering confidence in my abilities.

You know, I really think I could come to love this man.

I might already be pretty close.

I HATE that I'm about to cry.

I hate that Finn can tell I'm about to cry.

We're standing outside his hotel and there's a black cab waiting for me. Once I get into it, that'll be it for us.

We spent the entirety of Saturday night together, pretending like his flight back to New York wasn't looming over us. But we can't pretend anymore. His flight is in a few hours and this is it.

I blink back the tears threatening to spill over. It's really not fair.

"I'll be back soon, Amber," he murmurs, and the only solace I can take from all this is that he looks just as miserable as I feel.

"Not soon enough." And it's true. With his busy schedule once he gets back to New York there's no telling when he'll next be able to come back to London. We both know it, even if we won't say it out loud.

"You're not getting rid of me that easily, sweetheart," he says, cracking a weak smile. "Trust me. Give it a week and you'll be tired of seeing my name blowing up your phone."

I laugh at the irony of it all. I can't imagine the Amber of three months ago wanting nothing more than to see Finn Hawthorne's name at the top of her call list. "Never. Call me anytime."

"I will." He steps forward and pulls me into a tight hug. "Thank you, Amber."

"What're you thanking me for?" I'm glad my face is buried

in his shirt, because the tears have finally started to fall.

"Everything." He pulls back, brows furrowing as he spots the tears sliding down my cheeks. He brings a thumb up and wipes them away. "You've made me a better man, honestly. More thoughtful. Considerate. Trusting. And my life is infinitely brighter with you in it."

But I'm not going to be in for much longer, am I? "Stop. This is the kind of thing you say to someone you don't plan on ever seeing again."

"Fine," he says. "Then I'll just say this. I'm going to miss you, sweetheart." He pulls me in for a deep, long kiss, and it's most definitely the kind of kiss you share with someone when you know without a shadow of a doubt that this is it. This is the last time you're going to see each other.

When we break apart, I'm pretty sure there are tears in his eyes too.

"WOW."

"Mhm."

Bailey shoves a handful of popcorn into her mouth and chews thoughtfully. "But what if he's *The One?*"

We're sprawled across my living room, sitting on the bean-bags I swiped from The August Room on my last day since the sofas I ordered still haven't arrived. Bailey is sitting on my one, and I'm on Finn's. It still smells like him, which is maybe a tiny bit creepy, but I can't bring myself to care.

"There are three thousand, four hundred and ninety-one miles between us right now," I say with a scowl. "So if he's *The*

One, then someone up there is playing a very horrible trick on me."

"Should I be worried that you apparently know that number off the top of your head?"

"No. Yes. I don't know," I groan and sink into my beanbag. "It's just not fair. Whether he's *The One* or not, there was definitely something there. Would've been nice to see where it could've gone."

"I'm sorry, babe." She slides across the floor with her beanbag and gives me a one-armed cuddle. "If it's meant to be, it'll happen. Have you spoken since he left?"

I nod. "Every day, actually." It's been a week since he left London and I've woken up to a *good morning sweetheart* text — sent before he goes to bed — every day and gone to sleep after a short FaceTime call with him most nights.

"Did you guys ever talk about trying long distance?" Bailey asks. "I know it's not easy, but it might be worth it for the right person."

I shake my head. "We never spoke about it, and I didn't want to bring it up. We only knew each other for three months, and we didn't really start having any kind of relationship until at least the halfway point. I felt like it was maybe too new to ask him to commit to me like that."

Bailey shrugs. "Maybe, but if there's one thing this trip has taught me, it's that time really doesn't mean anything. I've known Cash for most of my life and look at us."

I chew on a handful of popcorn. She might be right there. Up until a week ago, I would've sworn that Cash hated her but apparently we were both wrong about that. "Do you think he's *The One*?"

"He might be," Bailey says honestly. "It's too soon to say, but he's definitely *something*." A soft smile creeps over her face. "He treats me so well, Amber. It's...it's not weird exactly, I'm just not used to it, you know?"

If I ever have the displeasure of seeing her ex-boyfriend again, the man who single-handedly shot down Bailey's self-esteem, I swear I'm going to punch him squarely in the face. And even that will be too good for him.

"Well, I'm a fan," I tell her. "Maybe I'll meet my own Cash one day soon."

Bailey rolls her eyes. "You've already met him, babe. It just sucks that he's three thousand miles away."

"*Three thousand, four hundred and ninety-one* miles away."

"Why don't you go and visit him?" she asks. "You've got a bit of free time now."

I snort. "A bit of free time" is an interesting way to say I quit my job at Zensi Designs, and I'm currently in a period of gardening leave, so I can't technically start working on looking for my own clients unless I want to feel the wrath of Cynthia's legal team if she ever finds out. Luckily, I'm being paid my full salary for the next two months, and I have a relatively comfortable savings nest to bounce back on, so I don't have to worry about my bills going unpaid. But that doesn't mean I can afford a flight to New York on a whim.

"Things just didn't line up for us," I say after beat of silence. "It sucks, but that's life. I'll move on eventually, and I'm sure he will too."

And maybe if I say that enough, I'll actually start to believe it.

24

FINN

"Mama, why does Uncle Finn look like that?"

"Like what, sweet pea?"

Maya makes a truly gruesome face. She sticks her bottom lip out and makes her eyes go all wide and watery. "Like this."

Nel snorts and even I can't help but crack a smile. She's a real character that kid.

"I don't look like that," I yell from my spot on the couch.

"No, I think it's a pretty accurate depiction," Nel says. She hovers over me and levels an unimpressed look. "If you're going to insist on coming around here moping, can you at least be helpful and help me get dinner ready? These vegetables aren't going to prepare themselves."

I want to say no, but she's got a look in her eye that says she's about five seconds away from putting me in a headlock. "Fine," I grumble as I drag myself off the couch. I'm well aware that I'm acting like a moody teenager and not a respectable 32-year-old man, but I can't bring myself to care. It's been a week since I left London, and I've been miserable every single day. I even called out of work — something I didn't even do when I got a really bad case of the flu last year — and blamed it on jet lag. I follow Nel into the kitchen with Maya hot on my heels.

"What's wrong, Uncle Finn?"

"He's lovesick," Nel says with a roll of her eyes. "Isn't it disgusting?"

"Yuck," Maya says in agreement.

"I'm not lovesick," I mumble as I rifle through Nel's fridge, pulling out the vegetables she needs chopped and diced for this meal. "I'm just—"

"You just miss your girlfriend."

"You have a *girlfriend*?" Maya squeaks. "Mama, does Uncle Finn have a girlfriend?"

"Yes, sweet pea."

"No, princess."

Maya glares at both of us. "Liars."

"Uncle Finn's the liar, sweet pea."

"Amber is *not* my girlfriend," I say firmly. Although I wish she was. I wish I'd said something before I left, asked her if she wanted to give this a try — give *me* a try. But it hadn't felt right. I don't know how to label what it was that we had back in London, but I know that it was still new. Too new to ask for a commitment like that.

I lift Maya up onto the kitchen counter and pull out the child safety knives I got her a few months ago so she could help out in the kitchen. I hand her a cucumber and she happily starts slicing.

"Is she pretty?" Maya asks, tongue poking out in concentration as she butchers the poor cucumber.

The question catches me off guard. "Is who pretty?"

"Your girlfriend."

"Yeah," I say without thinking. "She's beautiful." We've FaceTimed each other most nights, and every time her smiling face fills my screen, my heart starts to beat a little faster.

"Good," Maya says with a stern nod. "Can we meet her?"

"No, princess," I say sadly. "You can't meet her."

"Why not?" The question comes from Nel this time.

"Because she lives in London," I say, glaring at my sister. "And I don't know if you've noticed, but we're not currently in London."

"We're in New York!" Maya supplies helpfully.

"Exactly."

"So fly her out," Nel says, like it's the simplest solution in the world.

"I can't just fly her out."

Nel opens her mouth, closes it, then opens it again and shakes her head. "Maya, sweet pea, can you please go and find your apron? I don't want you to get your T-shirt messy."

Maya nods and I help her down from the island. Once she's gone, Nel crosses the distance between us and angrily prods my chest with a wooden spoon. "What the fuck is wrong with you, Finn?"

I frown at her. That wasn't the energy I'd been expecting. "What?"

"'*I can't just fly her out*'." She puts on a stupid voice and mimics the face Maya had made earlier. "Of course you can. Buy her a ticket, send it to her, and she'll be here within a day."

I start to protest, but Nel holds up a hand.

"Listen, Finn, I love you, but I'm getting tired of the excuses.

You finally found someone to pull you out of the ten-year funk you've been in—"

"It hasn't been that long."

The hand goes up again, and I mime zipping my mouth shut.

"You've found someone who gets you. Who makes you happy, and *don't* try to deny it. I've seen the way you smile whenever your phone buzzes and it's a message from her. You love that girl."

My throat goes dry.

Love?

Do I *love* Amber? There are so many little things about her that I love, but do I love her? Am I *in* love with her?

Yes. The answer floats to the front of my mind without a second thought.

Yes, I'm in love with her. I think I've been in love with her for a while now.

"Oh, great." Nel shakes her head. "So this is the first time you've realised that you're in love. Cool. Whatever. Not my problem. My point still stands. Either you fly her out or you head on right back to London. I don't care which one it is, but you need to stop moping around my house. Even Maya's starting to notice."

"What if she says no?" My voice is quieter than I'd like, betraying the genuine worry I can feel simmering beneath the surface. What if she doesn't want to come? What if *I* turn up on her doorstep and she sends me away?

Nel's gaze softens slightly and she prods me again with the spoon, only a whole lot gentler this time. "She won't say no."

"You don't know that."

"No, I don't," Nel concedes. "But you do. *You* know she's not going to say no, Finn. But she can't say yes if you don't give her the chance."

Nel is right of course. She's rarely wrong — something she gloats about every chance she can get — but I don't even mind the smug smirk she gives me now, because an idea is forming in my mind.

It might be a terrible idea and Amber might hate it with every fibre of her being, but I don't think she will.

"What're you thinking?" Nel asks. "You've got that look on your face that says you're about to do something very, very stupid."

"I am," I tell her with a shrug. "But I think it's going to work out. And I'm going to need your help."

***

WE'VE FaceTimed almost every night, but I've never felt as nervous as I do now. It rings a few times and then her face lights up my screen. Her hair is wrapped in a colourful silk scarf and it's clear she's ready for bed.

"Hey," she says, and I can hear the tiredness in her voice. "Didn't think you were going to call tonight."

"Sorry, sweetheart. Got caught up with a few things."

"Work?" She frowns. "You're supposed to be having some time off."

"Something like that." I swallow and try to inject a casual air of indifference into my tone. "Speaking of work, I've got a lead for you."

She sits up a little straighter. "A lead? Finn, you know I can't take on any clients while I'm on gardening leave. If Cynthia finds out, she could sue."

"You can't take on any clients in the *UK*," I tell her, and I should know. I spent several hours poring over her frankly awful employment contract with Cynthia. "She can't stop you from taking on international clients. No court in the world would allow that."

"You've got an international client for me?" she asks uncertainly. "I don't know..."

"My sister is a realtor," I tell her quickly so she doesn't talk herself out of it before I've even begun. "And she's got a property on the books that's just not selling. It's in a really beautiful location and could potentially sell for a couple million, but it needs a lot of work."

"Not seeing where I come in here, Finn."

"She wants to work with a designer to get it presentable," I explain. "Nothing *huge* but enough so potential buyers can see that it's actually worth something. She mentioned it over dinner last night, and I immediately thought of you."

"Finn, I don't—"

"It'd be an easy job for you to add to your portfolio."

"I know," she groans. "But I hate working virtually — it's so hard to get a feel of the space when you're only seeing it through a camera. I wouldn't want to do your sister a disservice."

"Come to New York then."

She doesn't say anything, and for a second, I think she's frozen.

"Amber?"

"I heard you, I just—" She gives me a weak smile. "I'd love

nothing more than to fly out to New York right now, but I can't afford it and—"

"Flights are paid for as part of your fee."

"What about accommodation? I'll need to get a hotel and—"

"Amber." I cut her off and raise an unimpressed brow. "Obviously you're staying with me."

Even in the low light of her bedroom, I can see her face flush.

"Obviously?"

"Obviously. Say yes, sweetheart. Say you'll do it. One last job, for me."

A slow but bright smile spreads across her face. "All right. When does she need me over there by?"

"How does tomorrow sound?"

25

AMBER

Finn is hiding something and, the funniest thing is, I'm pretty sure he thinks he's doing a good job at it.

When he calls me an hour before my flight to make sure I've gotten to the airport safely and that I'm enjoying the lounge privileges that come with the obscenely expensive last minute first class ticket he bought, I can tell immediately that something is up.

He's smiling like he physically can't stop himself, his grin stretching from ear to ear. Someone else might put this down to him just being excited about my imminent arrival in New York, but there's something else there.

It's in his gaze, the way he steadfastly refuses to meet mine like he's afraid if we look into each other's eyes I'll spot what he's hiding. It's in his gestures and voice that don't quite match up. The gestures are too wide and dramatic for the deliberately light and airy tone he's putting on, like he can't quite decide how he wants to play this and keeps bouncing between the two extremes.

What're you hiding Finn Hawthorne? And why has it got you smiling like that?

I'm desperate to know, but I'm also enjoying the unintentional performance he's putting on. And it's a good distraction from the maelstrom of doubt currently swirling in my mind.

As eager as I am to see Finn again, as much as I've spent the entirety of this last week missing him with every fibre of my being, one thought stays bouncing around my mind.

Why are we doing this?

Against my better judgement I've ignored the fact that it's obvious that this whole '*my sister has a property she wants you to design*' thing is nothing more than a flimsy excuse to see me, and I allowed myself to get caught up in the romance of it all.

Because it is romantic, isn't it? This man misses me so much that, after just a week apart, he's willing to fly me out on a first class ticket to see him. I should be swooning right now. And I do, for a little while. But then reality comes crashing over me like a wave, and suddenly I'm drowning in doubt.

What happens after this? Once we've enjoyed this time together and I'm sitting on a flight back to the UK, what happens when we decide we miss each other again? How many times can he conjure up a job opportunity to convince me to come and visit before we both have to admit that this isn't sustainable?

We both deserve something permanent, not just lust filled trysts every now and then just because he happens to be able to afford the airfare.

It feels like we're just delaying the inevitable. It might not happen on this visit, or the next, or even the one after that, but it *will* come crashing down on us eventually. When we realise that we both want more, and neither of us are in a position to give it.

Would he leave New York for me? I frown and let the question roll around in my mind. No, I don't think so. His work is over there, his family too – and I'd never ask it of it him.

Not for something so new.

Maybe if we'd had more time together. If these three months had been three years and I hadn't spent half of them hating him, maybe then we'd have something to build on.

Would *I* leave if he asked me?

The thought makes my stomach twist and I know immediately that I wouldn't. Not now. I'm entering a new chapter in life – I've just bought a house, I'm *finally* striking out on my own at work, and I think I'd probably end up resenting him if he asked me to give it all up to come and stay with him.

Bailey thinks I'm being ridiculous.

"You can't design houses in New York?" she asked, incredulous, when I voiced these thoughts to her.

I can, technically, but it would be an uphill battle. This industry is one that thrives on connections and word of mouth, and I don't have any of that in New York. It's going to be difficult enough building my own client list in London, I don't want to make things any harder.

This thing that Finn and I have going on clearly has an expiration date and we're racing towards it.

I wonder if he realises it.

A voice crackles out of the overhead speakers and announces that boarding has begun for my red-eye flight. The sound snaps me out of my increasingly depressing thoughts and

I force myself to lean back into the excitement I'd been feeling earlier.

"See you in..." I glance at my boarding pass. "Just over eight hours."

Finn smiles, and it's his real smile this time, the one that makes my heart stutter and my cheeks warm. "I'll be there to meet you. Have a safe flight, sweetheart."

My phone buzzes as I sink into my cushy first class seat.

BAILEY

Have a safe flight, babe. Let me know when you land.

And stop spiralling. ENJOY THE MOMENT.

Despite everything, I can't help but smile. Bailey knows me so well.

AMBER

I'm trying!!!!

The rich bitch vibes are definitely helping though.

I send her a photo of the little cubicle I've got to myself, along with the complimentary flute of champagne and I laugh when her immediate response is rows and rows of groaning emojis.

BAILEY

Omg. Jealous. Need to find a brand that will fly me and Cash out first class.

Better get used to this life, babe. You're dating a millionaire now.

He's not a millionaire.

Or is he? I'm actually not quite sure. Finn isn't overly flashy, but he carries himself with the quiet confidence of someone who's never had to subtly check their bank balance at a bar before placing an order.

BAILEY

You sure? Flying you out first class with less than a days' notice seems like pretty strong millionaire behaviour to me.

AMBER

...Shut up.

And we're not dating.

BAILEY

Not officially, but I give you guys three days.

Countdown starts...now!

I roll my eyes, put my phone onto airplane mode, and enjoy the perks that flying first class brings. Mostly the fact that, once we're in the air and the captain turns off the seatbelt sign, I'm allowed to recline my seat all the way back and turn my cubicle into a little makeshift bed. I've always struggled to sleep on flights, but I doze off quickly this time. When I open my eyes again, a flight attendant is hovering over me with a small smile and she lets me know we'll be landing shortly.

It takes me barely any time at all to get through Customs and Baggage Claim and, as I wheel my suitcase out through the arrivals gate, I keep an eye out for broad shoulders and a head of sandy blond hair. It's easy to spot him. He's standing front and centre in front of the arrivals gate, and a genuine grin stretches from ear to ear as he locks eyes with me.

If I didn't have my suitcase, I'd run to him. Sprint, even. As it stands, I have to settle for a brisk jog but he does me a kindness and meets me halfway. He sweeps me up into his arms and barely gives me the chance to get out a breathy '*hey*' before his lips are slanting over mine.

God, I've missed his touch. It sets my skin ablaze as he swipes his thumb along my jaw and pulls me in even deeper. I can't get enough of him, and I claw at the hairs on the nape of his neck, desperate to get closer.

In this moment, it's only the two of us. The rest of the airport fades away and all I can hear, feel, touch, and taste is Finn.

I nip at his bottom lip and he groans into my mouth. That's a sound I'll never tire of. I bite down again and relish in the way his entire body shivers. A hand drops down to my waist and settles on the small of my back. Even through my clothes, each touch burns like fire.

He pushes down firmly, pulling me flush against him. I can feel every perfect hard ridge of his chest against mine, and there's an unmistakable hardness pressing against my lower belly. I grind into it, a reflex more than anything else, and he hisses out a desperate moan. He pulls away, mumbling something that sounds a lot like '*not here, sweetheart*' but I lean forward, still chasing his lips.

He laughs as he wraps an arm over my shoulders and tucks me into his side. "I missed you too. But, unless you want to get added to the no-fly list, I think we should probably head out."

I lean into his touch and let him guide me out of the airport. It's an entirely innocent action, but the casual intimacy of it stokes the fire in my core. I think he's feeling it too. The hand on my shoulder doesn't stop tugging at my sweatshirt, like he's desperate to peel back the layer and feel for himself the heat radiating off me.

"How was your flight?" he asks as we step out into the car park.

"Great," I say honestly. "I slept most of the way thanks to the extra comfy seat. You didn't have to spring for a first class ticket, by the way. I've would've been fine in economy."

"And give you yet another reason to call me cheap?" He pretends to look affronted as he shoves my suitcase into the back of his car. It's an expensive looking model, black and sleek with tinted windows. "I don't think so, sweetheart."

It's remarkable how quickly we slip back into the swing of things, like there hasn't been an ocean between us for the last seven days.

"I haven't called you cheap in weeks. But—" I cock my head to the side and flash him a teasing grin. "If you wanted to beat the cheap allegations, you should've chartered me a private jet."

He comes to stand in front of me and gently boxes me in against his car. "I'll remember that for next time." His voice is low and gravelly. I follow his gaze as his eyes dip to my lips.

"Next time?"

He hums like he's barely listening before he swipes a finger against my jaw. "Next time."

I don't have the chance to think about the implications of *next time* and the fact that Finn and I desperately need to have a serious conversation about *us*, because his lips quickly cover mine and we're right back where we left off inside the airport.

His dick is still painfully hard. I drop a hand to his crotch and palm it through the soft cotton of his sweatpants. He doesn't break the kiss as he groans into my mouth. The feel of it reverberates down my throat and rumbles through every inch me. His hands trail down the length of my body and settle on my ass. He squeezes my cheeks like he can't resist, and then dips down a little further so he can lift me up. I wrap my legs around his middle and arch into his touch, desperate to get even closer.

A small voice in the back of my mind tries to remind me that we're still in a public place and that anyone could walk past right now and witness Finn pushing me up against his car, my legs wrapped tightly around his waist.

Annoyingly, I listen to the voice.

I break the kiss and laugh when he moans at the sudden absence of my lips on his. "How far is your place from here?"

He pulls a grimace. "Too far."

"Better get going then." I purposely roll my hips and brush against the tip of his still hard dick.

Something flashes in his eyes and the grin on his face is downright devilish. "Or..." he says slowly as he shifts so he's holding me up with one arm. Now that the other hand is free, he uses it to reach for the backseat door closest to us. "Or we could make very good use of these nice, tinted windows here."

An electric thrill shoots through me.

"What do you say?"

I roll my hips again in response, angling them just right to grind my warm core against his entire stiff length. His fingers dig into my hips hard enough to bruise, but then something akin to panic flashes across his face.

"Fuck."

"What?" I whip my head around in every direction, suddenly worried that someone's been watching us the entire time.

"I don't have any condoms on me." He groans and lets his head fall forward to land against my collarbone. "I wasn't expecting to be seduced as soon as you landed."

I bite my lip. "I have an IUD."

He looks up immediately.

"And my last test was about six months ago, I think. But there's been nobody since then. I'm pretty sure I have the results in my inbox somewhere, I can dig them out and—"

"Me too," he says breathlessly. "My last test was about four months ago. I'm all clear." He pulls back a little, his gaze seriously and searching. "Are you sure?"

I nod, then nip at his earlobe, enjoying the way he hisses beneath me. "Now, hurry up and fuck me in your fancy car."

26

FINN

IF THERE'S ONE SIGHT I CAN BE SURE I'M NEVER GOING TO tire of, it's this one.

Amber, naked, aside from a thin pair of green panties, grinding on me like there's nowhere she'd rather be right now than on my cock. I take one of her perfect breasts in my mouth, my tongue tracing aimless little circles around her stiff nipple. She lets out a half sigh, half moan as she folds over on me, her head coming to rest in the crook of my neck.

"Did you make me take off all my clothes just to tease me?"

"No," I say truthfully. I run my hands along her side, determined to commit every curve, every dip, every inch of her to memory. "But you know I'm easily distracted."

And what a distraction she is.

She sinks her teeth into the nape of my neck, right over the marks she left last time that have only just begun to fade. My girl is territorial, though I doubt she'd ever admit it out loud. She trails her tongue along my neck and up my jaw. "I'm here for two weeks," she whispers against my lips. "Plenty of time for distractions later."

Two weeks isn't nearly enough time for everything I want to do with her.

I'm starting to think that a lifetime wouldn't be enough.

But I'll take what I can get for as long as she's willing to give it to me.

I slip a hand between us and run my fingers along the thin strip of fabric separating her pussy from my touch. It's soaked through. "Look how wet you are, sweetheart."

She bucks her hips into mine, simultaneously riding my hand and rubbing against my throbbing erection. "Are you going to do something about it?"

Famous last words.

Her surprised squeak echoes around the car as I slide her off my lap. Before she can question anything, I wrap an arm around her lower belly and flip her onto her knees. I don't waste anytime tugging her lace panties down to her knees.

I hover over her and start trailing hot kisses down her body. "You're so beautiful, Amber. So—" I plant a kiss along the faint row of freckles on her collarbone. "*Fucking*—" Another kiss, this time in the little divots that appear in her lower back as she arches into my touch. "Beautiful." I give the glistening folds of her pretty pussy one long kiss. "*Everywhere.* Every part of you is beautiful."

"*Finn*," she breathes as she turns around to glare at me. "Please. Stop. Teasing."

I laugh, give her pussy one last kiss, then lean back onto my haunches. I pull my sweats and boxers down far enough to free my straining cock.

"Tell me what you want," I say as I line myself up with her entrance and slide the tip of my cock along her slick folds. "Anything you want. You just have to ask."

She rolls her hips, desperately trying to force my cock inside. I grip her hips with my free hand and hold her in place.

"I need to hear it, sweetheart. Tell me."

"I want *you*."

The confession seems to startle her, but I'm not sure why. Doesn't she know I'm already hers? Now and forever. There's no one else. There's never going to *be* anyone else. From the moment we first met, it's always been her.

"You already have me," I say as I slowly push into her. "I'm yours."

She moans and slams a hand against the window to brace herself. The tinted windows offer us a sense of privacy that's immediately obliterated by her loud, needy cries. I bring my hand up to cover her mouth while I strike up a steady rhythm.

"*Fuck*." Her voice is muffled by my palm, but I can still make out the curses as she bounces her beautiful ass on my cock, perfectly matching my rhythm. "*Finn*."

"You're doing so good, sweetheart," I whisper, leaning forwards so my breath tickles her ear. "You're taking me so well. I wish you could see yourself right now. See how beautiful you look bouncing on my cock like this."

"*Finn*—"

I drop my hand. I don't care who hears us at this point. Everyone needs to know that this beautiful, beautiful woman is *mine*. "Say it again."

"*Finn*."

I'm never going to get tired of hearing her same my name.

Especially when she says it like *that*. Like uttering my name is the only thing keeping her grounded right now.

Fucking hell, she's amazing.

Between the sounds she's making and the feel of her soft ass bouncing against me as she pushes herself back, eagerly meeting my every stroke, I'm on the cusp of losing it. But I can't, not yet.

I bring a hand down to her pussy and feel for her clit.

"Oh my fucking God."

She brings her hand down to meet mine, covers it, and starts guiding my finger until we find a pace that makes her start to shake.

"I'm so close. Please—" The hand she has on the window drops and she slumps downwards. I wrap my free arm around her waist, holding her up as best I can in the limited space. "Please don't stop, sweetheart."

And—

Fuck.

Hearing *her* call *me* sweetheart might just be what does me in completely. I crowd over her, press my lips against her shoulder and murmur three words I wish I could say out loud.

I'll tell her eventually – the words are practically clawing at my throat, desperate to be heard – but not now. Not in the back-seat of my car while she fucks my cock and fingers at the same time. I've got a plan and I intend on sticking to it.

Her body stiffens slightly and I catch a glimpse of her face reflected in the window in front of us. Her eyes are squeezed shut and her mouth is slack as she lolls her head backwards to rest against my chest.

"Come for me, love."

And she does, like she was simply waiting for my command.

"*Finn.*"

My groans and her cries mix together until they're practically indistinguishable as I bury myself as deep as I can and come inside her.

She forces herself onto her haunches, pushing me back onto mine, and finds my lips with a hunger I easily match.

"I missed you," she murmurs in between kisses. "I missed you so much."

"You're here now," I whisper. And in two weeks she'll be gone again. The thought makes my stomach twist, but I push it out of my mind. "Let's go home."

———

AMBER'S EYES roll back and she breathes out a satisfied sigh. "This is *so* good."

"I told you," I say with a grin. "Best pizza in the world."

She takes another bite of her slice – there's no hot sauce, but it's spicy sausage and mushrooms, so it's *almost* just how she likes it – and gives me another pleased little hum. "It's definitely up there. *Rosa's* could give this place a run for its money though."

We're taking a brief detour before we head over to my place, and I'm fulfilling a promise I made back in London. We're tucked away in a tiny restaurant in the heart of New York City. It's squashed between several larger establishments, all with brightly coloured signs outside and long lines spilling out of the door, but nothing beats *Louie's*. It doesn't matter that the only seats available are a handful of uncomfortable white plastic chairs and tables, or that the menu is functionally useless, or even the fact that I don't think the air-con has worked once in the ten years that I've been coming here – *Louie's* has the best pizza in New York. Maybe even the world.

It's my favourite secret, but I don't mind sharing it with her. There's a lot I wouldn't mind sharing with Amber.

I still can't quite believe she's here, and I keep catching myself reaching for her hand or sidling closer to her as if I'm trying to reassure myself that this is real. This is happening. Amber is here in New York with me.

"Why're you smiling like that?"

"Like what?" I try and school my expression into something neutral but, judging by the way she narrows her eyes, I'm not succeeding.

"Like you're up to something."

A laugh gets lodged in my throat. She doesn't know how right she is. Or maybe she does. Her gaze narrows even further and I hold up my hands. "Can't a guy admire a beautiful woman sitting in front of him without being accused of having an ulterior motive?"

"Not when you're the guy, no."

"Harsh."

She shrugs. "If that's what it takes to get you to tell me what you're planning."

"Why can't you just enjoy the journey? Let me surprise you."

Something flashes in her eyes and she gives me a triumphant grin. "So you *are* planning something." She leans in, places her hand over mine, and starts tracing soft circles on my palm. Her tongue darts out to wet her lips and she looks up at me through hooded lids. "Can I have a hint?"

She's trying to seduce the truth out of me and the realisation sends a jolt straight to my cock. I snatch my hand back and glare at her. Or, at least, I try to. The way she leans back into her seat and smirks tells me I've not quite hit the mark.

"You're not playing fair."

She quirks a brow in faux innocence. "Not ready for round two?"

My cock twitches and I return the smirk. "That's definitely not the problem."

"Then what is?"

"The fact that you're incredibly impatient."

"*You're* incredibly irritating."

I flash her a wide grin. "Say it like you mean it, sweetheart."

She rolls her eyes. "You're really not going to tell me whatever it is you're planning?"

"Not yet."

"When?"

I shrug. "A couple days? Maybe three? Four?"

If I'd had things my way, everything would have been ready from the moment she landed. But, as Nel keeps reminding me, good things take time and besides, I'm in perfectly safe hands with my sister.

Debate flashes across Amber's face before she gives me a begrudging nod. "Four days. But I've got my eyes on you."

"I wouldn't have it any other way, sweetheart."

27

FINN

Amber stretches out on my couch like she belongs here. Like she's been here countless times before and will find her way again.

I lift her legs and drape them over my thighs as I settle into the empty space next to her. "How're you feeling?" She responds with a yawn and I open up my arms. "Come here."

She crawls into my lap without hesitation, and I'm starting to realise that maybe I've got a territorial streak in me too. Because she's wearing an old sweatshirt of mine like it was made for her, and suddenly I don't want to see her in anything else again.

"Don't let me fall asleep," she murmurs, even as her eyelids flutter shut. "I need to make it a few more hours so jet lag doesn't kick my ass."

My fingers flex against the fabric of my sweater as she gets comfortable on my lap.

Work has been the number one priority in my life for as long as I can remember. All I've cared about is rising to the top and silencing the whispers and gossip that follows me. Outside of that, I've never felt empty or like I was missing something, but Amber has quickly filled a gap in my life I hadn't even realised was there.

I could get used to this. If she'll let me.

Would she let me?

I think, once she finds out what I've been planning, that she might.

Eventually.

I press a kiss to her temple. She doesn't stir. I should wake her up, but I don't. I want to sit in this moment and savour it for a little longer. Her head is right above my heart and the steady rhythm of her breathing quickly lulls me to sleep alongside her.

When I wake, I'm alone on the couch and I can hear laughter coming from the kitchen. I frown and sit upright. The laughter sounds familiar.

"...grab the album. There's definitely a few photos in there of him during his mohawk phase."

I leap off the couch and storm into the kitchen just in time to see Amber and Nel collapse into a fit of laughter.

"Told you he was up," Nel says with a smirk.

I scowl at my sister and make my way around the island. Amber is sitting on a stool and, to my surprise, Maya is perched happily on her lap. They both look up at me as I approach. Maya's face splits into a toothy grin and there's a soft twinkle in Amber's eye as her lips lift at the corners.

"*Uncle Finn!*" Maya cries, scrambling out of Amber's lap and into my ready and waiting arms as soon as I'm close enough. "Mama said not to wake you up. You were snoring real loud."

"That's a lie," I scoff. "Uncle Finn doesn't snore." I lean in and press a quick kiss against Amber's cheek. "I thought we weren't going to sleep?"

"No," Amber says, and I wonder if I'm imagining the slight blush creeping up her neck. "I told *you* not to let *me* fall asleep. Great job with that, by the way."

"How long was I out?"

"Not long. Nel and Maya got here about an hour ago."

"An *hour*?" I narrow my eyes at Nel. "Anything she told you is a bold-faced lie."

"That's good to know. She was mostly just telling me about what a great brother and uncle you are." Amber shrugs. "But if she's such a liar, I won't pay it any mind."

Nel barks out a laugh. "I like her."

"Me too," Maya pipes up. She's managed to scale me like I'm her favourite climbing frame at the park and is now sitting on my shoulders, forcing me to march around the kitchen. I knew it was a mistake to watch *Ratatouille* with her.

I cock a brow at my sister. "Didn't know I needed your approval."

And I don't need it. But it is nice to have.

"Nel was just about to tell me about the house I'm here to work on," Amber says.

I freeze on the spot and snap my head around. Nel meets my frantic gaze with a smirk and an almost imperceptible shrug.

Relax, the look on her face tells me. *Your secret is safe with me.*

"I was," Nel says out loud. "But then we got onto the topic of photos, and I got a little distracted."

"That's right," Amber says, a look of pure glee etched onto her face. "I believe I was promised some mohawk photos?"

I've never felt so betrayed. "Look how they're teaming up against me, princess" I groan as Nel pulls a thick, leather-bound book out of her bag. "It's not fair, is it?"

"I wanna be on Amber's team," Maya says plainly.

"Ugh." I drop Maya down onto the island and clutch at my heart, knowing how much she likes the theatrics. "Traitors. All of you."

I can't help but smile though. A warmth starts to spread through me knowing that my two favourite people in the world like my new favourite person just as much as I do.

"What is this?" Amber asks, ignoring my dramatics in favour of gently tapping the large book Nel has dropped onto the table.

"It's for Nanny and Grandad," Maya says. She scampers across the island, ignoring Nel's sharp '*Maya. Shoes!*' and kneels in front of Amber. There's not a hint of shyness or hesitation in her actions, like she's already firmly labelled Amber as someone she knows she can trust. That feeling of warmth has taken over me almost entirely. "For their birthday."

"*Anniversary,*" Nel reminds her. "It's their anniversary gift. Part of it anyway."

I come up behind Amber and brace my hands against the island, bracketing her in as she flips through the book. It's filled with photographs of our parents and us.

The first photo is a baby picture of my mother, dressed in a white gown. It's in black and white, but you can plainly tell that she's screeching her lungs out as my grandfather hands her to the priest to be christened. The next photo is the earliest one we could find of my father. He's about Maya's age, grinning cheekily up at the camera as he sits in a bucket filled with what we hope is mud.

The photos continue on, alternating between pictures of my mother and my father in various stages of their childhood, right up into adulthood when we finally get the first photo of them together.

"She was actually dating his neighbour when they met," Nel tells Amber as she pauses over the slightly grainy photo of them sitting side by side on a lawn swing. She covers Maya's ears for a second and then whispers conspiratorially, "Mom swears she ended things before she met Dad, but apparently it was *quite* the scandal back in the day."

Amber snorts and continues flipping through the pages. There's Mom and Dad on their wedding day, their honeymoon, moving into their first home, Mom pregnant with me, Dad cradling me in his arms, Mom pregnant with Nel, Dad holding the both of us, and hundreds more. It took us the better part of three months – with Nel doing most of the legwork – to pull all these photos together.

Amber stops on a photo of the four of us one Christmas. We're all wearing matching cheesy sweaters, but that's not what has her laughing.

"So you weren't lying about the mohawk phase."

"Believe me," Nel cackles. "I wish I was."

"Ha, ha," I deadpan, reaching forward to flip to the next page myself. Several more embarrassing photos follow – the mohawk really outlived its welcome – before we get to Nel, pregnant with Maya, and all the holidays and quiet moments we've captured since.

"This is beautiful," Amber says quietly as she gets to the last page. It's a photo we took together a week before I left for London.

"Mom loves sentimental stuff like this," I tell her.

Nel nods. "Last Christmas she burst into tears when she opened a snow-globe with Maya's face in it."

Amber laughs, but it doesn't sound like her usual one. I lean over her shoulder, and my heart plummets into the pit of my stomach when I notice there's a teary shine to her eyes. I give her side a gentle squeeze and feel a tiny bit of relief when she leans into my touch and sighs softly.

If Nel notices the sudden change in Amber's disposition, she's doing a great job of pretending otherwise.

"It's their 35th wedding anniversary this weekend, so we knew we had to go all out. Well, *I* knew we did. This one—" She shoots a dismissive nod in my direction. "Just wanted to get them a two-week cruise around the Caribbean."

"That's part *two* of the gift," I explain. "Sentimental stuff for Mom. A fun trip and some new memories for them both."

"It's great," Amber says, forcing an airy nonchalance into her tone. "Are you doing anything else to celebrate?"

Nel frowns. "The party? You're coming, right?"

Amber stiffens in my arms and I feel a sheepish grin tug at my lips.

"He hasn't told you, has he?" Nel shakes her head.

"*Nope*."

"I didn't mention my parents' anniversary party?" I ask innocently. I'm avoiding eye contact but I can feel the heat of Amber's glare on me. "My mistake."

Nel shakes her head and then slides off her stool, yanking Maya off the island as she goes. "Come on, sweet pea. Uncle Finn's got some apologising to do." Maya starts to protest, but Nel scoops her into her arms and marches towards the door. "It was lovely meeting you Amber, and hopefully we'll see you on Saturday." She turns and gives me a mock salute. "Good luck, Finn."

"*Saturday*?" Amber asks, brow arched. "As in, two days from now?"

"Oh yes," Nel laughs before she gives us one final wave and disappears down the corridor.

Amber waits until she hears the front door open and shut before she swivels around on her stool and glares at me. She's trying to look serious, but there's a lovely blend of amusement and frustration painted across her face.

"Is this what you've been hiding?" she asks. "Your parents' wedding anniversary?"

No.

"Yes." Truth be told, I'd honestly just forgotten to mention it to her, taking it for granted that she'd be coming. "They're having a party to celebrate on Saturday and I was hoping you'd like to come."

She exhales a deep breath and runs a hand through her hair. The action unsettles me. It's something I notice she does when she's uncomfortable or nervous about something, and I hate that I'm the one making her feel like this right now.

"I'm not sure that's a good idea."

"Why not?"

"Your family won't think it's weird if you show up with some random woman on your arm?"

I give her a wry look. "You're not some *random woman*, Amber."

Uncertainty flashes across her face. "Then what am I?"

I hesitate. There are so many things I could say to answer that.

I could tell her that in three short months she's somehow burrowed her way into the very depths of my soul and claimed herself a permanent seat in my heart.

I could tell her that having her by my side adds a brightness to my life, like she's my own personal sun.

I could tell her that I love her with every fibre of my being and the amount of time I've spent daydreaming about the life we could have together – the kind of life that might result in our future children spending three months searching for photographs for *our* 35th wedding anniversary – is truly becoming alarming.

And I'm going to tell her all of that and more.

But not just yet. I've got a plan and I still need a little more time to pull it off.

I try and think of an answer that'll placate her until then, but my silence must put her on edge because she says, voice tight, "Meeting your family is a big deal."

"You've met Nel and Maya."

"Exactly!" Frustration oozes from every syllable. "You shouldn't introduce me— I shouldn't be meeting people — especially Maya — if I'm not going to stick around. It's not fair. On them. On you. On me."

Alarm bells start ringing in my head. "You're not going anywhere, sweetheart."

She gives me a sad smile. "That's not your decision to make."

Okay. Fuck the plan. I'll say anything to wipe away the

cloud of doubt on her face right now. "Then let's make it together." I pull her in close. "Go on, say it."

"Say what?"

"Everything you've been holding back since I picked you up
at the airport." I tap the side of her head gently. "I know it's been
swirling around in there, slowly driving you mad. Get it out. Get
it all off your chest, and we'll figure it out together."

The smile she gives me is equal parts relief and nerves. She
takes a moment to find the words, and then says, "I don't think
this is sustainable."

It feels like an arrow to the chest, but I give her a nod and let
her carry on.

"You can't just fly me out whenever you're horny."

"I wasn't horny until you started—"

"I'm serious, Finn." Her voice is quiet, barely a whisper, and
she dips her head. "We both deserve more than that."

"I can give you more."

Her eyes shoot up to meet mine again.

"I'll give you whatever you want, sweetheart."

"It's— It's too soon," she chokes out. "We've only known
each other for three months. I couldn't ask you to do that. It
wouldn't be fair—"

"Why does that matter?"

"Because long distance is *hard*, Finn," she says. She sounds
like she's desperately trying to convince herself. "It's not just
FaceTiming every night and flying to see each other every
couple of months. It's a real commitment." She takes a deep
breath. "It's having faith in us that we're willing to go through
this for however long because we know that when it's all over,
we're still going to want each other. That's too much to ask for

right now. I wish we had more time together. That we'd been able to build—"

"Sweetheart." I cut her off and bring her hand up to hold it against my heart. I hope she can feel each steady, deep beat. I hope it calms her. Let's her know that I'm right here with her and I'm not going anywhere. "When we first met, you told me that you like a client who knows what he wants. I know what I want, and I want *you*."

"I want you too." The words spill out seemingly without her permission. But then her lips curl into a small grin and she says, a little more forcefully this time. "I want you too."

I mirror her smile. "Then we'll work this out. Together. At the end of this, whenever that may be, you're the one I want by my side. And an ocean and three thousand miles—"

"Three thousand four hundred and ninety-one."

"And three thousand four hundred and ninety-one miles isn't going to change that. You're mine, sweetheart."

"You'll go bankrupt from the plane tickets alone."

"It would take a lot for me to go bankrupt."

"Just because you've got money, doesn't mean you have to be stupid with it."

"If I'm spending it on you, then there's nothing stupid about it."

She laughs at that, and I can practically see the anxiety and tension wafting off her. "Whatever you say."

I reach for her hand and twist our fingers together. "So we're doing this?"

"I—Yes," she says firmly, giving herself a little nod. "If you want to?"

"There's nothing I want more."

"Then, yes. We're doing this." She lifts her head like she's about to kiss me, but then she throws her shoulders back and laughs. "Oh, God. Bailey's going to love this."

28

AMBER

I don't think I've ever been this nervous before. I'm pretty sure I didn't even feel like this on my first day at Zensi Designs. But here I am, sitting passenger side in Finn's car, nervously chewing my bottom lip as he drives up a winding road with huge white houses on either side.

Finn's parents live about a forty-five minute drive out of the city. Nel and Maya are in the back and they've been a welcome distraction from the maelstrom of nerves swirling around my mind for the entire journey. It's easy to forget that I'm about to meet Finn's parents with Maya loudly singing along to a playlist of nursery rhymes Nel apologetically asks us to play. And when Maya eventually drifts off about twenty minutes into the drive, Finn and Nel serve as another convenient distraction.

It's interesting watching them. Each interaction is filled with sibling banter and insides jokes that make them both roar with laughter.

Nel makes a crack at Finn's driving when an old lady cuts him off, sticking her middle finger up as she zooms past us, and he immediately responds by telling me all about how it took Nel seven tries to pass her driving test. I'm only half-heartedly listening to Nel defend herself — *"the first six fails weren't my fault!"* — too focused on the sudden pang of longing that shoots through me.

Would Noah and I have this kind of relationship if we were closer in age. Or, at the very least, if our mother would let us? It's been nearly a month since I last saw her, and she's made no effort to reach out and mend the rapidly growing divide between us. Maybe it's beyond mending.

The funny thing is, it doesn't really bother me as much as it probably should. I don't feel a sense of loss or a burning desire to reach out. Not for her anyway.

Noah's absence in my life has been weighing on me. I wonder what she's told him. If he's asked about me or where I am. If he misses me.

I don't realise I'm pulling at my hair, a few strands twisting around my forefinger, until I feel a hand on my thigh. The touch snaps me out of an unexpected spiral.

"You okay?" Finn's got his eyes on the road ahead, but his fingers squeeze my thigh in gentle comfort.

"Yeah."

He squeezes again, a little harder this time. He doesn't have to use his words for me to understand what he's trying to tell me. *I don't believe you.*

A quiet laugh escapes through my nostrils. I don't think I'll ever get over how easily he reads me. Like I'm his favourite book he's memorised from front to back and there are no secrets hiding between my pages. I place my hand over his. "It's just family stuff." I'm painfully aware that Nel is only a few inches away and, as much as I like his sister, I don't think I'm ready for her to know all the embarrassing drama surrounding my family right now.

He nods, jaw ticking slightly.

"But I'm fine now," I say. And I am. His touch has pulled me out of the cloud of anxiety, nerves and worry that was rapidly beginning to suffocate me. His gaze slides over to me for a brief second, just long enough to catch the truth in my eyes.

He nods again and, this time, it comes with a smile.

By the time we arrive at his parents' home, I'm feeling more at ease. The house is a huge, blindingly white colonial style mansion with a sweeping lawn and a queue of fancy cars in the driveway.

"You grew up here?" I ask incredulously. Finn's loft style apartment in the city is nice, but this is a hell of a lot nicer. I'm suddenly wondering if I'm underdressed. The knee length floral dress I'm wearing is definitely 'meet the parents' appropriate but, from the size of their house, I'm wondering if I should be in a gown. The cute bouquet of flowers I'd picked up on the way as an impromptu gift also seem silly now.

"We didn't move here until we were teenagers," Nel says as she unstraps Maya from her seat. "But we didn't grow up far from here."

"You're rich," I say, the realisation hitting me unexpectedly hard. "Like. Really rich." Bailey was wrong. This isn't millionaire money – it's definitely a whole lot more.

Finn laughs. "You just realised?"

"And I've been calling you cheap this whole time."

"Love that," Nel cackles. "Keep him humble."

"Our grandfather founded a pharmaceutical company years

ago," Finn explains as we walk up the driveway. Maya's in his arms, still half asleep. "It's always done well, but not as well as it's been doing since Dad took over as CEO."

"You didn't want to work with him?" I ask with a frown. It's clear Finn makes good money at The August Room, but I can't imagine it holds a torch to what he could make with his father. Though I suppose he's already set for life. He must have access to a trust fund or some kind of bank account with an obscene number of zeroes.

He shakes his head. "Wanted to get out from under my dad's shadow."

"And he stepped right into good ol' Uncle Ernie's one," Nel says, sarcasm lacing every word.

Finn's smile tightens and now it's my turn to give his hand a squeeze. He shoots me a grateful smile but doesn't have time to say anything else before the front door swings open.

"*Cornelia!*" a woman coos as she launches herself out of doorway and into Nel's arms. "We were just wondering where you'd all gotten to."

"Hey, Mom," says Nel. "Happy Anniversary."

"And *Phineas!*" their mother cries, turning to Finn. His cheeks immediately turn pink and my laugh gets so choked in my throat, it comes out as a strangled cough. She pulls him into a backbreaking hug which is quite impressive for someone of her size. She maybe just about clears five foot, and part of that is definitely helped by the sweeping bun of brown-blonde hair atop her head.

"*Mom,*" Finn groans as she takes a step back, her eyes shining with happy tears.

What it must be like to have a mother who's genuinely happy to see you.

She good-naturedly ignores him and instead scoops Maya into her arms, peppering her now fully awake and giggling granddaughter with kisses.

While she's distracted with Maya, I raise a brow at Finn and Nel. "*Cornelia* and *Phineas*, huh?"

They both pull an identical pained face.

"Don't start," Finn mumbles.

"She's the only one who calls us that," Nel says. "Even Dad just goes with Nel and Finn these days."

"You were named after my grandmother and Henry's great grandfather," their mother chimes in, a look of faux sternness etched onto her soft features. "Two beautiful names. I've never understood what the problem is."

"Cornelia's not bad," says Finn. "But *Phineas*, Mom? *Phineas?*"

She shrugs, like this is a conversation they've had thousands of times before, and then her gaze lands on me. For a second, I stop breathing. She's got Finn's dark-green eyes and they zero in on me with a strange intensity. But then her face splits into a smile as wide as the one she gave to Finn and Nel and, before I know it, she's hugging me like this isn't the first time we've met.

"You must be Amber! It's so, *so*, lovely to meet you." She pulls back a little, her hands still squeezing my shoulders. "Phineas has told us so much about you—"

"*Mom.*"

She happily ignores him. "I'm Juliette."

"It's lovely to meet you too. Happy Anniversary." I hand her the bouquet and she gushes over them like they're the most beautiful thing she's ever seen. "Your home is amazing."

The inside is just as stunning as the outside with beautiful high ceilings, oak wood floors, and a lovely blend of modern and traditional design.

"Thank you," Juliette beams. "Phineas mentioned that you're an interior designer. You and Cornelia should really discuss doing a few projects together. She's a realtor, you know?"

I frown. "That's why I'm here actually. I'm going to help Nel—"

"Mom, where's Dad?" Finn cuts across us loudly.

"Yeah," Nel joins in quickly, her voice equally as loud. "We've got a gift for you two."

Juliette's eyes light up as she spies the green gift bag in Nel's hands. "A gift? Children, you shouldn't have."

Finn rolls his eyes. "That's what she said on their thirtieth anniversary." He leans in and says in a loud, conspiratorial whisper, "There's a reason we went all out this year."

Juliette swats a playful hand at her son and then crouches down in front of Maya. "Go and find Grandad, sweet pea."

Maya nods seriously and then scampers off yelling for her grandfather. While we wait, Juliette directs us into the kitchen. The island in the middle is filled with trays and dishes and my mouth immediately waters at the sight of it.

"How many people are you expecting, Mom?" Nel asks, hoisting herself up onto a stool.

"Maybe fifty or so?" Juliette says as she lifts the foil on one of the trays and sneaks a cocktail sausage. "That's just from the RSVP's, I'm sure a few others will turn up. You know Marion and Ernest didn't RSVP, but she messaged earlier and said they're on their way."

Finn stiffens slightly beside me. "Ernest is coming?"

The atmosphere in the room changes. It's a subtle difference, but it's palpable. Even Juliette's smile wavers slightly.

"Yes," she says. "Your uncle is coming."

"Does Dad know?" Nel asks.

"Does Dad know what?" Henry Hawthorne lumbers into the kitchen. Maya is on his shoulders, cackling with delight, and I get an almost mirror image of Finn – just thirty years older. His blond hair is clipped short, his dark eyes are kind and warm, and the look on his face when he spots Finn and Nel is filled with nothing but love.

He jogs around the island and pulls both his children into deep hugs. When he gets to me, his brows crinkle for a second. I watch as he and Finn share a glance, some kind of silent communication that has Finn's lips twisting into a goofy grin. When he turns back to me, Henry smiles. "Amber, I presume?"

I nod. "It's so nice to meet you."

"Amber's an interior designer," Juliette jumps in. She comes to stand beside her husband and presses her hand idly against his chest. Henry immediately leans into her touch. It's clearly a familiar action, one they must have done thousands of times over the last thirty-five years and requires no thought to it. "I was just saying, she might be able to work with Cornelia on a few—"

"Ernest's coming tonight," Finn says loudly.

I narrow my eyes. That's the second time he's done that and while the others might fall for his clumsy attempt at a distraction, I don't.

Henry's features twist into a grimace. "Lovely."

"He's your brother-in-law, Henry," Juliette scolds gently. "And today is our wedding anniversary. I'm sure you two can manage to be civil for one night."

"*I'm* always civil," Henry grumbles.

"Try a little harder." Juliette kisses him on the cheek then sidles over to Nel and plucks the gift bag from her hand. "Now onto happier topics. *Gifts*." She takes the photo album out and spreads it on the island. "Oh. Oh, *children*. What is this?"

"It's a photo album of some of our most cherished and important memories as a family," Nel explains softly. "Think of it as a timeline of your love."

Finn nods by my side. "Everything in there is because of you two."

As they predicted, Juliette promptly bursts into tears as she flips through the album. Even Henry's eyes get a little watery at some points.

"This is beautiful," Juliette whispers. She's coming to the end of the album now, but something makes her pause. "*Oh*. Amber. You look gorgeous, and you both look so happy. You'll have to teach me how you got Phineas to smile like this for a photo."

I frown and lean over. On the last page of the album there's a photo that definitely wasn't there the other day. I recognise it instantly, although this is the first time I've actually seen it.

It's me and Finn on Primrose Hill. His arms are around my middle and I'm smiling shyly up at the camera, like I can't quite believe how much I'm enjoying being in his arms. His head is gently resting on my chin, and the smile on his face could rival the sun.

I blink and feel a tear start to slide down my cheek.

"What— Why—"

Finn presses a kiss right where the tear has begun to fall. "Like Nel said, these are some of our most important memories as a family. The moments we want to look back on in twenty years and remember."

"But—"

"You're a part of this family now, sweetheart," he says firmly. "You belong in this album, just as much as we all do."

And then I take a note from Juliette's book, and promptly start to cry.

29

AMBER

THERE ARE DEFINITELY MORE THAN FIFTY PEOPLE IN THIS house right now. It feels like every inch of the large space is packed with smiling faces, everyone eager to grab hold of Juliette and Henry for a second or two to share their congratulations and well wishes.

I glance across the room. Finn had been doing a good job of staying by my side and proudly introducing me to his extended family and his parents' friends and co-workers, but Maya is the only child here and she's got her uncle wrapped tightly around her little finger.

They're both sitting at a bright pink children's table squashed in the corner of the living room. Maya's pouring some imaginary tea into a plastic mug while Finn sits on the tiny chair, long legs pressed up against his chest, happily indulging her fantasies.

"She absolutely adores him," Nel murmurs, coming to stand beside me. She's got a plate full of fancy looking hors d'oeuvres and she angles it towards me. I snatch up a salmon bite and chew it as I watch the two of them play.

"I can tell." It's incredibly sweet to watch and I have to actively stop my brain from running wild with thoughts about the kind of father he'd be.

"Maya's father was never really in the picture," Nel tells me. "But he officially dipped out for good about two years ago."

"I'm sorry."

"Don't be," she scoffs. "I can't call him my biggest mistake, because I got Maya out of it. But we're definitely better off without him. She's happy. I'm happy. It's all good." We watch them in silence for a few moments. Maya quickly tires of whatever game they're playing at her table and starts dragging Finn towards the garden where her grandparents have a little jungle gym set up just for her.

He catches my eye just as they reach the back door and gives me a pretend grimace. "You good?" he mouths. I give him a nod and he lets Maya pull him out through the door.

"So," I say once he's gone. "Are you finally going to tell me about the house?"

Nel gives me a quizzical look. "The house?"

"The one I'm supposed to be redesigning for you." I arch a brow. "The whole reason I'm here."

Nel snorts. "I've known you for all of 72 hours, Amber, but I know you're smarter than that." She pops another salmon bite into her mouth. "You know you're not here just for the house."

"So there *is* a house?" Thanks to Finn's constant interruptions whenever anyone mentioned the property I'm supposed to be here to design, I was beginning to think he'd made it all up.

Nel looks like she's on the brink of bursting into laughter. "Of course there's a house."

"Can you show me a photo?"

"Nah." I glare at her, but she just shrugs like it doesn't bother at all "I promised Finn I wouldn't ruin the surprise."

"Will you at least tell me if it's a good surprise?"

She looks at me closely for a long beat. Her brows pinch in the middle and she pulls her bottom lip between her teeth. Eventually her features relax. "It's a good surprise, Amber. You'll love it. I guarantee—" A tall woman and a slightly shorter man step into the room and Nel's attention is suddenly on them.

The woman has platinum blonde hair, wide blue eyes, and a strained smile stretched across her cherry red lips. The man makes no attempt at a smile. His face is grim and downturned and it's clear he'd rather be anywhere but here.

"That's Aunt Marion and Ernest," Nel tells me quietly, gaze still trained on them as they swan around the room. Marion embraces an older woman I vaguely remember being introduced as Henry's cousin, while Ernest stands stiffly to the side.

On the other end of the room, Henry spots them both and his eyes narrow immediately. Juliette puts a placating hand over his and whispers something I can't hear.

"What's the deal with them?" I ask. "Your dad and Ernest? Why so much bad blood?"

Nel chews on her bottom lip and then shrugs. "I have a theory, but Finn doesn't agree."

"Why not?"

"Because, if I'm right, it's an incredibly petty reason."

I watch as Marion and Ernest approach Henry and Juliette. Marion pulls her brother into a fleeting hug while Ernest gives both Henry and Juliette a brief nod. His lips move almost imperceptibly and I have to assume he's saying 'congratulations' because Henry gives him a stiff smile in response.

"What's your theory?" I ask.

"Years ago, Ernest wanted a job at Dad's company, but Dad said no. He said Ernest didn't have that *spark* he was looking for in someone to work for him. Kind of a shitty thing to say, but I get it."

I blink, waiting for her to continue. "That's it?" I think about how miserable Finn had been every time he got off a call with his uncle. How he kept chasing his approval but never got it, even though he delivered a phenomenal end product. How Ernest didn't even send a congratulatory bottle of wine, let alone come and support him on the day of the launch. "There's got to be another reason." Surely one man wouldn't be so petty.

"That's it," says Nel. "Ernest has hated him ever since, and Dad's never been his biggest fan I guess."

"Why not?"

Another shrug. "From what I've heard? Ernest wasn't the best boyfriend to Aunt Marion back in the day. I think Dad still holds a bit of a grudge, even if she's forgiven him."

"And what does she think about their feud?"

"She pretends like she doesn't notice it. It's quite fun actually, seeing how much she's willing to ignore. One Thanksgiving they nearly got into an actual fight over the dinner table. Mom had to literally force Dad to stay in his seat. Aunt Marion didn't even flinch. She just sat there, picking at her turkey. Oh no." Nel sucks in a breath and fixes a strained smile onto her face. "Watch out. They're coming over."

Marion sweeps across the floor, cutting through the crowd

with ease. Ernest trails after her, his displeasure obvious. I've only been in his presence for all of ten minutes but I think if I were ever to see him smile, I'd worry he was about to have a heart attack.

"There's my beautiful niece," Marion coos in a manner that reminds me strangely of Cynthia. There's something in her tone that puts me on edge. It's sounds phoney, like she's forcing herself to pay Nel a compliment. "It's been so long. And who is this?" She turns to me, her eyes narrowed as she looks me up and down.

I stick my hand out. "Amber. It's lovely to meet you."

"She's Finn's girlfriend," Nel fills in, and I don't miss the way both Marion and Ernest frown slightly at the mention of his name.

"Finn's here?" asks Marion. She ignores my still outstretched hand. "I thought he was still in London doing his little launch."

His *little* launch.

Anger starts to bubble in my stomach, but I force it down.

I don't think Nel's got it right. Marion isn't ignoring the feud between her husband and Henry — she's stoking it. "The launch happened over a week ago actually," I tell her stiffly. Ernest's deep blue eyes flicker over to me. "It went well. *Really* well. You should be proud of him. I know I am."

"And you are?" Ernest asks.

"Her name is Amber," Nel says sharply. "She *just* introduced herself."

A wave of gratitude washes over me. Nel reminds me of Bailey a little bit; she's definitely a ride or die.

Ernest ignores her. "The launch was satisfactory."

"It was *brilliant*," I snap. A few people around us glance over in our direction, but I pay them no mind. "He did an amazing job pulling everything together in such a short space of time. The launch was featured in every major newspaper and magazine, and you can't scroll through Instagram these days without seeing an influencer posing inside the club. That's a hell of a lot more than just *satisfactory*."

He stares at me curiously, like he's actually seeing me for the first time since this whole conversation started. "He did what was required of him. Nothing more, nothing less."

Marion puts a gentle hand on Ernest's arm and gives me a condescending look. "Finn's a good boy, but he needs a little more direction. I'd hoped that working for Ernest would give him a bit of a *spark*—" Her bright red lips curl and suddenly everything falls into place. This has been a revenge plot years in the making, and Finn has become an unfortunate casualty. "But alas."

"Yes, it's been a shame," Ernest says with a smirk. "But that's what happens when you ride the coattails of your family name for too long. There's no chance for real talent to form."

"What the *fuck*?" Nel hisses, any pretence of politeness towards her aunt and uncle long gone. She's practically shaking with barely concealed anger. "How dare you."

I was right. Definitely a ride or die.

"Watch your mouth, Cornelia," Ernest says dryly.

"You watch yours," I snap.

Ernest and Marion both look at me like I've slapped them.

I wish I had. Instead, I take a step forward and poke Ernest squarely in the chest. "Finn has more talent in his pinky finger than either of you have combined."

From the corner of my eye I spy Finn re-entering the room with a tired looking Maya. I should stop before I embarrass both of us, but I don't. My anger is fuelling me and I'm on a roll.

"He might just be the most driven man I've ever met. Everything he's done throughout the last few months has been to impress *you*."

I think about all the early mornings and late nights he spent hunched over his laptop, making sure every last detail was perfect. It annoyed the hell out of me, but I understand it now.

If I had people like this actively working against me, willing me to fail, I might be a little annoying too.

"And this is how you talk about him when he's not around? Just because you're still mad at his dad for not hiring you how many years ago?"

Ernest's cheeks colour. "You don't know what you're talking about."

"I think I do," I say. "I think I know exactly what's going on here. And you're pathetic. The both of you."

"Who the *hell are you*?" Marion snarls. She whips her head around frantically. "Who is the girl? Where has she come from? And *where* did she get the audacity to—"

Finn suddenly looms over us. I can spy barely concealed anger simmering away underneath his stony expression. "Enough. I've heard enough." He loops an arm around my waist and pulls me in tight. "Honestly, I don't care what you have to say about me, or what kind of games you're using me for. But you don't talk to her like that. *Ever*."

A thrill shoots through me and heads straight to my core.

"Tell *her* to watch how she speaks to us," Marion spits. She wrinkles her nose and looks down at me. "I don't know where you found her, but—"

I don't hear whatever it is she's about to say, because Henry's booming voice cuts across her.

"Marion. Ernest." His tone is cold and void of any of the love I'd heard earlier. "A word?"

Finn uses the the opportunity to quickly pull me away from the both of them and into the kitchen. As soon as we're alone, he bends down slightly and cups my face in his hands. I see worry reflected in his eyes as he searches my face for something.

"Are you okay?"

"*Me?*" I splutter. "I'm fine. A little embarrassed. I should probably apologise to your parents for causing a scene at their party. But yeah. I'm fine. Are *you* okay? I'm so sorry you had to hear that."

His shoulders slump. "Wasn't the nicest thing to hear, but it's what I've suspected all along. It was nice hearing you defend me like that though."

"Of course," I tell him. "What else was I supposed to do? Just let them tear down someone I love like that? I had to say something."

The smile on his face right now could light up a small town. "Someone you love?"

My heart skips a beat or two, and then decides to make up for lost time by pounding against my ribcage. I meet his gaze head on. "Yes. Someone I love very much."

He reaches for my face again, tilting my chin upwards. "*Sweetheart.*"

"I love you, Finn." The words jolt out of me unbidden, but I don't regret them.

285

"I love you too," he murmurs before he closes the gap between us and kisses me. I've lost track of the number of kisses we've shared now, but this one will forever be my favourite. "I've been wanting to tell you for a little while now."

"You should've."

"I had a whole plan," he says. "I wanted it to be perfect."

"This *is* perfect."

"You two are sickening."

We pull apart to find Nel leaning against the doorframe. "Can you stop being so cute and horribly in love?"

"Nope," Finn says with a grin. "Is everything all right back in there?"

"Marion and Ernest have gone. Dad looked like he wanted to fight both of them, but Mom stepped in asked them to leave. She wanted to come in and talk to you guys, but I said I'd check in on you two first."

"She's not mad at me, is she?" I ask, suddenly nervous. Have I ruined the whole party and tainted Juliette and Henry's view of me forever.

Nel snorts. "No, not at all. I told her what happened, and she's just glad you defended Finn. We both are. Thank you."

"You don't have to thank me,"

"I know I don't have to, but I want to." She crosses the distance between us, effortlessly shoves Finn out of the way, and pulls me into a deep hug. "You're good for him, Amber."

"He's good for me too." *So good.*

Nel clears her throat when she pulls away, and I pretend like I don't notice that her eyes are a little glassy now. "Feel free to re-join the party if you want to, but..." She fumbles around in her pocket and pulls out a set of keys. Finn's brows shoot into his

286

hairline the second he spots them. "I think it's probably about time Finn tells you what his big surprise is." She tosses the keys to me and gives me a wink. "Enjoy."

Curiosity tinges through me. "What does this open?"

Nel just laughs and Finn glares at her retreating form as she leaves the kitchen.

"Finn?"

He sighs like this is quite possibly the worst thing that could ever have happened to him, but there's a light in his eyes that betrays him. I think he looks excited. Or is that nerves I see? Maybe a mix of the two? He reaches for my hand and squeezes it tightly. "Come on, sweetheart."

"Where are we going?"

"Do you trust me?"

"You know I do."

I trust him implicitly with my heart and everything else that comes with it.

"Then keep on trusting me, just for a little while longer."

30

AMBER

WE'RE ABOUT AN HOUR'S DRIVE FROM HIS PARENTS' HOUSE, coasting down a quiet road that cuts through a thick, dense forest. There's a wall of lush greenery on either side of us, and the rapidly setting sun casts a beautiful orange glow over the landscape.

It's stunning, but I'm struggling to appreciate it. My mind is racing like never before as I stare at the set of keys in my hand. I've been squeezing them so tightly, I think they might leave a permanent imprint on my skin.

"You're not even going to give me a tiny hint?"

"Nope."

"This is very unfair."

"I know," Finn says cheerfully.

We drive for another fifteen minutes or so before he turns into a side road so small, I definitely would've missed it in the rapidly encroaching darkness. His car shakes as we drive up the gravel road and a large house emerges from the thick trees.

Maybe *house* is the wrong word for it. It's a huge two storey lodge with beautiful wooden panelling interspersed between the large windows that wrap around the front. Finn pulls the car up at the edge of the property, and I can spy a lake stretching out behind it.

"What are we doing here?"

"Remember the house I said Nel needed you to redesign? This is it."

I frown at him. "This is my surprise. Work?" I love what I do, but...*really*? I don't know why, but I'd been expecting more.

He shrugs and I don't miss the way the left side of his mouth starts to twitch.

"What's so funny?"

"Nothing!" he says, and he looks so earnest, I almost believe him. *Almost.* "I just want you to like it." He comes round to my side of the car and opens the door for me. "Come, let me show you around."

He pulls the keys out of my hands and guides me up the pathway.

"There's seven bedrooms, four and a half baths, a large rec room..." He trails off and clicks his tongue. "An office. A fitness room. There's a dock around the back that leads out to the lake. And there's a tennis court somewhere on the land. I think this property accounts for about 10 acres or so. Sorry, I'm probably forgetting a few things. Nel was supposed to be here to tell you all of this."

I'm not entirely sure why *he's* telling me it in the first place.

He unlocks the door and steps aside for me to enter.

Honestly? It's underwhelming inside. The décor is very dated and it's easy to tell why Nel's been struggling to shift it. But there's potential — *so much potential*. I feel a little giddy as I

289

walk around and take in the high ceilings with stunning oakwood accents, and the view of the lake from the living room takes my breath away.

"What do you think?" Finn asks quietly. We've nearly finished the tour, and we're standing outside the only room he hasn't taken me inside yet. His hand is resting on the doorknob, fingers flexing nervously against the handle every few seconds.

I frown for a brief moment, but then my lips morph into an easy and genuine smile. "It's going to take a lot of work, but it's definitely an exciting project. I should probably arrange to meet up with Nel as soon as possible so we can talk about what her clientele typically goes for. I've got a few ideas already, but it would be good to tailor them a bit more."

"I could just tell you."

I frown. "Do you know?"

He nods and takes a deep breath before pushing open the door. I follow him into the room. It's a bedroom - the master bedroom, I think - and it's empty for now, save for the large, ornate mirror resting against a wall.

My heart skips a beat, and then another.

Because I know this mirror. It's been very carefully cleaned, but I *know* this mirror. It's been burned into my mind since the first time I saw it at the Interiors Fair. My holy grail item.

"What—"

Finn cuts me off, still looking strangely nervous. "The house will have to be bright and airy. Lots of natural light." He comes to stand by my side and threads our fingers together. I stare at our reflections in the mirror. My eyes are wide, my chest heaving.

"She likes something called *modern organic*."

She?

"That's when you blend together modern aesthetics with nature's beauty."

My throat feels like it's closing up, and my next words come out sounding choked. "*I* know what *modern organic* means, Finn." I force down the lump in my throat. "How do you know?"

"You told me," he says with a nonchalant shrug. "Back at that restaurant the day we picked up the chandelier. She's going to want warm, neutral tones, something that makes the space feel inviting and comfortable from the second you walk in."

"Who are you—"

"And it's got to be very expensive. That was one of her requirements."

Something clicks in the back of my mind.

The mirror I said I wanted for my dream home and—

It'll be something on a lake and very expensive.

"Finn," I say slowly, realisation dawning on me. "Who am I designing this house for?"

"For us," he says simply. "I bought this place for us."

"You—" The world around me starts to spin. My voice comes out sounding strangled. "You *bought* this? *When?*"

"That night I asked you to come here," he says sheepishly. "It *has* been on the market for a while, and when Nel showed me some photos I knew that it would be perfect for you."

"For me?" I hear what he's saying, but the words aren't making any sense.

"For you, sweetheart." A pause. He gives me a sheepish smile. "For us."

He's bought me a house.

He's bought me my *dream* house and even set things up so I can design it exactly how I want to.

"*Why?*" My voice comes out as a croak. I don't need to look in the mirror again to know my eyes are filling with tears.

"I'm going to marry you one day, Amber." He says it so simply, like it's a given fact of life.

The sky is blue, the Earth is round and, one day, Finn Hawthorne is going to marry me.

"I thought it made sense to get a start on our dream home."

If the world was spinning before, now I'm in a vortex. I stumble against the nearest wall for some stability and take deep, calming breaths.

He bought me my dream mirror.

He bought me a *house*.

He wants to marry me.

He—

"I love you, Amber."

I shake my head and a hysterical laugh bubbles from my lips. "You are the most *frustrating* man I've ever had the pleasure of meeting."

"Not the response you want after an 'I love you'," he says with a soft smile. "But I'll take it."

"I love you too, Finn. I *do*. But this? This is too much." I shake my head, *I've* just bought a house. I've got bills to pay. A *mortgage*. We don't even live in the same country, we—"

He lifts my hand and presses it against his lips. "I don't care how long I have to wait. I'm not asking you to move out here and marry me right away. Go back to London, start your business, do what you need to do. I'll be cheering you on from the sidelines, and we can make it long distance; I know we can. And when you're ready, I'll be here for you."

I blink and tears quickly begin to fall. "You didn't have to buy me a house to tell me that, you know? You could've just said it. It would've had the same effect."

"Doubtful." His expression turns anxious. "What do you think?"

What *do* I think?

I prod my finger into his chest and glower up at him. "I think that this is simultaneously the most romantic and most selfish thing anyone has ever done for me."

He bows his head and I have to poke him again to get him to look at me.

"Marriage means being a team." I can see as the hope starts to return in his eyes. "It doesn't mean deciding things on your own and buying million dollar houses on a whim."

"Two million."

I have to bite the inside of my cheek to stop myself from laughing. "It *means*," I say a little louder. "It's means that we talk about things like this and we make those decisions together."

He nods. "I know. I know that this was—"

"A lot?"

"A hell of a lot," he says with a wry grin.

"You'll really wait for me?" I ask. "Because I can't move here just yet. I need to get something off the ground for myself back home."

I tense slightly, because there's a chance that his next words might bring everything crashing down around me. He could just ask me to quit trying to start my own company back home, to sell my house, and fly out to be with him. And if he does, I think that might just spell the end for us.

"I know how much your work means to you, sweetheart."

I brace myself. Here it comes. The beginning of the end for us.

"And I'd never ask you to drop everything for me."

The tension in my body seeps out of me like a popped balloon almost instantly. Why was I worried about this?

"All I want for you is to be happy. And if that means staying in London for a while and getting AWH Interiors off the ground—"

"AWH Interiors?"

He flashes me a grin. "Amber Wyatt-Hawthorne Interiors."

I snort and smack his chest gently. "Just AW Interiors, thank you very much. You may have bought me a house, but I don't see a ring on my finger."

"Sweetheart, I would have a ring on your finger by the end of the day if that's what you really wanted. But I'm not in a rush. I just needed you to know how serious I am about you. About us. I'm in this for the long haul."

I lean into him and rest my head on his shoulder. "You bought me a house."

He chuckles. "I did."

"This is going to be our home."

"It is."

"I still can't believe this."

He shrugs, his lips lifting into a smile. "There's a lot of that going around today. I can't believe you love me."

"I think I've loved you for a little while now," I admit.

"Me too," he says. He tilts my chin up and kisses me softly, sweetly. "We're going to have a good life together, sweetheart. I promise you that."

My heart swells so much, I'm surprised it doesn't shatter my ribcage. "I'm going to hold you to that."

He huffs out a laugh and leans in for another kiss. "I hope you do."

31

EPILOGUE: FINN
TWO YEARS LATER

"We're going to be late."

"And whose fault is that?" Amber's voice floats out of the bathroom.

I grin at my reflection in the mirror. "Definitely yours."

She pokes her head out from behind the door and glares at me. "That's not how I remember it." Her towel is still wrapped around her body and the scent of her perfume wafts out of the newly opened door.

"I can come back in there and refresh your memory if you'd like?"

Temptation flashes in her eyes. "How late are we?"

I glance at the watch on my wrist. "Right now? Already twenty minutes."

She groans and disappears back into the bathroom, pulling the door shut firmly behind her. I laugh, turning my attention back to the mirror so I can finishing tying this tie. Once I'm done, I navigate through the maze of cardboard boxes and suitcases strewn across the floor and flop down onto Amber's bed.

"Want me to get started packing some of this stuff away?" I call. There are two piles of thick, coffee-table type books on the floor. "The books? Are they all coming with you?"

"Just the left pile," she shouts back. "I'm donating the right pile."

I nod to myself and slip off the bed. We've spent the last week going through her house sorting things into piles, deciding what she's giving away or throwing out, and what's coming with her to New York.

I can't stop the silly grin that splits my face as it hits me again: Amber is moving to New York with me.

These last two years have flown by in a blur thanks to the steady routine we developed. I've been flying to London once every six weeks, staying for two weeks, and then flying back home. Once a quarter Amber will fly over to the States to stay for two weeks too. It's been tricky working out the logistics of it — having to plan around Amber's increasingly busy work schedule now that AW Interiors has taken off — but we've made it work.

Things have been helped by the fact I no longer work for The August Room or my uncle anymore. After the mini show-down at my parents' anniversary party, I knew that there was nothing left for me in that company, and that Amber had been right all along. I needed to branch out and do something for myself. Something not attached to my last name.

And that's what I did. Sort of.

It very quickly became apparent that escaping the Hawthorne name was easier said than done, but that didn't have to be a bad thing. Thanks to my decade at The August Room *and* my last name, I had a contact book full of names of people in high places, and I realised I could do some good with that. So I started up a mentorship scheme for recent graduates from underrepresented backgrounds in the corporate world; kids without a contact book full of connections but who are as equally talented and deserving of getting a foot in the door.

The scheme has done really well, and we've helped secure over 100 graduates an entry level job at a company that otherwise would've been inaccessible to them.

It took me a while, but I think I've finally found my passion. At least when it comes to work.

My first passion comes striding out of the bathroom, and I idly wonder if I'll ever get tired of the sight of her. It's doubtful. She's wearing a fitted green dress, but she could be wearing nothing at all and she'd still take my breath away.

Her move to New York has been a long time coming. We've been planning it for the last year and have managed to time it with a new contract she's secured from a high-end restaurant chain in the city to design their new location.

She's also been slowly working on the house I bought us on the lake, and it's finally finished and ready for us to move into. *Together.*

The thought makes my heart leap in the best possible way.

I abandon the pile of books and make my way to her. She's standing in front of the mirror, slipping a pair of gold earrings on, and she lets me slip my arms around her waist without any protest.

"We're going to be late," she reminds me as I lean in and press a kiss to her exposed neck.

"We're already late."

"Bailey's going to get annoyed."

I trail my hands along her sides, over her thighs, and give her ass a squeeze. "She'll understand."

Amber laughs and swats me away. "Not today she won't. Come on—" She backs herself into me, deliberately grinding her ass against my rapidly growing erection. "We'll have plenty of time for this later."

I bite back a groan and hold her hips in place. "We have time now."

She snorts and slips out from beneath me before I can do something stupid like tear her pretty new dress off and throw her onto the bed. "We absolutely do not." I think she must feel at least a little bit sorry for me, because she leans in and presses a quick kiss against my lips. "But we've got a whole lifetime ahead of us. I think you can wait one night."

A whole lifetime with her. The thought makes me smile. There's no ring on her finger yet — she made me promise not to propose until she's settled in New York — but that doesn't matter.

We're on same page.

I remember the promise I made two years ago.

We're going to have a good life together, sweetheart.

I smile and pull her in for one last selfish kiss. I really can't wait to make good on that promise.

32

EPILOGUE: AMBER

THE PARTY IS IN FULL SWING BY THE TIME WE ARRIVE. There's a big white sign outside the door to the restaurant that reads:

WE'RE ENGAGED!

BAILEY & CASH

My face splits into a wide grin. My best friend is engaged to the love of her life and I couldn't be happier. As soon as we step through the doors, the bride-to-be accosts us, her brows knit together in an uncharacteristic glare.

"First you steal my maid of honour and drag her halfway across the world with you. *Then* you have the audacity to show up late to my engagement party?" She crosses her arms and shakes her head. "Not gonna lie, Finn. It's not looking good for you right now."

Finn laughs and holds up his hands. "Won't happen again, Bailey."

"Good." She drops the whole '*I'm annoyed with you*' act and laughs with him. Their friendship has been an unexpected but pleasant development over the last two years. "I'm glad you guys could make it. I know it's been hectic with the move."

"Wouldn't miss it for the world," I say as I sweep her into a hug. "I'm *so* happy for you. Where's Cash? I need to give him the whole '*if you hurt her, you'll have me to answer to*' speech."

"You've not done that yet?" Finn asks, pretending to look surprised. "Bailey gave me the speech the first time we met."

Bailey beams, looking incredibly pleased with herself. "That was just part one of the speech. Don't worry, Finn, I've got an extra special round two locked and loaded for whenever you pop the question."

"Give me a couple months," Finn says with a grin.

"Ooh," Bailey throws me a wink. "Back to back weddings, I like the sound of that."

I roll my eyes. "Tonight is about *you*. And Cash. Wherever he is."

Bailey nods to the large table that cuts across the middle of the room. They've hired the entire restaurant out for the night and rearranged the seating so everyone can fit on the one table. Cash is standing near the top end, nodding politely to something Bailey's father is saying.

As if he can sense her seeking him out, he looks up suddenly and catch his future wife's eye. It's sweet watching the way his face immediately lights up when he spots her. He excuses himself from the conversation with her father and practically sprints across the room to get to Bailey.

He slides an arm around her shoulders as soon as he's within touching distance, tucking her into him. From the look on her face, there's nowhere she'd rather be.

"Amber's got a threatening speech for you," Finn says helpfully after we've gone through a round of hugs and congratulations.

Cash laughs. "I'd expect nothing less, but there's no need. Dane's already given it to me."

"That doesn't count," I say. "Dane might be her brother, but he's also *your* best friend. He's playing both sides."

"What am I playing now?"

Dane shimmies into the little circle we've made. His eyes are bright, his face is sweaty, and I'm pretty sure there's a lipstick stain on the collar of his shirt. I'm not the only one who notices it, because Bailey rolls her eyes and scoffs.

"Some poor girls heart, I bet." She flicks his collar and scowls up at him. "You've been here for less than an hour. Do I even want to know whose lips have been all over you?"

Dane grins. "Doubt it."

"I hope it's one of *your* friends," Bailey murmurs to Cash who only laughs, too desensitised to Dane's antics by now.

Finn and I leave the newly engaged couple to float around the restaurant and greet the rest of their guests and grab ourselves some food. They've got a buffet style counter set up and I bump into Bailey's mother while I'm scooping rice onto my plate.

"Amber, my lovely!" She kisses both my cheeks and then wiggles her brows as she looks Finn up and down. "And this must be your boyfriend? Bailey tells me you're moving abroad to live together soon?"

"In two weeks," I tell her. It's come up so fast, but I don't feel any nerves when I think about this impending move. It feels right.

So right.

"How exciting!" She claps her hands together and smiles. "How're your parents feeling about the move? Have they planned a trip out to see you?"

I feel myself stiffen slightly, but any hint of tension or anxiety immediately washes away the second I feel Finn's hand come to rest on my waist. I let myself sink into his touch and give Bailey's mother a polite smile. "We haven't spoken in a while, actually."

"Oh— I'm so sorry to hear that."

"It's fine," I say with a shrug, because it absolutely is. I've long since stopped mourning my lack of a relationship with my mother.

My focus has been on doing my best to make sure the door remains open for Noah once he's ready and old enough to reach out without her hovering over his shoulder.

I still send him presents every birthday and Christmas, still send him birthday cards packed with money and a message filled with love, but I've never gotten a response. I don't even know if she lets him know I've sent him anything, but I keep at it. Not speaking to him has been hard, but all I can do is hope that once he's old enough he'll seek me out himself.

Bailey's mother frowns. "What hap—"

"You must be so excited with all the wedding planning," Finn says smoothly, cutting across her before she can ask the question that makes my stomach twist. "Do you know if they've settled on a date yet?"

He knows they haven't, but it's an easy way to get her off the topic of me and my mother.

God. I love this man so much.

We spend the next ten minutes politely indulging Bailey's mother as she shows us some of the Mother of the Bride dresses she's been looking at and then starts getting a little teary eyed when she turns and sees Bailey and Cash swaying gently on the dance-floor.

We use that as an opportunity to hurry away over to the table and slip into a pair of empty seats next to Dane. He's got a plate of food in front of him, but it doesn't look like he's touched it. He's staring straight ahead, thick brows pulled into a slight frown as his dark brown eyes follow the photographer Bailey has hired to capture the evening.

She's pretty, with a mane of roughly blown out black hair, and what looks like a permanent lazy smile etched onto her face. I shake my head and huff out a quiet laugh. Dane has been a player since we were kids, and it's oddly refreshing to see that apparently nothing has changed.

He moves to stand up, the legs of his chair scraping roughly against the floor in his haste, but two perfectly manicured hands quickly come down on his shoulders and push him firmly back into his seat. "Don't even think about it," Bailey says sharply.

"Think about what?"

"I've seen you making googly eyes at Eliott all night."

The aforementioned googly eyes flit across the room and land on the photographer again. "I don't know what you're talking about," Dane lies.

Bailey's not buying it.

I'm not buying it.

I'm pretty sure *he's* not even buying it.

"I'm serious, Dane. Eliott's a phenomenal photographer and she gets booked out a full year in advance."

"And what does that have to do with me?"

"We haven't confirmed the wedding date yet, but I want her to do it. And she's not going to if you sleep with her and then never call again."

Behind her, Cash snorts and Dane shoots his best friend a glare.

"Go find whoever gave you that lipstick stain and bother her again," Bailey continues. "But. Not. Eliott. All right?"

Dane deflates in his seat. "Not that I was going to do anything—"

"Dane."

"But fine. I'll leave your photographer alone."

Satisfied, Bailey pulls Cash back over to the dance-floor and they immediately start gyrating to the beat. Cash's personal dance lessons with her have clearly come in handy, because they both look like borderline professionals.

It's nice watching them dance. Cash doesn't take his eyes off her, a goofy smile plastered on his face as his hands skirt up her back.

"They look so happy," I murmur, leaning into Finn. He drapes an arm over me. "I'm going to miss them."

"I'll fly them out anytime."

"Cash hates flying." I've been trying to convince the two of them to join me on a trip to New York for the last two years. Bailey's flown out with me once, but Cash hasn't taken me up on the invitation yet.

"Then we'll fly here," he says with an easy shrug. "Are you

—" He swallows. "Are you regretting the move? We can push it back if you want to be here for all the wedding planning?"

I turn around to face him. "Never. It's sweet of you to offer, but no. I'm ready for us to start our life together."

These last two years have been a necessary evil, giving me the time to set up my business and for us to deepen our relationship and bond with each other.

But I'm ready now.

I've been ready for a while.

"I'm tired of there being an ocean between us. I want you. I want *us*."

He leans in and holds my chin between his thumb and forefinger, pulling my face closer towards his. "Me and you, sweetheart," he breathes against my lips. "Forever."

"Forever," I agree.

"It's going to be good," he promises me.

I shake my head. "It's going to be great."

THE END

WANT MORE?

If you enjoyed Amber and Finn's story, read on for a sneak peek
of **ONE MORE SHOT**, the next book in the Flights and
Feelings series!

Coming soon!

ONE MORE SHOT follows Dane Clarke and Eliott Rayne...

ONE MORE SHOT
CHAPTER ONE

ELIOTT

I have one goal for tonight and one goal only: I, Eliott Rayne, am going to have an orgasm.

Sasha, my roommate and best friend, cheers loudly. "That's the spirit, girl!" Some of the Prosecco in her glass spills over onto my bedsheets as she flops down onto my bed. "Positive vibes only."

It feels like I need more than just positive vibes right now, but I appreciate the sentiment all the same. Because, despite having just turned twenty-seven, I've never managed to *get there* with a partner. Not for lack of trying, mind you.

Committed relationships, one night stands, friends-with-benefits, men, women, both at the same time – I've tried just about every combination possible and not a single one has resulted in the kind of happy little moans I can hear coming from Sasha's bedroom every time her boyfriend, Wes, stays the night.

It's borderline sickening in a ridiculously sweet kind of way.

I put the finishing touches on my make-up and step back from the mirror. Sasha has already downed her glass of Prosecco and has swiped mine off the bedside table to sip on. I ignore the thievery and turn to face her.

"How do I look?"

She grins. "Fucking stunning."

Sasha would stay that if I stumbled out of bed at 5am wearing last night's make-up and a bin bag, but that doesn't mean it's not true right now. Leather pants, corset top, my favourite walkable yet sexy heels – this is a tried and tested outfit. Make no mistake about it – someone is coming home with me tonight.

"So, what's the plan?" Sasha asks, swinging her long legs over to the side so I can drop down onto the bed with her. I snatch my glass away from her and she gives me a pretend pout before reaching for the bottle to refill her own glass.

"No plan," I say in between sips. "Unless '*Find someone hot. Bring them back home. Have an orgasm*' counts as a plan?"

Sasha rolls her eyes. "Yes, that's a given, obviously. But beyond that, what're we looking for? Just because they're hot doesn't mean they know how to fuck, and since we can't just ask them—"

I snort into my drink. "Oh yeah, that'll go down well. Excuse me hot person, how would you rate your sexual prowess on a scale of one to ten. One being '*couldn't find the clit if I beat you over the head with it*' and ten being—"

"Your sex game is so good; you'll ruin me for everyone else for the rest of my life." She sighs happily and a playful grin tugs at her brown lips. "I miss Wes."

"It's been a week," I tell her dryly. "And you're seeing him tonight."

Wes is a DJ and has been on tour with an artist around the country for the last week. As much as I like him, it's been nice not having to hear Sasha's bed-frame rhythmically rocking against our shared wall every other night.

Don't get me wrong. Wes is a great guy and I'm happy that Sasha's found someone who can apparently pinpoint every single one of her many pleasure points in ninety seconds or less, but all it does is remind me that I've never had someone who knows and loves my body like that.

It's not like I've never had an orgasm before. My very well loved vibrator can always be counted on to get me where I need to go, but it always feels flat. Like I'm on the edge of something amazing but can't quite reach it.

"It's been a *long* week," Sasha giggles. "Shirley has been working overtime."

Shirley being the vibrator I bought her as a joke last year when Wes was overseas for two months.

"But back to you and Mission: *Get Eliott Laid*."

"Getting laid isn't the problem," I say, and *God*, do I wish it was. If that's all it took, I wouldn't be in this position right now – desperately trying to find someone to, as Sasha so helpfully put it, *ruin me for everyone else*.

I'm starting to think that I'm broken, and that's just not the kind of thing *positive vibes* can fix. At this point, I need a divine intervention.

"You're right," Sasha says, nodding seriously. "I'm changing the name to Mission: *Big O*." She gives me a mock salute and some more of her Prosecco spills onto my bedsheets. A jolt of irritation pulses through me, but I shove it away. "I'll be the best wing woman you've ever had."

Being the only person I've ever felt comfortable sharing my struggles in the bedroom with, Sasha's the *only* wing woman I've ever had. We met at university nearly ten years ago now – two lone black girls in the middle of England desperately trying to find a shop that sold products that worked with our hair types – and we've been pretty much inseparable ever since.

When I worked up the courage, about four years into our friendship, to tell her that I'd never had an orgasm with a partner before, Sasha didn't laugh at me or judge me or run and whisper behind my back like I'd feared. She immediately jumped into *'well, let's fix that'* mode and she's been stuck like that ever since.

I think the day I do finally have an orgasm; Sasha might be happier than me.

My phone buzzes, and I glance at it. In the space of about five seconds, my screen lights up with a quick stream of notifications.

LEANNE

ELIOTT!!!!!

PLEASE HELP

EMERGENCY. 999.

ELZZZZZZZZZ

ELIOTT

What? What's happened? Are you okay?
Where are you?

No response.

Oh God.

I feel my Prosecco start to climb back up my throat and my mind starts swimming with worst case scenarios. My baby sister, injured in a ditch somewhere, alone and afraid.

ELIOTT

Leanne????

Please answer.

LEANNE

soz, jen just sent me a snap and i had to reply

So *not* dying in a ditch then. Great.

ELIOTT

Jesus fucking christ, Leanne. I was worried about you.

You said it was an emergency.

LEANNE

it IS an emergency

can u send me £50 plssssss

promise i'll pay u back

as soon as my student loan drops

A paragraph of about one hundred praying emojis come through next and I resist the urge to hurl my phone at the wall.

Leanne is seventeen and enjoying her last summer before she starts university in September and barely two days can pass without her hitting me up for money, a ride, or some other kind of favour.

> **ELIOTT**
>
> Ask Mum.

LEANNE

she said to ask u

Of course she did.

> **ELIOTT**
>
> What do you need it for?

LEANNE

travel. i don't have enough in my account to get to work until i get paid next week

can u spare the lecture this once and just let me borrow it???

i PROMISE i'll pay u back

pinky swear

She won't, of course. She never does and I doubt she ever will.

> **ELIOTT**
>
> This is the last time.
>
> And we need to have a serious talk about your money management.

LEANNE

THANK YOU!!!!

lifesaver

love you xoxo

> **ELIOTT**
>
> Love you too.

I send over the money and the finish the rest of my Prosecco in one gulp, wincing as the alcohol leaves a fiery trail down my throat.

"You good?" Sasha asks, shooting me a sideways look.

"*Great*." I try and shake off the sudden wave of irritation I'm feeling, but it lingers. "You ready to go?"

We're heading to an event hosted by the artist Wes has been DJing for all week. He'll be behind the decks tonight, which means we're guaranteed a good time.

Sasha finishes off her glass and then stands up. Just like me, she's also dressed to impress in a hot pink mini-dress, her long black hair falling in waves to the middle of her back – but Wes is the only man on her mind.

Irritation makes way for a pang of jealously, but I quickly brush it away. Orgasm first. Then we'll work on the whole loving life partner thing.

Sasha turns to me and grins. "Mission: *Big O* has officially started."

AS SOON AS we step through the doors, we're met with chill R&B, the smell of barbecue mingling in the air, and a crowd that's just the right kind of tipsy.

Sasha immediately spots Wes behind the DJ deck and drags us through the crowd to meet him. It gives me a chance to scope out what I'm working with tonight. A beautiful girl with braids that fall all the way down to her knees winks at me as we squeeze past her, and my heart does a little flutter. I make a mental note to find her again on the dance-floor at some point tonight, along with the tall, broad shouldered man with the striking green eyes that follow me as we cut across the room.

"He's definitely into you," Sasha murmurs, her quick gaze darting to Green Eyes for a half a second before it finds me again. "And did you see the guy giving you the once over when we walked in?"

I shake my head and resist the urge to glance over my shoulder to see if I can spot anyone else looking at me.

"Well, he was nice. Oh, and there was a guy with locs checking you out. He was *hot*."

"You talking about me?"

I can practically see all thoughts of being my wing woman fly out of Sasha's mind as Wes leans over the DJ deck and grins down at her. She doesn't hesitate diving across the deck and pulling him into a long kiss.

"He was hot, for *Eliott*," Sasha clarifies as they pull apart. They're both wearing identical goofy grins and Wes doesn't seem to mind at all that Sasha's left a lipstick stain on his cheek.

Wes grins over at me and I match his smile. Over the last three years we've become friends in our own right, and there's no one I'd trust with my best friend's heart more than him.

"Got your eye on anyone?"

I'm pretty sure Sasha hasn't told him the extent of my bedroom troubles, but Wes has never once judged me for cycling through partners and has even offered to set me up with a friend of his once or twice. I've always declined, too afraid that my inability to orgasm might start to get round our circle of friends, but I've always appreciated the offer.

Sasha and I point out the few people we've spotted so far,

and Wes wishes me luck and kisses Sasha again before he has to return to his set.

"Alright. Game plan," Sasha says as we move through the crowd again and head to the bar. "We'll get some drinks, and then start working the room. Give us an hour, and you'll be dragging someone out of those doors and into your bed. How's that sound?"

It *sounds* great and, in theory, it should be.

In practice? Not so much.

Turns out, the girl with the long braids is in a relationship and they're looking for a third. Her partner is equally as attractive as her, but the one threesome I had a year or two ago didn't do anything for me and it's not an experience I'm eager to revisit.

Green Eyes is inexplicably already far too drunk by the time we reach him, despite the event only starting an hour or so ago. The other guy Sasha spotted checking me out seems promising at first, but he keeps calling me *Ellie* – a nickname I've always loathed – even after I ask him to stop, and any thoughts of heading home with him dry up relatively fast.

We can't find the guy with locs she spotted when we first came in, but we do see a few mutual friends about two hours in and agree to momentarily drop the plan for a while to just enjoy the night and dance with them.

It's fun for a while, but then Wes takes the music into an upbeat dancehall segment and the dance-floor is suddenly filled with sweaty bodies gyrating against each other. I don't mind dancehall, but I'm more of a soca girl myself. Sasha, however, *loves* dancehall. She's standing directly in front of the decks, putting on a show for Wes like they're all alone and not in a packed warehouse somewhere in East London.

I consider asking her to come with me, but she looks like she's having a good time (and Wes is definitely enjoying the show) so I leave her to it and step outside to get some air.

The small outdoor space is mostly empty aside from a few smokers in the corner and a tall guy leaning against the nearest wall. He's standing directly below a light, and the warm amber glow illuminates him against the night sky.

And fuck *me*. He's hot.

Warm brown skin, a defined jaw covered in just a little bit more than stubble, thick brows, full lips, and chin length locs pulled into a messy bun with a few strands falling in front of his face.

I wonder if he's the guy Sasha caught checking me out earlier. I hope so.

He pays me no attention, his undivided gaze on the phone in his hands, as I inch further into the space. He's wearing a shirt with the first few buttons popped open and I get a glorious glimpse of a well-defined chest.

Sasha's not here, but Mission: *Big O* is officially back in action.

I casually lean against the wall, leaving enough space between us that it's not awkward, but also not so much that he can't ignore my presence. His thumbs stall against his phone, and I feel a little thrill shoot through me as his gaze slides in my direction.

I pretend to look through my purse, giving him a moment to unabashedly look me up and down. He must like what he sees, because he stuffs his phone into his pocket and clears his throat.

I glance up at him and raise a brow, like I'm not sure why he's bothering me.

He grins and, *wow*. It's a very nice smile. Slightly lopsided, but warm and friendly. The kind of smile that makes you want to smile right back. I don't, though. I keep my expression a careful balance between wary and intrigued, not wanting to play my cards too early.

"I was hoping to bump into you."

I bite the inside of my cheek to stop a pleased smirk from spreading across my face. He *was* the guy Sasha saw. "Do we know each other?" I ask, cocking my head to the side.

"Not yet." He takes a bold step towards me, closing the tactical gap I'd left between us. "But we can fix that pretty quickly."

He's hot *and* he's smooth. I give him two *ticks* on my mental checklist.

"I'm Dane." He sticks out a hand.

I pretend to hesitate for a second, and then reach out and grab it. "Eliott." I linger for a beat too long, letting my fingers trail slowly along his as I pull back. "It's nice to meet you."

"Likewise." He grin widens, showing off a dimple on his left cheek. "You're not into dancing?" He nods over his shoulder back to the still heaving dance-floor. Sasha's nowhere in sight and, since she hasn't messaged me, I can only assume that means she's gone behind the DJ deck with Wes.

I shrug. "Just waiting for the right song."

He shoots me a curious look. "And what song would that be?"

"Something a little slower than this. What about you?" I ask. "How come you're out here all alone?"

"I was actually just about to head out. I only came as a favour to a friend, but I'm not a big dancer, so this isn't really my scene." He looks me up and down again, and then his grin morphs into a small smirk. "Glad I stayed, though."

"Oh, really?" I ask, feigning confusion. "Why's that?"

He chuckles, like he can absolutely see right through me but is more than happy to play along. Another *tick*. "Just met a gorgeous girl, and I'd like to see where things go."

I pretend to giggle and duck my head to disguise my eye-roll.

Dane speaks with the well-practiced charm of someone who has said that exact same line about a hundred times before. There's no hesitation in anything he says. No fear of backlash or rejection. It's like he's got it down to a science and he knows exactly what he needs to say and when to have me fawning all over him.

He's got *player* written all over him. Not exactly my usual type personality-wise, but there's a confidence there and I'm wondering if he can bring that to the bedroom.

The dancehall music blaring inside morphs into something slower. I don't recognise the song, but I catch Dane's eye and give him my own well-practiced sultry smile. "Come on. I love this song."

He doesn't protest, just threads his fingers through mine and lets me drag him back onto the dance-floor. I quite like that. How he's happy to defer to me and let me lead, although it's clear that he's usually the one in charge.

Another *tick* for Dane.

I pull him to a stop in the middle of the dance-floor and press my back up against his chest. He's tall enough that he has to crouch slightly so I can wine my waist against his, but he doesn't complain. Instead, he brings his hands down to my waist and pulls me flush against him.

He wasn't lying when he said he wasn't much of a dancer. His movements are slightly awkward, like he can't quite catch the beat no matter how hard he tries, but he seems content with letting me guide us.

He drops his head onto my shoulder. "Where'd you learn to move like this?"

I laugh as I roll my hips to the beat. "It's not hard."

He hums, his grip on my waist tightening slightly. "Maybe you'll have to teach me. Do you do private lessons?"

I have to hand it to him; he moves very fast, and I'm not mad at it.

"Is this your game?" I ask, tilting my head slightly so we can make eye contact. "Pretending that you can't dance and asking for *private lessons* back at some girl's place?"

"I'm not pretending." He grins, and there's that dimple again. "But let's just say it is my game. Is it working?"

The song switches and I pull away for a brief moment, only to spin around so I'm facing him. I loop my arms around his neck and he resettles his around my waist.

"Maybe," I lie. Because it definitely is working. All I need is the *Sasha Seal of Approval* and then Dane is coming home with me. "Tell me more about you."

"Dane. Twenty-nine. Business owner. Allergic to bananas. Terrible dancer. Great at..." He wiggles his brows. "...*Other things.*"

I snort and roll my eyes. "Ugh. And you were doing so well. I've never met a guy who said something like that who could actually live up to the hype."

He drops his eyes to my lips. "You've never met me until tonight."

Fair point.

"Your turn. Tell me more about you, *Eliott*." He says my name slowly, like it's something to savour.

I pretend to think my answer over as I look around the room, desperate to spot Sasha and get her thoughts on him. "I'm twenty-seven. I'm a photographer – weddings specifically. No allergies, that I know of. But I really hate tomatoes."

"Tomatoes are like, 90% water," he scoffs. "Impossible to hate."

"They're disgusting. Especially when they're in sandwiches."

He laughs. "Noted. Keep tomatoes away from you. Anything else I should know?"

I bite my lip. What about *'I've never had an orgasm and I'm hoping you're going be the one to change that'*? No. Can't say that. It'll scare him off before we've even really gotten things started. Instead I settle for looking up at him through my eyelashes and strategically biting my bottom lip. "I live about a fifteen minute Uber ride from here."

Something flashes in Dane's eyes. "Good to know."

We dance like that for a little longer, sharing mundane pieces of information that we'll both most likely have forgotten by tomorrow morning. I learn that he has his own construction business, his favourite colour is blue, he likes to cook and, he likes watching quiz shows in his spare time. Doesn't matter the show or the format, he'll get into it somehow. I end up sharing that I'm the eldest of three children, *my* favourite colour is yellow, I'm definitely a dog person, and I have to wear socks to bed because my feet are always cold.

By the time I eventually spot Sasha sliding out from behind the DJ deck, her gaze inquisitive as she scans the crowd for me, Dane and I have been wrapped in each other's arms for at least an hour.

"I've just seen my friend," I say, reluctantly unwinding my arms from his neck. "I'm gonna go and let her know I'm good."

I move to step away, but he trails his hands up my side, along my arms, and then skims a hand over my jaw.

"Dane—"

Then his lips are over mine and he's swallowing the rest of my question. As first kisses go, it's not half bad. It's great, actually. I try and focus on the feel of his lips – soft and surprisingly gentle – on mine, or the way his hand cups my jaw like I'm the most precious thing in the world to him and not some girl he just met. But my mind starts to drift. I can taste rum on his lips and wonder if he can taste the cherry flavoured cocktail I'd been drinking earlier on mine. Does it bother him? Does he like it? Is he enjoying the kiss? Am I using too much tongue? Not enough tongue? I will my mind to stop racing with pointless questions, but it doesn't listen. It never does.

He pulls away, hand still on my jaw, and gives me a smile that is somehow a strange mix of both shy and smug. "Just giving you a reason to come back."

There was no way I wasn't coming back to find him, but that just sealed the deal. "I'll be five minutes," I promise before I drift back into the crowd.

When I get to Sasha, she's grinning from ear to ear, clearly having seen Dane and I on the dance-floor. "Who's the hottie?"

I give her the rundown on everything that's happened since I first left the dance-floor and, by the time I'm finished, she's practically vibrating with excitement.

"I *knew* it'd be him," she says, glancing over my shoulder to get another peek at him. "When we walked in, I said there was a guy with locs checking you out, didn't I? It was him! You think he's got what it takes?"

"I hope so."

Dane chooses that moment to look over in our direction. He meets Sasha's gaze and, to his credit, doesn't look away. Sasha surveys him for a long moment before giving him a small nod and turning back to me.

"I like him. He's got balls."

Anticipation shoots through me and I bite down on my lip to try and temper the eager smile I can feel on my face. "He's got the *Sasha Seal of Approval*?"

"Hell yeah." She starts gently shoving me back in Dane's direction. "Let me know when you get back home and when he leaves— *If* he leaves. And Wes and I are only ten minutes down the road if you need us."

Dane quirks a brow as I approach him again. "I'm guessing your friend gave me the okay?"

Sasha has all the subtlety of a brick to the face and I don't need to turn around to know she's still got eyes on us. "She did." It's my turn to raise a brow. "Is that a problem?" Some guys can get funny about the measures women have to take to stay safe on a night out and if he's one of them – ridiculously handsome or not – then I'm calling it quits right now.

"Nah. You do what you've got to do. And besides—" He

reaches for my hand and I let him pull me into his chest. "I'm assuming her approval can only mean good things for *us*."

He tilts my chin up and steals another kiss, one I'm more than happy to give. It's been a while since I've been with someone like Dane. Someone who doesn't second guess themselves and just oozes confidence the way he does. I like it.

"You said your place is only fifteen minutes away," he murmurs against my lips when he eventually pulls back. "Is that offer still on the table?"

I nod eagerly – probably too eagerly, but I don't care at this point. I want him. I want him so bad my entire body has begun to tingle with anticipation.

"Good." His lips are still barely grazing my own and I feel, rather than see, his smile. "Lead the way."

ALSO BY ANISE STARRE

One Week in Paradise

A steamy fake dating contemporary romance

Order on Amazon today!

ABOUT THE AUTHOR

Anise Starre is a born and bred Londoner who now travels the world with her husband. She loves writing sweet romances with a hint of steam and spice to get the heart going.

Keep up with her on Instagram @authoranisestarre or on TikTok @anisestarre

Printed in Great Britain
by Amazon